Readers love *SERE* by JOHN

"A little gem that glittered for me just like that magenta apartment sign."
—Sinfully Sexy Books

"I absolutely loved this book… If you are interested in a sweet love story and quite a bit of humor, I highly recommend this book."
—On Top Down Under Book Reviews

"I was completely won over by this book… I totally and completely recommend you read this book when you've hit angst overload and need to remember how to smile."
—Love Bytes (The Blog of Sid Love)

"I loved the way the author takes the reader on this rollercoaster experience… If you are looking for a fun story filled with eccentric, quirky characters as well as tender sweet moments, I recommend *Serenading Stanley*."
—Live Your Life, Buy the Book

"Run to get this book. Totally worth it. And please, please—someone pick this up and turn it into a sitcom or a rom-com movie. This is the kind of thing I'd gladly watch on the big screen!"
—My Fiction Nook

"My cheeks were hurting from all the smiling I did throughout the story. Mr. Inman, I love your sense of humor, and I'm looking forward to reading more of your books."
—The Novel Approach

"The romance was sweet, and the characters were absurdly entertaining, which made *Serenading Stanley* an all-around great read."
—The Romance Reviews

"Call this one funny, charming and a joy to read."
—The Romance Studio

By JOHN INMAN

A Hard Winter Rain
Head-on
Hobbled
Jasper's Mountain
Loving Hector
Paulie
The Poodle Apocalypse
Shy
Snow on the Roof (Dreamspinner Anthology)
Spirit

THE BELLADONNA ARMS
Serenading Stanley
Work in Progress

Published by DREAMSPINNER PRESS
http://www.dreamspinnerpress.com

Work In Progress

THE BELLADONNA ARMS
JOHN INMAN

Dreamspinner Press

Published by
DREAMSPINNER PRESS

5032 Capital Circle SW, Suite 2, PMB# 279, Tallahassee, FL 32305-7886 USA
http://www.dreamspinnerpress.com/

This is a work of fiction. Names, characters, places, and incidents either are the product of author imagination or are used fictitiously, and any resemblance to actual persons, living or dead, business establishments, events, or locales is entirely coincidental.

ISBN: 978-1-63216-195-6
Digital ISBN: 978-1-63216-196-3
Library of Congress Control Number: 2014944918
First Edition October 2014

Printed in the United States of America
∞
This paper meets the requirements of
ANSI/NISO Z39.48-1992 (Permanence of Paper).

For John B., who puts up with me on a daily basis and, amazingly, keeps on smiling.

Chapter 1

HI. MY name is Harlie Rose.

Let me tell you about the time I fell in love. I mean, *really* fell in love. Oddly enough, it all started with me standing in a rainstorm with a broken heart. Yeah, see, you're confused already. But I didn't say I wanted to tell you about the *first* time I fell in love. I said I wanted to tell you about the time I really really *really* fell in love. There's a difference, you know. There's a *big* difference.

But anyway, back to the rainstorm. And jeez, what a rainstorm it was!

You never really expect to see a monsoon in San Diego. You never really expect to see palm fronds scattered to hell and back and torrents of rainwater sluicing down the gutters. Not in this town. You also don't expect to see people in cutoffs and sandals (San Diegans *never* know how to dress) leaning against a wintry wind with their dripping hair sticking straight out behind them like the fins on a '69 Cadillac, while they try to slog their soggy asses down the sidewalk without being picked up by said wind and tossed over the border into Tijuana.

And you never really expect to see a fat old drag queen clutching his periwinkle blue dressing gown around him as he hauls the trash out to the curb, or see him daintily sidestepping all the puddles so as not to ruin his size twelve marabou-feathered house slippers with the four-inch heels that might have been swiped from Carole Lombard's dressing room on the Fox back lot about a hundred years ago (if Carole Lombard had worn size twelves) and which now looked like a couple of drenched chickens, what with all the sopping wet feathers. And how the hell can a three-hundred-pound man walk in those damn things anyway?

You also never expect to see a drag queen, young, old, or in-between, wearing a transparent plastic rain bonnet on his head (the kind that ties under the chin) to ward off the deluge, especially when he doesn't have any hair on his head. Not one single hair. And besides, those plastic rain bonnets just aren't chic enough for a respectable drag queen. Are they?

This was the kind of stuff rattling around in my mind while I stood at the curb in the frigging downpour and watched the old drag queen, who was actually kind of charming in a *Ripley's Believe It Or Not* sort of way, as he trundled the barrel of trash out to the curb to park it next to six other barrels like it.

Shivering in the wet and cold, I continued to watch as the gigantic man in the periwinkle blue dressing gown and the plastic rain bonnet disappeared back inside the rundown apartment building from whence he came, clattering up the stone steps on those ridiculous heels and panting like a steam engine while he did it. And since the old queen didn't return, I figured that was the end of the show.

Hearing a clanking noise, I craned my head back and squinted through the slanting rain to the top of the six-story apartment building the old queen had disappeared into. What I saw was a rusty neon sign perched on top of the structure, still lit in orange at this late hour in the morning, banging and rattling and leaning rather precariously in the biting wind gusting off the San Diego Bay.

The neon sign read Belladonna Arms. One of the *l*'s was flickering like maybe it was about to give up the ghost. And while I stared at the sign, the whole thing suddenly flickered out. Apparently the old queen had flipped a switch somewhere inside, hoping to save a few bucks on the light bill, maybe.

I tugged my coat collar snug to cut off the tiny rivulet of rainwater dribbling down my back. I wasn't wearing a hat or carrying an umbrella, which further proved San Diegans are *never* prepared for anything but sunshine, so my hair was as sopping wet as the old queen's marabou feathers.

I looked back at my battered Buick station wagon parked at the curb behind me to make sure it hadn't been swept away in the tsunami of trash-laden gutter water splashing and gurgling down the hill I was standing on—the only hill in downtown San Diego, in fact. The car was safe and sound, of course. It was also clean and shiny for the first time in living memory, thanks to the downpour which had started yesterday and hadn't let up since.

For the last four months, I had been all over the place in the old Buick. Deserts, prairies, purple mountain majesties. Thirty-two states in all. No kidding. I was like a regular nomad. And aside from the occasional flat tire, the ugly gas-guzzling beast had never failed me once. And it was still not failing me. There it sat at this very moment, packed to the roof with everything I owned, which in the grand scheme of things wasn't much, I supposed. But still it was all mine. Computer, clothes, books. And reams of notes taken on my pilgrimage, from which I had just returned this very minute to reclaim San Diego as my home.

Yep. It was time to finally settle down and pull those notes together. And time to somehow squeeze The Great American Novel out of them. I was home now to do exactly that, or I *would* be home as soon as I found a home to settle in.

That's why I was standing in the rain in front of the Belladonna Arms. The old sign had caught my attention while I was tooling aimlessly down Broadway looking for a place to light. Broadway, by the by, is San Diego's main thoroughfare. It bisects the city from east to west, and at the moment I could see it a bit down the hill from where I stood.

But back to the sign. When I first spotted it, I had immediately liked the cheesy orange lettering on the rattletrap neon contraption. I even liked the way it stood slightly askew atop the boxy, less than elegant 1940s-era apartment building the old drag queen had ducked into. The whole misaligned package of tattered neon and weathered construction, perched one upon the other on this out-of-place hill on the southernmost tip of the California coast, somehow shrieked *home* to me. Go figure.

So there I stood. Drenched. My ass still asleep from driving all night. A million ideas about my upcoming book ricocheting around inside my soaking wet head, waiting for me to put down a couple of roots long enough to type them into foreverness.

Remember that broken heart I mentioned earlier? Well, a sudden heart-wrenching vision of my ex-lover, Dan, suddenly rose out of the ashes to make a cameo appearance, squeezing itself into my head like a

pushy dinner guest hogging the best chair. But I was used to that. Dan
had been making those mental cameos ever since he threw me out of
his life four months ago, which was the stimulus for *beginning* my
four-month nomadic trek across the country in the old Buick wagon to
start with. Soothe a broken heart, get away for a while, spend a little
time alone, gather some background material for my next book.

Hide and lick my wounds. Shit like that mentally shook the
interloping thought of Dan out of my head. Then I shook my actual
head too, just to dislodge some of the rainwater clinging to it. It didn't
do any good. My hair was soaked again in less time than it took to
shiver away the cold. Or try to.

Still standing on the sidewalk, staring up at the Belladonna Arms
in front of me, I jumped when the old queen poked his head back out
the front door and screamed down the stairs, "Honey, whatchoo doing
standing in the rain like a nimrod? If you're looking for an apartment,
come on inside before you fucking drown!"

I felt the blood rushing to my face. I supposed I did look pretty
stupid.

I raised my hand in greeting to the old queen while he held the
door open for me, kindly and patiently offering asylum from the
elements. While he waited for my pokey ass to join him, he plucked the
plastic rain hat off his head, gave it a businesslike shake, and stuffed it
in the pocket of his periwinkle blue dressing gown.

I jogged up the steps and found myself on a broad roofless porch
where lounge chairs were parked all in a row, like on the *Titanic's*
promenade deck before the iceberg came along. Each and every one of
the lounge chairs in front of the Belladonna Arms was determinedly
empty at the moment, since the weather wasn't exactly conducive to an
afternoon siesta in the fresh air for anyone not wearing a wetsuit and a
fucking snorkel.

While the old queen graciously ushered me inside, tutting all the
while like he had never seen a dumber human in his life, I gave myself
a final massive shake like a drenched dog before ducking through the
doorway to get out of the downpour.

Still dripping, I stood there checking out the lobby. It didn't take
me long to conclude the inside of the Belladonna Arms was about as
chic as the outside. A bank of rusty mailboxes was embedded in the
wall to the right with an overflowing wastebasket sitting on the floor in

front of it. The wastebasket was stuffed with flyers and assorted junk mail nobody wanted. Straight ahead, a wide, banistered staircase headed off to parts unknown, both up and down. And finally, to the left, a couple of beat-up high-backed library chairs sat huddled around a plastic *Ficus benjamina* that stood about eight feet tall and looked like it hadn't been cleaned since it blew here from Oklahoma during the Dust Bowl. The ficus was currently decorated with a bright pink feather boa which someone had flung among the branches.

"Even the tree's in drag," I mused, staring at it.

The old queen saw where I was looking. "Oh, that. That's left over from New Year's Eve."

I blinked. "But this is April."

"Yeah, well."

The queen closed the door behind me, blocking out the roar of wind and rain. He tugged the dripping marabou-feathered house slippers off his fat, hairy feet, and gazed at the slippers with a wounded expression. "I guess feathers and biblical floods don't mix," he mumbled.

I finally turned to study the man up close. He was probably in his late fifties, needed to go on a diet pronto, and should never have been in drag without some serious removal of body hair first, like *all over* body hair except for the top of his head, which was as bald as a watermelon, as I mentioned earlier. What makeup he wore on his big round face had obviously been applied the day before and had suffered greatly in the process of being slept on. His black morning beard stubble rose through the weathered pancake on his fat cheeks like a crop of young rice poking through the Nile's mud plain after the first Inundation, and let me be the first to say, it wasn't exactly alluring. In truth, the man looked a little like an obese and aging version of Heath Ledger's Joker in *The Dark Knight*, only not nearly as cute. Poor man.

Strangely enough, I liked him immediately.

I liked him even more when he stuck out a humongous hand and offered me a friendly smile. "I'm Arthur," he said.

"I'm Harlie. Harlie Rose."

We shook hands, and I nodded toward the soaked high-heeled slippers the man still cradled in his other paw. "You might try a blow-dryer on those feathers. Put it on low so they won't get all splintered and frazzled."

The old drag queen brightened. "You think?"

I shrugged. "Don't see why not."

The two of us appraised each other for a moment. If the man was embarrassed to be caught in a periwinkle blue dressing gown with marabou-feathered house slippers in his hand and yesterday's makeup slathered and smeared across his rain-spattered face, he certainly didn't show it.

"Looking for an apartment?" Arthur asked. He obviously had no intention of apologizing for the way he looked, and truthfully I saw no reason why he should. Even weirdoes have a right to be weird. This is America, after all.

So I grinned, liking Arthur a little bit more than I already did. "Maybe," I said. "Are the apartments furnished?"

"Sure, honey. Furnished, newly painted, reasonably priced. What more could you ask?"

"Any gay people in the building?"

Arthur looked down at himself, then gazed back at me with a perfectly arched eyebrow cocked high on his forehead. "What do you think?"

I laughed. "Maybe two or three?"

"Maybe. Although it would be simpler to count the straights."

"And how many are there of *those*?"

Arthur made a great show of counting on his fingers, rolling his eyes in concentration, mumbling incoherently to himself while gazing at the ceiling, then finally announced, "One. And he's living with a man who'll soon be a woman. One of these days they'll be getting married."

I considered that. "Then I guess I'll fit right in."

Arthur giggled girlishly, eyeing me up and down and not looking too disappointed at what he was seeing. "I thought you might," he breathed in his best Marilyn Monroe impersonation, which was really bizarre. Then he dropped the Marilyn impersonation, thank God. Even he seemed to realize it simply wasn't working, what with him weighing three hundred pounds and looking the way he did and being dripping wet and all. "Moving in alone, Harlie? Or do you have a boyfriend out there hunkered against the rain waiting for an invitation to join the party?"

I couldn't have stopped the flash of sadness from crossing my face if I had wanted to. I felt it creep over my skin like a fog bank rolling in, but I was powerless to stop it. I tried to cover it up by giving myself another wet-dog shake, but Arthur saw right through me.

A hand the size of a meat loaf came out to gently pat my cheek. "I'm sorry, honey. You're just getting over a broken heart. I can see it on your face. And don't look so surprised. I can spot a broken heart from fifty paces. God knows I've had enough of 'em to be an expert on the subject." He shook out his nonexistent hair like Rita Hayworth. "Well, not to worry. We just had a spate of love affairs come to blossom in this place, and looking the way you do, I see absolutely no reason why it can't happen to you too."

Ignoring the compliment, it was my turn to roll my eyes. "Not interested. I think I've had my fill of love for a while."

Arthur blessed me with a profound look of disbelief. "That's what everybody says until it hits them between the eyes."

"Yeah, but I mean it."

"Of course you do," Arthur smirked. "Just remember, honey, if you can't find a lover looking the way you do, then what hope is there for someone who looks like me?"

I stumbled around for something to say, but before I could get it out, Arthur pressed a perfectly manicured fingertip coated with blood red nail polish to my lips and tutted me to silence. A glimmer of resigned sadness crossed Arthur's face, which I found a little heartbreaking to witness. (Like my heart wasn't broken enough.) But when Arthur finally spoke, he didn't seem to be finagling for a compliment. He was simply telling it like it is.

"I know how I look, young man. I know I'm ridiculous. But hell, why should I try to be someone I'm not? My chances of finding someone to love are practically nil anyway. Might as well be myself while I'm waiting."

I gave him what I hoped was a gentle smile. "Don't cut yourself short, Arthur. I'll bet there's somebody out there right now who'd dig the hell out of a big brawny bear like you. Maybe all you need to do is make a few wardrobe changes. Experiment with a little repackaging. Try to be a bit—well—*butcher*."

Arthur threw his head back and laughed, and while he did it, he clutched his soggy periwinkle robe a little tighter around his paunch. Laugh or no laugh, when he leveled his eyes back to my face, there was a sudden gleam of hope there, buried in amongst the disbelief. I could almost hear Arthur's little wheels turning in that massive head of his, as if he was suddenly considering what I had said.

"Me? Butch? You think so? You think I could pull it off?"

I studied him, wondering what sort of Pandora's box I had opened. "Clothes make the man, or so they say. Won't know until you try, I guess."

Arthur pondered that. Then a lecherous glint sparked his eyes. Again he looked me up and down, from the crown of my dripping head to the toes of my dripping shoes. "So do *you* like big old fuzzy bears?" he asked hopefully. He spat up a grumbly growl from somewhere deep in his mountainous chest, which I suspected was meant to be sexy.

I blushed, sorry I had steered Arthur's train into the wrong siding. "Nope. Not me. Sorry."

Arthur harrumphed good-naturedly and barked, "That's what I thought!"

Then with a smile, Arthur clutched me gently by the crook of my arm and steered me toward the staircase. "Come along, honey. Forget about this old queer. I'm a lost cause anyway. Let's talk business. Those blossoming love affairs I told you about left me with a slew of vacancies, what with everybody joining forces and moving in with one another all over the place. Let's show you what's available. The quicker we find an apartment you like, the quicker you can get out of those wet clothes and begin the process of *not* looking for another lover, bear or otherwise."

"Wiseass," I muttered, but I smiled a little anyway at Arthur's incorruptible good humor.

Arthur tittered with glee as if to *prove* his good humor was ironclad, even if his heart wasn't. He led me up the stairs on bare feet, leaving watery size twelve footprints glistening in his wake like Bigfoot spoor. Arthur's soggy Carole Lombard pumps still dangled, dripping, from his hairy paw.

Halfway up, Arthur stopped and gazed back to where I was trailing two steps below. "Butch, huh? You really think butch is the way for me to go?"

I was beginning to shiver in my wet clothes, but there was such an earnest look in Arthur's eyes when he asked the question, and no small amount of hope there as well, I decided to honor the question with an honest-to-God answer.

"Sure. Why not? If the current demographic you're shooting for hasn't responded to your bait, then it's time to shoot for an alternate demographic. And sprucing up the bait can't hurt either."

Arthur's face lit up. "Ooh. You mean more makeup?"

I narrowed my eyes. "Less."

Arthur's face fell. "Less?"

"None, actually, would work best."

"None? You mean *no makeup whatsoever?*"

I shrugged. "Sorry, Arthur. It's a dog-eat-dog world out there, and if you want to be a Rottweiler, you can't go around looking like a French poodle."

"Pithy," Arthur grumped.

I eyed him up and down, as Arthur had done me. What I saw wasn't promising. I squinted my eyes in thought. Then I snapped my fingers. God, I was smart.

"Construction worker! That might work. Or, wait. Maybe a cowboy! A big, butch, hairy cowboy."

Arthur frowned. Worry lines dug trenches into the veneer of pancake #10 smeared across his brow. "Horses and guns scare the sillies out of me, honey."

I laughed. How could I not? "Christ, Arthur, I'm not asking you to join a posse or have a shoot-out behind the saloon with Jesse James and the gang. I just mean *dress* like a cowboy. Get some jeans, boots, a hat. Maybe some open-assed chaps." I eyed Arthur's three hundred pounds—as seen through periwinkle blue chiffon that really didn't cover nearly as much of Arthur as I wished it would—up and down again. "Well, maybe not open-assed chaps, Arthur. But for Christ's sake lose the chiffon. A nice checkered lumberjacky shirt with snap buttons and maybe a bolo tie would be nice. What d'you think? And the first thing you need to do to be butch is stop calling everybody 'honey' and saying words like 'sillies.'"

"I like 'honey.' I like 'sillies.' And chiffon is so comfortable. It breathes. It *flows.*"

I grunted. "It might be best if you didn't say things like that either."

"Can I at least put a feather in the hat?"

I tried not to groan as I remembered the feather boa in the plastic ficus in the lobby. "As long as it's only one and as long as it isn't pink and as long as it's not a fucking ostrich plume, I guess it's okay."

Arthur's face fell. "Darn. Who knew butch people had to follow so many rules?"

I figured this conversation was only going to get worse, so I thought nipping it in the bud might be the best thing I could do with it. Conversational euthanasia. That's what was called for.

I cast my eyes past Arthur and let them travel wistfully up the stairs. "Umm. About that apartment?"

Arthur looked like he was blinking himself back to reality, or what I suspected was the nearest thing to reality Arthur would ever know. "Right. Of course. Come on, honey. Oops, sorry. Come on, *Harlie*. Let's show you what I've got. One of the units ought to suit your needs. And hopefully it'll be one on a lower floor. I hate these goddamn stairs."

"In that case," I said, sympathizing with the man and at the same time freezing my ass off in my soaking wet clothes, "got anything on two?"

Arthur beamed. "Oh lord, honey. Aren't you the sweetest thing! Yes! Yes, I do! Come on, I'll show it to you right away! You'll love it! I know you will. It's a bit weatherworn, but it has a little slip of puce carpet on the floor, and new curtains, and you can have a pet if you want as long as it's not a giraffe or something. I'll even knock a few bucks off the rent for giving me sartorial assistance with my wardrobe, and by the way, this unit has a brand new refrigerator and, oh, the bathroom! Wait'll you see it! It's got—"

Arthur was still talking twenty minutes later as I signed a one-year lease for Apartment 2A, which was just as cute and darling as Arthur said it was. As for being weatherworn, which it most certainly was with its painted-shut windows and hazy bathroom mirror and ancient wall heater in only one room—well, what the heck? After thinking about it for a couple of minutes, I decided those faults weren't faults at all. They were character traits. Old world charm, so to speak. Like the extremely limited closet space, which must be how people lived eighty or ninety years ago when the Belladonna Arms was built. That was a character trait too.

And with those rationalizations clearing the way, suddenly I was happy as hell to call the Belladonna Arms my new home. In a spurt of gratitude, I gave Arthur a hug and thanked him profusely, all of which made Arthur blush all over like a red-hot pot-bellied stove.

I spent the rest of the day dashing from car to apartment in the pouring rain, arranging my meager belongings in my new home exactly the way I wanted them. As the apartment gradually took shape, I began to wonder where my life would go from here—and if another love really might manage to worm its way into my damaged heart as Arthur implied it would.

Standing in a steaming shower to wash away the chill of the storm still raging outside my tiny bathroom window, a crush of loneliness suddenly settled over me. I wept a little, remembering Dan. The way Dan once laughed before the laughter stopped. The way he once loved me before the loving stopped.

The way Dan had walked away on that last day we were together—had walked away without even once looking back.

That thought was such a soul killer, I squeezed my eyes shut to block it out for what must have been the thousandth time, fiercely focusing my thoughts on my unwritten book instead.

My book, I thought, desperately clinging to the possibilities it offered. *That'll be enough to get me through this first lonely day of my new existence. I'll work on my book.*

But I wasn't dumb. I knew even the book wouldn't be enough to fill the avalanche of empty days bound to follow this one.

Cranking the squeaky shower handle to OFF, I rubbed myself down with a towel. No longer dripping, but still depressed as hell, I studied my naked reflection in the bathroom mirror.

I WAS a pretty good-looking guy. Everyone said so, and I had to admit it. Hell, even Dan had said I was cute before he stopped noticing. Not to say I could be a model or anything, but at least I wasn't troll material. I didn't exude snail slime when I walked. Or reek to high heaven or make unfortunate noises when I sat down.

I stand five ten and wear my straight-as-a-string reddish blond hair past my collar and perpetually in my eyes, which are blue and slightly astigmatic. Dan used to tell me I had the skin color of golden sand baking on a sun-drenched beach. That was before he told me to fuck off and get the hell out, of course. I also sport a smooth chest with nary a hair in sight except for a tiny trail of reddish fuzz leading down from my belly button to my crotch. My entire body, from toe to crown, is carved in the slim, neat lines of a long-distance runner. And like a runner's, my legs are strong and sculpted, if I say so myself. They are also nicely coated with a brushing of pale hair, and every trick I have ever entertained in my life has told me they were the most beautiful legs they had ever seen.

Not that I let it go to my head, mind you. In truth, I was neither unhappy with my body, nor particularly proud of it. I thought it was nice enough as bodies went, as long as everything was working properly, but it didn't hold a candle to countless others I had seen.

Take Dan's body for instance.

Always attracted to darker men, I had fallen hard the first time I saw Dan in running shorts at the San Diego Marathon, where we first met three years back. Dan's long, graceful frame, dusted with dark hair across his chest and another smattering of dark hair trailing down across his belly and disappearing beneath the waistband of those sexy-ass shorts he had worn that day, was everything I had ever fantasized about in a man. Long, hairy legs, a luscious fuzzy ass, and a smile that could melt aluminum when the guy really turned on the high beams.

Keeping pace through the cheering crowd that day, we had chatted each other up and down during the long run. Two hours after the race ended, we were in bed together, sipping electrolytes, trying not to let our legs cramp up, all the while foraging happily on each other's naked bodies. Before the sun set on that first day, through lips that tasted of come and Gatorade, we were talking about moving in together.

Two weeks later we actually did.

Our love affair lasted until Dan coolly pulled the plug, without explanation or apology, two and a half years later. That was four months ago.

My long road trip had been little more than a coward's way to run from the pain. I knew that now.

So here I was. Starting over. Parking my ass in one place with an honest-to-God roof over my head and a carpet under my feet that wasn't a floor mat from Pep Boys and getting back to the business of living my life the way it was meant to be lived.

I stood in the cramped fifties-style bathroom with the green and brown tile on the countertops and the claw-footed tub with the plain green shower curtain surrounding it on a circular metal rod and stared at myself in the age-stained bathroom mirror. As unhappy as I was, I still watched a smile creep across the reflection of my face when I thought of my poor newly-minted landlord, Arthur. Jesus, now there was a guy with problems. As low as I felt when considering my own problems, the thought of Arthur could still bring a smile to my face. The guy was priceless. He really was. I wondered if I really *could* butch Arthur up a bit. Didn't seem likely. But then, you never know. Stranger things had happened. Although I couldn't think of any offhand.

Still, in the grand scheme of world events, it would probably be wiser to concentrate on my own problems rather than anyone else's. Wouldn't it?

My immediate bucket list of things to do, or *gets*, as I called them, wasn't that daunting. Get in touch with a cable company and get the computer online. Get to a supermarket and stock up on food. Get started on the book. Find a way to finally get over Dan. (Big exclamation mark after *that* one.) Get a part-time job to plug the holes in my income the scant royalties from my four other published books never quite filled. And finally, get my head out of my ass and start functioning like a responsible human being.

I supposed the part-time job should be one of the first problems I needed to tackle. Not that I was desperate for cash, really. Not yet. But I would be one of these days. Living on a budget didn't bother me much. I was used to it. Even living with Dan and sharing expenses, I had needed to watch my money. But still, writing the two-thousand-dollar first and last month rent and deposit check to Arthur had unnerved me a bit since I had been living in my car for the past four months, where the biggest expenditure I had faced was filling up the gas tank now and then.

I would grow accustomed to paying rent again soon enough. After all, I had been writing and slogging away at low-paying jobs for the past five years, which was how long I had been a published author.

Now, at twenty-eight, I took the part-time jobs in my stride, cashed the measly paychecks that came my way without worrying about my poverty level too much because I still had my royalty checks to fall back on. Still, I managed to keep my mind centered where it truly belonged—on my WIP. After all, writers are always worried about their WIPs. Works in Progress don't complete themselves, you know. Be they books, lives, or love affairs, we all have one or two WIPs we're trying to coax into shape at any given time. I might not have a love affair going at the moment, but I certainly had a book and a life in need of a little help.

I stopped ogling my naked self in the mirror and did a couple of jumping jacks to get my ass moving. It was time to get to work on that bucket list. I glanced through the bathroom window, which only moments before during a lull in the storm had offered a lovely, if hazy, view of the San Diego skyline off in the distance. Now all I could see was rain. Cold, torrential, pummeling rain.

Not that it bothered me. I liked rain, no matter how pummeling it was. Most San Diegans do, since they don't see it very often. Still, the middle of a deluge wasn't the best time in the world to be looking for a job. Maybe I'd hold off on that until the weather eased up. I had other things I could do, anyway. Plenty of them.

Still naked, I padded through the apartment on my bare feet, dick swinging pleasantly free, enjoying the air on my bare skin. I peered into the closets where I had just arranged my few articles of clothing, then scavenged through the kitchen cupboards and drawers, peeking into every single one before finding what I was looking for. A San Diego phone book.

I dug my cell phone out of the backpack where I had stowed it last and called the first Internet provider I found listed in the yellow pages.

When an appointment had been set for the following day, I flicked off the phone, said good-bye to my naked self, threw on some clothes and a coat, grabbed an umbrella I had forgotten I owned until I found it when I unpacked earlier, and set out to buy some groceries.

Lives don't write themselves any more than WIPs do. Nosirree. Might as well get started living mine right now. And to live it, I needed food.

I locked the apartment door behind me, taking a moment to brush my fingertips fondly over the 2A screwed onto the front of the door in something that resembled copper but probably wasn't. I trotted my way down the one flight of stairs to the front door, wondering if I'd see Arthur along the way, which I didn't.

I had a feeling I was going to like the Belladonna Arms. I wasn't sure why. The place was actually kind of a dump. *But hey,* I thought, popping open the umbrella and ducking underneath it as I strolled out the door and into the rain, *it's kind of a happy dump. And happy is exactly what I need right now. Christ knows I've been morose long enough.*

By the time I sloshed my way to the car, I was surprised to hear myself whistling. And wasn't *that* a stunning revelation.

With the first twist of the key in the ignition, the old Buick station wagon sucked in a gallon of gas, farted a flume of carcinogens, and roared to life, just as it always did.

As I pulled away from the curb with windshield wipers whapping out a cheerful drumbeat, I suddenly realized two words were repeating themselves inside my head—the same two words, over and over and over again, pecking away at my skullcap like a flock of persistent woodpeckers digging for termites in a hollow log. I had a feeling those two words had been echoing back and forth between my ears for a while now. Even before I noticed they were there. When I finally realized what the two words were, I smiled a little wider. When it dawned on me the words inside my head were written in big-ass capital letters, all flourishy and ornate and maybe even in Technicolor, I barked out a laugh, which *really* startled the crap out of me.

And still the words kept hammering inside my noggin.

Fuck Dan Fuck Dan Fuck Dan Fuck Dan—

Chapter 2

WHEN I returned from the store, laden with grocery bags and once again soaked all the way down to my socks and BVDs, I found a cat sitting outside the door to good old apartment 2A, my brand new home. The cat looked a little perturbed that he'd been forced to wait so long, which was a surprise to me since I'd never seen the cat before in my life. The cat was white with a black tail, one black ear, and a little black Hitler moustache, which made him look sinister. He was also fat. Really fat. Folds of cat fat were rolling off him in every direction like pictures I had seen of Mauna Loa upchucking lava. I figured if poor Arthur ever reincarnated into a feline, this was what he'd probably look like.

"Meow," the cat griped, pausing for a moment from licking his butt to look up and say it.

"Meow back atcha." I grinned.

"That's Ralph," a voice cooed behind me. The voice held a subtle Spanish accent, very lilting and sexy, very pleasant to the ear. I turned to see a cute Mexican guy with pink hair and another cute Mexican guy hanging on to the first cute Mexican guy's arm. The second cute Mexican guy had his dark hair braided in cornrows. Both were in their early twenties, small and fit and wearing cargo shorts and matching yellow muscle shirts. They were wearing them to great advantage too, showing off luscious, sexy arms and lean, fuzzy legs all wrapped up nicely in taut, lovely skin the color of sun-ripened filberts. Being a cross between a blond and a redhead, I envied their skin tone immediately. I also found it very attractive. But I let my intrigue begin and end there. The two young men were obviously an item, and I respected relationships above all else. Especially after the way my own had self-destructed a few months back.

Trying not to count the weeks in my head from the last time I had partaken of sex with anyone other than myself, I juggled the grocery bags in my arms and said "Oh, uh, hi."

"Hi," the two cuties echoed, giving me a thorough once-over before the three of us focused our attention back on the cat, who was once again licking his butt. He seemed to be enjoying it too.

"Reminds me of you last night," the first cutie said to the second cutie.

The second cutie nodded, pulling the first cutie a little closer. "*Ay*. Does it ever. Except I wasn't licking myself."

At this juncture, the first cutie had the good grace to blush. "No, precious, you certainly weren't." He then proceeded to wiggle his ass around as if fond memories had crawled down his pants and set up housekeeping, which spurred the other cutie to drag him even closer and start gnawing on his neck like a really hungry guy with a turkey leg.

"Ahem," I said, trying to head off a hard-on. Watching these two was enough to excite *anybody*. I again shifted the grocery bags around in my arms until I had a free hand, which I promptly stuck out in their direction. "I'm Harlie. I guess you two already know each other." Understatement of the century.

Both cuties ignored the outstretched hand and swooped in to give me a raucous hug, smashing my bread and spilling a bag of oranges, which went rolling and bouncing down the hall.

"Welcome to the Belladonna Arms! I'm Ramon," the pink-haired one said, releasing me to go chasing after the oranges.

"And I'm ChiChi. We live on six," Cornrows said, watching Ramon gathering up my fruit purchases with a grin on his face while his arms were still wrapped around me tight, flattening my bread a little flatter, and getting his shorts and T-shirt soaking wet since I was still dripping from the storm, which didn't seem to bother ChiChi at all.

And since ChiChi smelled really, really good hanging all over me, and felt all warm and fluffy to boot, I suddenly realized I was in dire danger of *another* hard-on if the guy didn't get the hell off.

Ralph didn't seem to be interested in any of it. With one leg now pointed straight out behind him like a ballet dancer at arabesque, he began applying every ounce of concentration he could muster into the act of licking his balls, a skill every human present undoubtedly envied, even if we hadn't known each other long enough to actually admit it out loud.

"So he's *your* cat, then," I said, reluctantly but firmly easing myself from ChiChi's embrace. I wasn't sure but I thought I felt a boner brush my hip when I did it, and the boner sure as hell wasn't my own. Not yet anyway.

"No," Ramon answered, returning with an armload of oranges and feebly flapping a limp wrist at the cat. "We just feed him now and then. We're not even sure his name is Ralph. That's just what we call him on those days he comes around to raid the fridge."

Ralph was now scratching at my door, demanding entry. I figured what the hell, and doing a little more juggling of grocery bags while ChiChi and Ramon looked patiently on, I plucked the door key from my pants pocket and jiggled it in the lock.

Tail high, proudly exposing a spit-moistened rear end for all to see and admire (which reminded me of Ramon being moistened by ChiChi, and damn, wasn't *that* a disconcerting thought!), Ralph waited for a crack to appear in the door wide enough to accommodate his massive ass, and as soon as one did he immediately flounced through it. He still seemed a little annoyed it had taken so long to get through the door. Like he'd been hanging around that hallway *forever*.

None too shy themselves, Ramon and ChiChi followed Ralph into the apartment sans invitation, Ramon still cradling his armload of oranges.

Since I was the only one left standing in the hall, I snipped, "Why don't you all come inside then," which was pretty much a waste of breath because Ramon and ChiChi and even the cat had already traipsed all the way through the apartment and were now milling around the kitchen. Ralph was sitting on the kitchen table as if he owned it. He was looking around with the supercilious air of an impatient diner trying to hail a lazy-ass waiter. Ramon carefully dumped his armload of oranges into the sink so they wouldn't roll all over the place. And ChiChi was once again chewing on Ramon's neck while he did it. Ramon and ChiChi seemed to be very affectionate. And they seemed to be very affectionate *continually*.

I eased my bags down onto the table, displacing the cat, which Ralph didn't seem to be too pleased about, and snipped again, "You guys just get married or something?"

"Nope. Not married," Ramon gasped. He gasped because at that precise moment, ChiChi had stuck his tongue in his ear. "But we just moved in together a while back."

I figured they must be part of the rash of new love affairs Arthur had told me about. "Well, congratulations."

ChiChi had Ramon pressed up against the sink, crotch to crotch, legs intertwined. They really were *extremely* affectionate. They stopped snogging each other long enough to turn and study me standing there looking out of place in my own kitchen. "Are we embarrassing you?" ChiChi asked.

Yes, I thought.

"No," I said, deciding *yes* would have been unneighborly. Although I really was getting horny watching them, and being horny was about the last thing I needed to contend with since I had no one to relieve the horniness *with*.

"Got a lover?" Ramon asked, as if reading my mind. Shyness apparently was not a problem Ramon coped with on any sort of regular basis, although he didn't look nearly as eager to hear my answer as ChiChi did.

"Not me," I blithely purred, feeling a blush rising to the back of my neck and hoping it wouldn't work its way around to my cheeks where everyone could see it. "I'm single. I like being single. I have no intention of becoming *un*single for a very long time." I had a vague suspicion I was protesting too much, not to mention lying through my teeth, but I wasn't about to admit it to myself or anyone else.

Ramon and ChiChi apparently suspected the same. I could tell by the way they snickered.

Then ChiChi explained why. "Don't get too used to being single. Everybody in this building falls in love sooner or later. I'm afraid there's nothing you can do about it, either. It's something in the air. Like mildew or asbestos poisoning. Or maybe it's in the walls. Like dry rot."

Ramon slapped his lover's arm. "*Ay, pendejo!* Those aren't very romantic comparisons!" He turned to me. "It's more like pollen, my handsome new friend. Yeah. That's it. Love pollen. Very sweet, very sticky. When you live in the Arms for a while, it sort of settles on you like dust. It crawls up your nose and into your heart, digs in under your skin and down your pants, gets you itching, gets you looking, gets you *wanting* to fall in love. Wanting it more than *anything*."

And Ramon immediately proved himself right by grinning and exposing two beautiful dimples, which I fell in love with immediately.

Mesmerized by those sexy-ass dimples, but not feeling too comfortable about it since the man was standing there in his lover's arms, for God's sake, I gave myself a shake and began unpacking my groceries. While I was doing that, Ralph the cat rooted through the bags, wondering if there was anything for him. Which there wasn't. Apparently Ralph didn't give a shit for romance. He just wanted sustenance. Which was actually the last thing he needed, the fat fuck.

Ramon and ChiChi were still standing at the kitchen sink wrapped in each other's arms. Watching me. Watching the cat. Then, eyes wide, they turned to study each other as if they had just been struck by the same thought at the very same time. ChiChi was wearing a happy, mischievous expression, while Ramon was beginning to look uncomfortable.

"But he's so cute," ChiChi said, eyeing Ramon with wide, teasing eyes.

"Please don't do this," Ramon whispered.

I stopped unpacking the groceries to study my two guests. "Who's so cute?"

ChiChi and Ramon were too busy eyeballing each other to put much energy into answering, although ChiChi threw me a tidbit of information like a tourist at Sea World tossing a three-dollar fish to a dolphin.

"The cat. We're talking about the cat."

"Yeah, that's right," Ramon hastily echoed. "We're talking about the cat."

I glanced at the cat, then back at them. "Whatever floats your boat," I said.

Still staring at his lover, ChiChi leered and gave Ramon a wink. "I'm going to go for it, with or without your permission. You know that, don't you?"

Ramon simply stared back. One word, barely audible, escaped his lips. "Slut."

"You bet," ChiChi said, giving me a glance. Then he turned back to Ramon. "Tell me you don't think he's cute."

Ramon nodded, but he didn't look happy about it. "All right. He's cute."

"Sexy."

Again Ramon dragged the words out. His brow furrowed as if he didn't like the way they sounded on his lips. "Yes. Sexy."

My ears were getting warm. "Are you guys talking about me?"

ChiChi flapped a dismissive hand in my direction. "Don't be silly."

Ramon stayed mute. But if looks could kill, ChiChi would have been dead a dozen times over.

Once again they spoke as if I weren't in the room, and it was starting to get a little annoying. For all they cared, I might have been a potted plant standing in the middle of my very own kitchen. "We could do it together," ChiChi said. "You never know. You might like it."

Ramon thought about that, or pretended to. I wasn't sure which. How *could* I be when I really didn't know what the hell Ramon and ChiChi were talking about to begin with? "If you don't want to participate, you can just watch and jack off. That might be interesting."

That got my attention. "Watch who? Jack off with who? You and the cat?"

"Yeah," ChiChi tittered, burying his face in Ramon's shirtfront and sneaking a peek at me while he was at it. "Maybe we'll ask him up to watch TV, Ramon. That should get the ball rolling."

Ramon narrowed his eyes. His voice was a desperate hiss when again he said, "Please don't do this, Cheech."

I blinked. What the hell were they talking about. Cats don't watch TV. Do they? And even if they did, who in the world would invite them over to watch it? And as for the jacking off part, I didn't even want to think about that.

ChiChi's face lit up. "This weekend. I'll do it this weekend."

"No," Ramon pleaded. "I only want *you* in my bed."

"You're taking the cat to bed?" I asked, getting more confused by the minute.

ChiChi's hand flapped me to silence. "Oh hush." Turning back to his lover, he said, "We have planning to do."

"I won't have it," Ramon blustered. But even I could see his bluster was falling on deaf ears.

Ignoring Ramon completely, ChiChi turned to me, all bright-eyed and cheerful and innocent. "Well. Gotta run, neighbor. Nice to meet you. Good luck with the cat. Love what you've done with the place. Don't take any wooden pesos."

And before I could even say good-bye, the two were gone, hustling themselves across the apartment and out the front door, Ramon being pulled along by ChiChi, limp and unresisting, while ChiChi was still giggling and whispering and conspiring at his side, although I still didn't know what about. Even with all the whispering and giggling and conspiring going on, I noticed ChiChi still had time to give Ramon's ass an affectionate squeeze before they disappeared through the door. But the second he did, Ramon slapped it away.

Ramon was pissed off, that much was clear. But I still didn't really understand why. Did I?

Needing a second opinion, I turned to the cat. "What was that all about?"

"Meow," Ralph said, scooting a can of tuna across the table in my direction with his nose.

"My God," I said, gaping at the can. "Don't tell me you can read."

Ralph refused to acknowledge that statement. He merely plopped himself down in the middle of the table like a flowerpot and waited for me to serve up the tuna.

Knowing I was in over my head, I started digging around for a can opener, which I had just bought. It was in one of the bags. By the time Ralph was gobbling up the tuna and adding another two or three ounces to his already chunky ass, I had forgotten about Ramon and ChiChi and their odd conversation.

Well. Except for the boner (*ChiChi's* boner) I was pretty sure I had felt brushing my hip earlier. And their legs. All four of their legs. Twined around each other, looking all fuzzy and tanned and scrumptious. I thought about those sexy buggers for the rest of the day.

I SPENT the afternoon on the living room floor, sorting through the countless index cards on which I had jotted down ideas for my upcoming book as I had tooled around the country for the last four months in my behemoth old Buick. Many of the cards didn't make any sense at all, while others I couldn't decipher because of my atrocious handwriting. Those I threw away. Still I ended up with hundreds of wrinkled, dirty, scrawled-upon index cards, many of which were stained and smudged and pretty disgusting looking from having spent the past few months being trampled into the gunk on the floorboard of my car.

Next I arranged the remaining mountain of index cards into three piles—beginning, middle, end—as if I were plotting a three-act play. When that was finished and I had three smaller hills of cards in front of me, I separated each one of those hills into separate piles, each pile denoting a chapter of the story. Thus I had a gradual unfolding of the plot that had been simmering in my head for weeks and weeks. This gave me a sort of half-ass outline with which to direct the writing when I actually sat down to do it.

As unlovely as it was, this was my system. This was how I worked. I was pretty sure other writers would simply pull out a gun and shoot themselves in the head if they had to work this way. But that was their problem.

Once I had twenty-eight piles of index cards in front of me, which was apparently how many chapters the story would take to complete, barring an infusion of fresh ideas along the way, I tapped the cards into alignment and circled each pile with a rubber band. I then tucked an unused index card into the top of each pile and numbered them sequentially. Chapters 1 through 28.

Sitting back and rubbing my aching back, I stared at the twenty-eight neatly aligned stacks before me. There. Now all I had to do was write the fucking thing.

A knock at the door brought me out of my reverie. I groaned myself to my feet and gazed around for Ralph. I spotted the cat sprawled on top of the refrigerator, head dangling over the side, sound asleep and snoring. The plate of tuna on the kitchen floor was squeaky clean. Ralph had eaten it all.

Another knock at the door got my ass moving. Trying not to creak after sitting cross-legged on the floor for the past two hours, I dragged myself across the room, molded my face into a semblance of welcoming piety, and pulled open the door.

The man standing on my doorstep was the most drop-dead gorgeous hunk of manhood I had ever seen in my life. Buzz-cut brown hair. Green eyes. The man had lovely hairy arms and a shadow of dark beard graced his sculpted jawline. An intriguing cluster of dark chest hair peeked out from the top of his white V-necked T-shirt, and boy, was that intriguing as hell. The man had such a perfect body—tall, slim-hipped, graceful—it made me almost breathless looking at it. And all those fantastic ingredients were topped off by the sweetest smile and the whitest teeth one could ever imagine, not to mention a bonus serving of dimples on either side. And how scrumptious was *that*? The entire package, with everything taken in toto, damn near made me pass out cold. Jesus God, the guy was hot! And Jesus God, I really had to get myself laid one of these days! I was turning into an absolute lech.

As soon as I could tear my eyes away from the vision on my doorstep, I noticed my caller wasn't alone. A little guy was standing next to him. The little guy had reddish blond hair sort of like mine and a friendly, elfin face. Geeky black glasses sat perched on the end of the elf's nose, and behind the glasses a pair of magnified pale blue eyes gazed out at the world with what appeared to be sweet serenity, which in my opinion befitted an elf perfectly. The little guy had his hand in the hunk's back pocket, looking proprietary as hell, and who in their right mind could blame him. He seemed to find my reaction to the first sight of the man standing next to him amusingly familiar. Perhaps he had had the very same reaction the first time *he* laid eyes on that perfect face. And body. And hair. And teeth. And dimples. Etc., etc. Of course, I didn't know *for sure* that was what the little guy was thinking, but I figured I couldn't be far from wrong.

While I pondered all this, it was the little guy who first stuck out his paw, giving me a hardy handshake. "I'm Stanley. This is my lover, Roger. We just stopped by to welcome you to the building."

The two men were dressed almost exactly alike in faded blue jeans and tees. Their feet were bare. The only adornment on either of them was a plastic bracelet on the little guy in the colors of gay pride. Well, no, that wasn't quite true. The biggest adornment the little guy sported was the stunning specimen of manhood standing next to him.

I trailed my eyes from one to the other, and as soon as I could tear them away from the one with the perfect dimples, I settled my gaze on the smaller man. "Well, aren't you the luckiest fucker in the world" I wanted to say, but of course I didn't.

What I did say was "I'm Harlie. Harlie Rose. It's nice to meet you both. Uh, come on in. The apartment's a wreck but come on in anyway."

"Thanks," the gorgeous hunk said, and I stepped aside as Roger tugged the little elfish guy through the door behind him. They were kind of a mismatched set, these two, but each man was so obviously devoted to the other it made me feel all warm and bubbly (and jealous as hell) just watching them. I couldn't help wondering if Dan and I had *ever* been that close.

Roger gazed around like a tourist while I ushered them all the way inside. Both men scoped out my messy apartment with imperturbable good humor. There were unshelved books everywhere, several stacks of index cards still scattered across the floor, and a collection of dictionaries, a *Chicago Manual of Style*, and several thesauruses piled high on the edge of my desk next to my computer. An open box of books on the coffee table caught Roger's eye. The author of each and every one of those books, or so it said on the covers, was Harlie Rose.

"Wow," Roger exclaimed, pulling his lover closer. "Look, Stanley. Harlie's a writer."

The little guy's face lit up. He picked up one of the books, flipped it over to peruse the blurb, then trained his sweet blue eyes on me. "I'm impressed. I'll have to read your books. We both will."

"Absolutely," Roger chimed in.

I laughed, honestly touched. I also tried desperately not to blush. "That's great. I just doubled my readership."

Roger snorted. "That bad, huh?"

I grinned. "Well, maybe not quite." I found myself really liking these guys. They were so damned *nice*. And now I was around them both for—what, two minutes?—I was finding the little guy as sexy as the hunk. Suddenly I understood their relationship completely. They honestly *belonged* together. Everything about them screamed "perfect match."

"Are we interrupting the creative juices?" Roger asked with a smile.

Just hearing the word "juices" coming from that gorgeous mouth made my hair stand on end. It was at that moment I decided I had best find a trick really soon to take the edge off my hunger for man flesh or somebody might come knocking on my door only to find the new resident of 2A self-incinerated into a little pile of horny ashes on the living room floor. Four months was too long to go without sex. *Way* too long.

Then I remembered there was still a question hanging in the air waiting to be answered.

"Oh. Uh, no. I seem to be a quart low on creative juices at the moment." I glanced down at the scattered stacks of index cards. "Just trying to get a handle on my new work in progress. Don't know if I'm succeeding or not."

Stanley pointed into the kitchen. "Look! There's Studley!"

All eyes turned to Ralph, who still lay sprawled atop the refrigerator snoring like a drunken sailor.

"Studley?" I asked. "I thought his name was Ralph."

"Depends on who's feeding him," Roger said. "Studley's not picky. He's an equal opportunity sponger. He sponges chow from anybody who lets him in."

"So who does he belong to?" I asked. "Arthur?"

Stanley giggled. "Arthur's the only one who *doesn't* feed him. Arthur's allergic to cats. Nope," Stanley explained, "Studley's a free agent. Nobody knows who he belongs to. Heck, maybe no one. Maybe he's just another resident of the Belladonna Arms. Sort of a pet-in-residence. Comes with the rent. Like bedbugs." Stanley saw my eyes pop open wide. "Kidding," he quickly added. "No bedbugs. No bedbugs."

"You didn't just feed him, did you?" Roger asked, still staring at Studley, or Ralph, or whatever the hell his name really was.

I shrugged. "Well, yeah. He was hungry. I gave him a can of tuna."

Roger's heavenly green eyes crinkled up in laughter. "So did I. Not more than three hours ago. I'll bet he picked out the can himself."

"Yeah, he did," I said, grinning back. "I think he can read. Maybe I should hire him to proof my next book."

"I don't think he's *that* smart," Stanley chuckled, eyeing the old reprobate still sawing logs on top the fridge. Oddly, Stanley didn't sound too convinced when he said it.

As if suddenly realizing he was being talked about, Ralph (or Studley) pried open his eyes and looked around. He gave himself a languid stretch, sniffed his ass to make sure it was still there, then dragged himself to his feet. Hopping down to the kitchen counter with a grunt, he dropped the rest of the way to the floor, which pretty much shook the whole building. He stalked past the three of us as if we weren't there and disappeared through the open door. The last we saw of him, he was heading up the stairs to three like he had been invited somewhere for brunch.

I cupped my hands around my mouth and yelled, "You're welcome. Come again."

Stanley was still holding one of my books. The latest one, in fact. When Studley was good and gone, he returned his attention to the book, studying the blurb on the back again. "This sounds great," Stanley said. "Can't wait to read it."

"Then take it with you," I said. "Bring it back when you're done. Or better yet, keep it. I've got boxes."

Roger plucked the book from Stanley's hand and returned it to the box on the coffee table. "I think we'd rather support the arts the old-fashioned way. We'll buy the books ourselves. That way the author can earn a little money so he can continue to feed all the other stray animals that come knocking at his door. I assume they're on Amazon. The books, I mean."

"Sure," I said, honestly touched. "Amazon. Barnes & Noble. Wherever. Thanks."

Stanley's eyes emitted a mischievous twinkle. "We will expect the author to sign them, of course."

And once more I felt the blood rush to the back of my neck, not because I was embarrassed this time, but because I was flattered. "Well, sure. I'd be happy to."

"Good," Roger said, once again extending his hand. When I raised my own hand to meet it, both Roger and Stanley took hold of it. A three-way handshake ensued. It was the first I had ever experienced. When it was finished and everyone had released their grasp on everyone else, I had the strangest feeling I had just made two new friends.

"We'll let you get back to work," Roger said, smiling when Stanley's hand slid back into his rear pocket. To me, he said, while laying a hand at the small of his lover's back, "We're up on five. In 5C. Stop by any time you want. And welcome to the building. Arthur *said* you were nice."

That surprised me. "Did he?"

They both nodded. Stanley added, "Arthur's nice too when you get to know him. A little eccentric, but nice."

"Oh, is he eccentric?" I asked.

Both Roger and Stanley howled with laughter at that one.

Even I couldn't keep a straight face. "I told him he should butch up his act if he wants to find a boyfriend."

Roger seemed to find that even more amusing than calling Arthur eccentric. "Yes, well, we'll just all hold our breaths and wait for that to pan out, shall we?"

The three of us giggled like a trio of schoolgirls gossiping on the playground.

Stanley waggled his fingers in my direction and tugged Roger further toward the door.

"Seeya," he said, making a final adjustment to the glasses on his face. Roger's hand was resting at the back of Stanley's neck now, and once again I thought how lucky they both were to be so content in each other's company.

Especially the little guy. My God, talk about winning the lottery!

I stood at my door and watched the two troop arm in arm up the stairs, speaking softly between themselves. They were a little classier than ChiChi and Ramon but, in their own way, just as affectionate.

Wow. Maybe the Belladonna Arms really *did* spit out some sort of weird-ass love pollen onto its residents. And maybe if I got lucky it would even deign to sprinkle a little on me.

I let that thought twinkle around inside my head for all of three seconds before I softly closed the door and dragged myself back to reality.

Locked away in my apartment, once again alone, I chuckled to myself. *Yeah, right,* I thought. *Love pollen. Put that in a book, why don't you? See how far it gets you.*

I scooped up the stacks of index cards still scattered across the living room floor and placed them neatly on the hand-me-down desk that came with the apartment. Moving to the window, I stared out at the rain.

The storm was still pummeling the coast. Rain was coming down in buckets, interspersed now with hail. The streets were awash with it. The hail had gathered in the gutters looking white and snowy and totally out of place for a Southern California April.

Somewhere back in the recesses of my brain, a flash of memory sparked behind my eyes. It was a memory of Dan. Naked. Clutching me tight. We had awoken in each other's arms at some point or other in the middle of the night during one of the early months of our relationship. It was back in the days when we still believed our love would be enough to keep us together forever.

Forever being a relative term apparently.

With my heart suddenly aching in my chest, I turned from the rain, and from the memory as well, and focused my eyes on my new apartment. The crummy furniture, the cheap rug on the floor, the smell of emptiness in the air like the place was still vacant.

I squeezed my eyes shut, blocking it all out. I listened to the storm battering the city through the window behind me. I could faintly hear the squeak and groan of the old neon sign on the building's roof clattering in the elements. And while I listened to the rain and the wind and the spatter and tinkle of hail on glass, I wondered what Dan was doing now. I wondered who he was with.

The first tear that skittered down my cheek was a surprise. It was also the last.

I stared down at my feet for a moment before raising my head and screaming, "Fuck you, Dan!" into the empty room. After that, I headed off to the kitchen to make a sandwich. By the time I got there I was feeling a little better.

I wondered how long that would last.

Chapter 3

I RAN like a greyhound fresh out of the chute—graceful, light, streamlined. At least that was how I ran inside my head. I suppose the truth of it might have been a little less poetic. No matter how I actually *looked*, I loved the sound of my feet slapping the pavement, loved the sparkling morning air washed clean by three solid days of downpour, loved the sporadic glints of dawn peeking through the leftover cloud cover. I even loved the ache in my legs that came from using muscles I hadn't used in a while.

If only I could enjoy being single as much as I enjoyed *running*.

Fucking Dan.

As the blocks rolled away beneath me, the day began to wake. The sun slowly rose to perch itself on the horizon, red and fat and gorgeous. The air blew fresh and crisp and cool through my hair and over my bare legs. I didn't entirely trust a huge bank of black clouds moving in from the west, but since the weatherman said it wouldn't rain again until evening, I decided to risk it.

I headed up Park Boulevard toward the park.

After three days in the Belladonna Arms, I had come to the conclusion that moving there had been a wise choice. The apartment was satisfactory, the neighbors friendly. I even had a cat of sorts. Well. Whenever the cat decided to come around. Not a bad combination of perks for such reasonable rent.

And speaking of rent, after my morning run I would set off in search of a job to supplement my writing income so I could keep myself solvent while I pecked away at my work in progress. *Both works in progress* actually—the damn book and my damn new life.

I wasn't a world-class runner. I'd be the first to admit it. I just liked to jog. At my own pace. I carried a hip pack with me, strapped down tight so it wouldn't bounce around too much, and in it I carried a few bucks, my ID, two pens (in case one ran out of ink), and my ever-present stack of index cards. You never knew when an idea might slap you in the face, and I knew better than anybody that books were made from such spur of the moment ideas. Best to write them down the minute they popped up, otherwise they were known to disappear as quickly as they came into being.

Following the curve of the boulevard, I passed San Diego High. The stately red brick edifice glowered at me, looking forlorn and spooky in the breaking dawn—abandoned, as if even the custodial staff had not yet arrived to crank it into life. Hard to believe in a couple of hours it would be a screaming hive of horny teenagers. I knew. I had attended San Diego High myself, and in my day I had been one of the horniest.

As I pounded past on my weathered Asics, the *thwack thwack thwack* of my footfalls thundered out across the empty football field on the morning air, just as it had thundered into the ether a decade earlier when I and a shitload of other miserable kids had headed out for gym class.

I gave a cluck at the memories my old high school stirred up. But by the time I began chuckling at myself for being so nostalgic about a period in my life I had absolutely detested, my long, loping strides had carried me past the school and past the football field until my memories were left behind in my wake where they fucking well belonged.

With the Navy Hospital complex looming on the right, I crossed the street. I scampered out of the way of a roaring city bus, the windows of which were packed full of gloomy faces, mindlessly staring out at the dawn, each and every one of them obviously less than thrilled to be heading back to work on this Monday morning.

I veered off the macadam and onto the park's perfectly manicured lawn, still wet with rain, where my footsteps were suddenly silenced. Here I was on the outskirts of Balboa Park, and I knew this park like I knew the contours of my own face. I should. I'd been playing in its canyons and promenades since I was a kid. Still played in it, in fact.

Going to the zoo, visiting restaurants, jogging (like now), or simply strolling along with nothing to do but think. It was a perfect place for thinking. Even being alone wasn't so bad in the park.

After ducking into the cool shadows under a copse of trees, I weaved my way into the heart of the park, leaving the sounds of traffic and city life far behind. Here, among the conifers and fountains, along the arbored walkways between silent museums not yet open for business, I let my legs carry me wherever they wished to go. Except for a few other morning joggers and bikers who were also taking advantage of the break in the rain, I had the sidewalks and roads and grassy expanses of Balboa Park all to myself.

On a stretch of lonely trail behind the Air and Space Museum, my echoing footsteps were suddenly joined by another's. The runner came up behind me before I even knew he was there, which pretty much startled the shit out of me.

Before I could turn to see who it was and what the runner was playing at, rushing up behind me like that, I heard a familiar voice with a lilting Mexican accent, albeit a little out of breath, crooning to me from behind.

"You run like a little rabbit, señor. No wonder your ass is so mouthwatering."

Startled, I stopped and whirled around. I stepped aside an instant before the jogger plowed into me, stumbling to a stop about six inches away.

I stood gaping at the man who was panting with exertion. Either he had been running really hard to catch up, or he was totally out of shape.

"ChiChi!" I cried, gasping for breath. "What the hell are you doing? You almost scared the pants off me!"

Looking disappointed, ChiChi pouted as he stared at the pants in question, which were actually my running shorts. Then his face brightened as his eyes trailed up and down, taking in my bare legs and heaving chest. And oddly, the pout returned, this time accompanied by a devilish glint in those smoldering Latin eyes.

"If only I had," ChiChi breathed.

"If only you had *what?*" I asked, wiping the sweat from my face with the tail of my shirt.

ChiChi giggled. "Scared the pants off you." Then ChiChi's eyes began a second reconnaissance of my body, this time beginning with the bare expanse of belly I had apparently offered up for view when I tugged my shirt up to my face. As ChiChi stared, he licked the corner of his mouth with a pink tongue. Sort of like a lizard. Or more accurately, like a happy, hungry chocoholic ogling a dessert cart packed with goodies. And I didn't much like it.

I studied ChiChi standing there in front of me, dressed in the same attire as I was: little running shorts, a white T-shirt wet with perspiration and clinging to the lines of his torso, and big clunky tennis shoes laced around his feet, spattered now with mud and grass clippings. The young Mexican's dark hair was no longer braided into cornrows as it had been a few days earlier. Now it hung loose and soft and windblown, framing ChiChi's handsome Latin face. ChiChi suddenly leaned forward with his hands on his knees and tried to catch his breath, and I had to admit the guy looked gorgeous even standing there all hunched over and gasping like a fish out of water. Still, it was pretty funny to see him panting away like that, since I was barely out of breath at all.

I tried not to dwell on the twinge of superiority I felt, knowing I was in better shape than the man in front of me. Instead, I used up a whole lot of energy trying to ignore the tremor of sexual excitement I felt pulsating from the base of my spine and shuddering its way south to the back of my legs. At the same time, a second tremor traveled north, sort of like a tiny rolling earthquake, and I tried to ignore that one too. The fact that the second tremor made the hair on the back of my neck stand up and wiggle around in the morning air, which in turn made me shudder all over again, didn't make ignoring it any easier.

Nor did the first sudden twitches of a waking erection, which very quickly began to stretch the crotch of my shorts. Crap. That was the last thing I needed.

If I hoped ChiChi wouldn't notice the growing bulge in my running shorts, I was soon disabused of that notion.

ChiChi glanced down and his eyes opened wide. Their heat intensified for a moment before he dragged them away from my crotch. When they were once again centered on my face, ChiChi smiled, flashing a mouthful of white teeth.

"My God, you're beautiful," he cooed.

I blushed, and it wasn't from embarrassment. It was from anger. "And you have a lover. What the hell are you playing at?"

ChiChi's smile twisted into a leer. Cute, but annoying. "My lover isn't here."

It was at that precise moment I decided I didn't like ChiChi very much. I didn't like being tempted by him. I didn't like being eyeballed and flirted with. And I didn't like being followed into the park. In fact, I was so annoyed I felt my burgeoning hard-on wither away to nothing and slip back into hibernation, which was certainly a step in the right direction. Damn thing.

ChiChi seemed to mistake my expression of relief for one of intrigue. Big mistake.

"Ramon hates to run," ChiChi said, his eyes still meandering south now and then to check out my crotch. "Maybe you and I can set up a jogging date. It's more fun with two. Running, I mean." Obviously that wasn't what he meant at all, but he wasn't very good at nuance. And even if he had been, I wasn't in the mood for it.

Nor was I in the mood for watching ChiChi tweak his nipple through his sweat-soaked T-shirt as he stood there in front of me with a lecherous simper on his face.

"Stop that!" I barked. I let out a sigh, knowing ChiChi wasn't about to stop it at all, and that realization really began to piss me off. The fact that I was tempted by ChiChi's offer pissed me off even more. Not only was I mad at him, I was also mad at me. "Like I said before. You have a lover. A very sweet lover who's crazy about you, from what I could gather the other day. Although I'm beginning to think maybe he could have done a little better."

"Ouch," ChiChi groaned with a snicker, all the while rolling his eyes like a burlesque comic. "That hurt." Then he smiled wide. "You're tempted. I can see it in your eyes." His eyes traveled south one more time to reconnoiter my sleeping dick. "And other places."

I only have a couple of rules I live by. One is to never mess with people who are in a relationship. The other is to never, under any circumstances, lie.

And sometimes, I had learned, it was really fun not to lie. Like now.

"Yes, Cheech. I admit I am tempted. Fuzzy Latinos are just my type. And no two ways around it, you're a good-looking guy. At least you were until you opened your mouth. Let me make this as clear as I can, okay? I don't fool around with another person's lover. Ever. I don't sneak around behind people's backs and do things I'd be ashamed of in the morning. Ever. And I don't leave myself open for looking like a raging asshole, *ever*, not intentionally anyway, which seems to me to be exactly what you're exceptionally adept at. So I'll tell you what, ChiChi Von Slutfuck. You tell me which way you're headed for your little workout, and I'll jog off in the *opposite* direction. That way we can act like we never saw each other at all. How's that?"

ChiChi's nipple tweaking hand moved to his crotch. Whatever he discovered there seemed to be in need of a tweak as well. He looked intrigued by my anger. Intrigued and turned on, which wasn't exactly the response I was hoping for. "What are you afraid of, Harlie?" ChiChi's eyes skittered into the bushes beside the trail. "Let's move into the shadows for a minute, and I'll show you what I'm talking about."

He reached out to grasp my arm, but I shook him off.

"I'm leaving now. I'd appreciate it if you wouldn't follow me."

Without waiting for an answer, I headed off in the same direction I had been going before ChiChi snuck up behind me.

This time ChiChi didn't follow. Although I did hear a chuckle or two as I disappeared around a bend in the trail.

Poor Ramon, I thought, once again dragging my T-shirt up to wipe the sweat from my face without breaking stride. *Poor fucking Ramon.*

SINCE ARTHUR had told me the Belladonna Arms was packed to the rafters with homosexuals, God love 'em, I was surprised to answer my door and find a lovely young woman standing on my brand-new welcome mat. (The mat was purchased at a thrift store down the street for ninety-nine cents. No one knows how to pinch a penny like I do.)

My visitor held out a plate of Toll House cookies. The delicious smell wafting off the cookies, obviously still warm from the oven, almost made me pass out cold.

"Holy crap," I mumbled. Sticking my face directly over the cookies, close enough to feel the heat, I closed my eyes and sucked in another whiff of heaven.

My visitor giggled.

"Don't be shy," she said. "They're all for you."

I opened my eyes and blinked. "Really?"

"Uh-huh."

"Gee whiz, thanks." I took the plate from my visitor's hand. It was warm to the touch. In fact they both were. The plate *and* her hand. "Golly. Cookies." I couldn't believe my good fortune.

My visitor stood maybe five four. She was dressed in skin-tight jeans and a baggy gray sweatshirt that read CPAs Do It On Paper. She had her collar-length brown hair pulled back in a ponytail and wore no makeup I could see. *No surprise there,* I thought. *She doesn't need any makeup. She's gorgeous the way she is.*

Still, I wasn't accustomed to gifts coming out of the blue. "What's the catch?" I asked, not rudely, just genuinely inquisitive. All the while, those cookies were smelling really, really tempting.

My visitor smiled very sweetly. "No catch. Arthur said you were new, so think of me as the Welcome Wagon."

"And the cookies?"

"Housewarming gift."

"Really?"

"Really. And cookies aren't the only thing I'm offering."

"What? You got a jug of milk and a gallon of ice cream?"

She laughed, and the sound of her laughter was like little silver bells merrily tinkling in the air. I grinned to hear it. Our eyes laughed at each other for a couple of heartbeats, and when those heartbeats were finished, I thought I might have acquired *another* friend. And wasn't that an astonishing development. The Belladonna Arms was the most amazing building indeed.

"I'm Harlie," I said, rather surprising myself at my own enthusiasm.

"I know. I'm Sylvia."

A flicker of memory sparked in my head. I remembered Arthur's words about the one straight tenant living with a man who was soon to be a woman. The sudden recognition flashed across my face, apparently, because my visitor's cheeks turned a very attractive pink.

"Arthur told you about me," she said.

It was my turn to blush. "Yes. A little."

"What did he say exactly?"

"Oh, this and that. I don't really remember."

Sylvia cocked her head to the side as another round of tinkling bells filled the air. "You're a terrible liar."

"I know. It's one of my greatest downfalls." Then I perked up. "You really want to know what he said? He said you were beautiful."

"Did he really?"

"Uh-huh. And he was right."

The pink in Sylvia's cheeks deepened to a lovely rose. "Thank you. I guess I'll have to make *him* some cookies next."

"Well," I hedged. "You might consider holding off on that. It's my understanding that Arthur is looking for a boyfriend. Maybe until his search has ended and he's actually snagged one, he should cut back on the calories a bit. Especially since I told him he should give up drag and start dressing like a cowboy."

Sylvia snorted. "You did?" Then she rolled her eyes skyward. "That's something I'd like to see."

I accompanied her snort with one of my own. "You and me both."

I stepped aside and motioned Sylvia inside. I couldn't stand it any longer, so as she passed, I quickly plucked a cookie off the plate and popped it in my mouth. When Sylvia turned back, I was blissfully chewing the damn thing with my eyes squeezed shut, or almost shut. Actually I could see her through my eyelashes. She looked away before I caught her staring and patiently waited while I finished. While I chewed and grunted in appreciation, slavering and gnashing away at my cookie like a happy werewolf gobbling up a particularly delicious villager, she studied the apartment, taking in the computer, the books, and the fat black-and-white cat lying on the sofa.

"Gizmo adopted you too, I see."

I swallowed hard and dragged myself back to reality. Damn, that cookie was good! I opened my eyes all the way to see what Sylvia was talking about. It didn't take me long to figure it out.

"Gizmo? Oh, you mean Ralph. I mean Studley. I mean the cat. Yeah. He likes my tuna. Lazy bugger."

I took Sylvia's hand and led her into the kitchen. Pulling out a kitchen chair from the table, I asked her to sit. When she was comfortably ensconced, I pulled up the opposite chair and laid the plate of cookies on the table between us.

"Cookie?" I politely asked, as if I had baked them myself.

Sylvia giggled and shook her head. "They're all for you."

Goody. Before she could finish her sentence, I had another one melting in my mouth. Around it I said, "Not to sound greedy or anything, but you mentioned another gift?"

Sylvia made a kissy face in the direction of the cat, and the cat said "Meow" back. As soon as that formality was over, she concentrated her attention back on me. If she was surprised she had only been in the apartment for fifteen seconds and I was already on my third cookie, she didn't show it.

"Jesus God, these things are good!" I groaned with most of my front teeth blacked out by chocolate. I could feel it. I could tell by the glimmer in Sylvia's eyes my seemingly toothless smile looked pretty funny, but she was too polite to mention it.

"I hear you're looking for work," she said.

I swallowed with an audible gulp. "Yeah, but not as a CPA."

A glint of confusion crossed Sylvia's face, and then she glanced down at her sweatshirt and giggled. "Oh, no. This is Pete's sweatshirt. Pete's my fiancé."

"Lucky man," I said.

Sylvia stared at me for a moment, then reached across the table and patted my arm. "Thank you, Harlie. I'll introduce you to him one of these days. Right now he's a little busy, what with it being April and all. Tax time, you know."

"Gotcha."

"No, the job I'm offering is restaurant work. Think you might be interested?"

"Well, I'm not much of a cook. But if it's waiting tables or bussing dishes, I've had some experience. Is it anything like that?"

Sylvia nodded, twisting her ponytail around the tip of her finger while she studied me. "It's exactly like that. And it's within walking distance from here. I'll be leaving next week, and they are looking for someone to replace me."

"Why are you leaving?" I asked.

And again, Sylvia blushed.

I jumped in my chair. "Oh. Of course. Your surgery. Is—is that it?"

Sylvia squared her shoulders and finally plucked a cookie from the plate for herself. She took a teeny nibble off the edge of it and said, "I see Arthur told you plenty."

"I guess he did." After a moment, while we both savored a bite of cookie, I asked, "When is the surgery scheduled?"

"In about a month," she said. "Pete wants me to rest up for a few weeks beforehand, so he insisted I stop working right away." She smiled sweetly. "He's a little overprotective."

"He must love you very much."

"Yes," she said. There was no doubt on her face at all, only a solemn acknowledgement that what I had said was the absolute truth. "Yes, he does."

"Are you scared? About the surgery?"

Sylvia seemed honestly surprised by the question. "No. Why should I be? I've been waiting for this my whole life. Thanks to Pete, it's finally going to happen. I can't wait for you to meet him." She gazed through the window at the darkening sky outside. It was starting to look like rain again. Almost idly, she asked, "Do you have a special love in your life, Harlie? I mean, do you have anyone you simply can't imagine living without?"

I followed her gaze, taking in the bank of black clouds sliding in from the horizon, seeing the branches of the eucalyptus tree stirring in the wind outside my kitchen window.

"I thought I did. But now, I guess—well, I guess I don't."

Again, Sylvia reached out to lay her small hand on my arm. "I'm sorry."

I nodded, laying my hand over hers. "Me too."

With a twinkle of mischief and a grin, she wagged a finger in my face. "You can't have Pete. He's taken."

I forced a laugh and was surprised to find it made me feel a little better. "Well, darn," I said. "And I was just about to put the moves on him too."

Remembering what happened on my run that morning, it was on the tip of my tongue to ask Sylvia's opinion of ChiChi and Ramon, but then I thought better of it. The last thing I wanted was for poor Ramon to find out what had transpired out there on that hiking trail. I wasn't sure why I felt guilty about it, but I did.

Instead, I slid another cookie off the plate, poked it in my mouth, and closed my eyes in bliss as Sylvia looked patiently on.

When the cookie had dissolved to another cosmic plane entirely, giving me a rush of sensory overload as it flittered away into the ether, I swallowed happily, opened my eyes, and said, "The job sounds great. When can I see your boss and what can I do to kiss his ass and make him want to hire me?"

Sylvia tittered a little laugh. "You won't have to do anything. Just look the way you look right now, although you might want to wipe the chocolate off your chin."

"Sorry," I said, grabbing a napkin from the napkin holder. "I don't quite understand."

Sylvia reached across the table and patted my cheek. "You are cute and my boss is gay. You do the math. In other words, just be nice to him."

I frowned. "You mean—?"

Sylvia immediately realized what I meant, and looking appalled, she gave a little jump in her chair. "Good lord, no! You don't have to *sleep* with him or anything. Just be *nice*. You know. *Polite*. Trust me, your looks will do the rest. Poor Mr. Burger is very sweet. And don't worry. He'll like you. I know he will."

"Why's that?" I asked.

Sylvia smiled across the table. "Because you're sweet too."

"Oh," I said, feeling another blush rise to my cheeks. "Uh, thanks."

Those little bells of laughter rang out again. I suspected she enjoyed embarrassing me, but that was okay. I didn't really mind.

I wondered if she knew how appreciative I was. "And thanks for the job lead! No kidding. This is great. I won't have to go hunting for work. If I get it, I mean."

"Don't mention it," Sylvia said. "And don't worry. You'll get it. I already talked you up."

"You did?"

"Yeah." She glanced around for a pen and paper to jot down the information I needed for the interview.

I plucked a blank index card and a ballpoint pen from my pocket with one hand while reaching for a seventh cookie with the other. "Why did you call him *poor* Mr. Burger? What's wrong with him? Is he a pain to work for? Does he crack a whip? Is he an old gay lech?"

Sylvia scribbled on the index card and answered my questions at the same time. "No, honey. He really is the sweetest man ever. He's just lonely, I think. He lost his lover a few months ago, and I don't think I've seen him smile since. That's why I called him poor Mr. Burger. It clearly broke his heart. I don't know what he'd do without the deli. It's his whole life now." Sylvia stopped scribbling and gazed deep into my eyes, holding the index card aloft. "All I ask is that you be kind to him. If you promise me *that*, I'll give you *this*." And she waved the card under my nose like a farmer dangling a carrot in front of a stubborn-ass mule.

I snatched it from her fingers before she changed her mind. "I promise."

"Good."

I deciphered Sylvia's handwriting while she went back to nibbling on her cookie. I remembered Arthur, and a germ of an idea wormed its way into my head.

I wonder, I thought. *I just fucking wonder.*

"You're looking sneaky," Sylvia said. "What are you thinking?"

"Uh, nothing," I said. "Nothing at all."

Sylvia didn't look like she believed me, but she let it go. She pushed herself from the table and plucked at her sweatshirt. "Pete will be home from work soon. I have to run. He's taking me out to dinner, and I have to get dressed."

"You look dressed to me," I said.

"Oh, pooh," she tittered. "Don't waste your nice on me. Save it for Mr. Burger."

And with that, she was gone, flitting through the apartment and out the door, leaving nothing in her wake but the teeniest whiff of cologne and the even more delicious aroma of freshly baked Toll House cookies, or what was left of them

So I snatched another one off the plate before they disappeared entirely.

When Ralph/Studley/Gizmo propelled his twenty pounds of feline flab into my lap to check out the cookies himself, I drew a line in my hospitality.

"Sorry," I growled. "These cookies are mine. You want cookies, go find your own."

The cat purred, then bumped my chin with his head. When neither of those subterfuges worked, he sprawled out in my lap and went to sleep while I polished off the cookies myself.

It was quite amazing really. I had been in the Belladonna Arms for less than a week, and I already had tenants lusting after me and more friends than I knew what to do with. Hell, I even had cookies. And a cat.

Sort of.

Chapter 4

THE BROADWAY Deli was in the perfect location for me. I had to admit that. I could walk to the joint from the Belladonna Arms in exactly six minutes. Imagine the money I would save by not pouring it down the Buick's bottomless gas tank every week. That thought alone made me almost giddy with excitement.

The deli was located on the corner of 10th and Broadway, right at the spot where a dozen city buses converged to drop off and pick up commuters. It was also three blocks from my old high school and four blocks from Beaumont University, whose sprawling campus I could look down on from my kitchen window back at the Belladonna Arms. The deli was also within spitting distance of half a dozen senior citizen high-rises and towering office buildings, not to mention a homeless squatter's camp tucked up under the freeway to the east. Even at this early morning hour, the deli was jumping with activity. What I had expected to be a small neighborhood deli with maybe five or six tables, a place where people mostly ordered takeout sandwiches, was in fact a full-fledged restaurant with upward of fifty tables and booths and covering a fourth of a city block.

Poor Mr. Burger, my ass! He was sitting on a gold mine! Peering through the establishment's windows, I saw a horde of diners perched in endless rows of red leather booths, all gazing out onto Broadway while chowing down on breakfast, slurping coffee, and psyching themselves up for the day ahead. The scents of bacon, eggs, sausage, and waffles, all hot off the griddle, made my mouth water and my stomach grumble before I ever put a foot through the door. Other scents wafted out to the street as well. Corned beef and cabbage, stewing for the lunch crowd to come. Prime rib roasting slowly on what, judging from the aroma, was a barbecue pit somewhere out back. To top it all off, breads and biscuits and muffins were baking somewhere in the bowels of the building. It all smelled so delicious I could feel my toes curling inside my shoes.

As I stepped in off the street, I spotted Sylvia. She was standing at the cash register by the door making change and smiling at a pair of customers who were paying their bill and smiling back. Sylvia and half a dozen other servers hustling about were all dressed in white shirts and black pants. *Cool,* I thought. *I already own a white shirt and black pants. I won't have to buy any new clothes to meet the dress code.*

On the inside, the restaurant looked even huger than it did from the outside. Huge and obviously very, very popular. Half the downtown workforce must wend their way through here at some point or other during the course of a day. It wouldn't be an easy job, but on the other hand, tips should be good. *Yay,* I thought. *Tips. I love tips.*

Spotting me, Sylvia beamed a wide smile to match my own, and she pointed over the customers' heads to a doorway at the back of the restaurant. She mouthed the words "He's back there—good luck," and I set off in the direction she indicated.

I eased my way through a swinging door that separated the dining area from the kitchen. If the dining area was bustling with activity, the kitchen was positively *teeming.* Two young men worked a broad electric grill, flipping eggs, rolling sausages, scooping up bacon. Another cook seared steaks over a wood-fired pit with a gigantic bonnet that hovered over the flames to suck up the smoke. Two teenage girls arranged serving plates and platters along a counter for the servers, who were flying back and forth through the swinging doors to snatch up their orders and cart them out to the customers while they were still hot. Another man, this one wearing a long rubber apron and fat rubber gloves, was sweating bullets as he sprayed steaming hot water onto a mountain of dirty pots and pans by the scullery, making a horrendous racket while he did it. Part of the racket was the aria he was singing from *Rigoletto* as he worked. His obviously trained tenor voice boomed out across the noisy kitchen, but no one paid any attention to it at all. When he finished one aria, he immediately began another. This one from *Aida.* Sounded like he had a pretty good repertoire. It was all I could do not to clap and toss him a quarter.

Amid this turmoil, all the way in the back of the kitchen, a tall, brooding guy in white baggy pants and a sleeveless white T-shirt stood in front of a bank of ovens. He too was sweating bullets as he shoved dough into one hot oven and scooped bread and biscuits and muffins out of the other. This was the baker, and my perusal of the establishment came to an abrupt halt the moment I laid eyes on him.

The baker was a tree. He stood maybe six feet four, had broad shoulders and heavy, rolling biceps I immediately longed to lick. He had a deep, broad chest pushing at the sweat-soaked T-shirt. And since the kitchen was about a thousand degrees, why the hell wouldn't his shirt be sweat soaked, huh? The baker had a thick mop of dark hair poking out from under a white chef's hat, and a crisp slice of bacon perched between his luscious lips like a cigar. He absentmindedly chewed on it as he worked. He had a glower on his face like maybe his puppy had just died. Somehow the glower only made him sexier. God, what a hunk.

I slavered over the guy for about half a minute before reality set in and I tore my eyes away to look for the man I had actually come to see.

I found Mr. Burger sitting at a metal desk in the corner, the only spot of stillness in this whirl of activity. The desk was strewn with papers and a foot-high stack of *more* papers were stabbed onto a lethal-looking spindle beside the splayed-open pages of a ledger, three dirty coffee cups, and a half-eaten, jelly-slathered croissant. Mr. Burger had his feet propped up in the middle of all this mess as he lounged back in a swivel desk chair with a phone pressed to his ear. He looked bored.

I approached, still trying not to google-eye the baker if I could help it. I parked myself at a respectful distance from my prospective boss because I didn't want the man to think I was eavesdropping on his telephone conversation, although I was. Writers are nosy people. Did I ever mention that? Well, it's true. They are.

"Yes, Julie," Mr. Burger was all but groaning. "I do get out. I went to the movies a few weeks ago. How's that? And yes, I realize a movie once a month doesn't constitute a social life, but I'm working, you know. I don't have a lot of time to...."

Mr. Burger's sentence trailed away as Julie (whoever she was) apparently continued to chew the guy a new butthole for not living life on the edge. Or at least for not getting out a little more often.

Burger was maybe in his high fifties. Sprawled out on the desk chair with his long legs propped up, he looked to be about as tall as the baker. Of course, that was where their similarity ended. The baker was gorgeous and young, maybe my age or a little older. Twenty-nine. Thirty tops. Mr. Burger was neither young *nor* gorgeous. And he was as skinny as a rail, although he had a pleasant enough face, not broody and sexy like the baker, I thought with a sigh. In fact, Mr. Burger looked like Sylvia had described him. Sad. Having some broad named Julie nagging him about his social life probably didn't help much to cheer him up either. Poor guy.

Remembering what Sylvia had told me about her boss losing his lover and all, I had to admit Mr. Burger didn't look gay. Of course, some of the best gay people don't. *I* don't. Okay, well *maybe* I do.

While I waited for Mr. Burger to hang up the phone on Julie's nagging ass, I had time to consider how much I really, really wanted this job. I wasn't dumb enough to think it was a career choice. Hell, I just wanted to make some extra income. Most restaurants even offer the help a free meal now and then. That would be nice. And who knows, maybe I'd even get to know the baker. And if I could get to know him *biblically*, it would be even better. No reason I couldn't do that, right? That didn't make me a bad person, did it? Huh? Did it? Shifting from one foot to the other, still waiting for Burger to get off the phone, I occupied my time ogling the baker from across the kitchen but trying not to *look* like I was ogling him. Not that it really mattered. The guy hadn't glanced my way even once. Hell, why should he? For all I knew, he was as straight as a two-by-four, which in my opinion would have been a bummer indeed.

So I stood there, swallowing back a continuing reservoir of saliva, lost to the world, slavering over the baker's magnificent biceps as I watched him knead and pound a massive lump of bread dough on a marble tabletop. His slitted eyes never left the dough. One would think he really hated that dough. As he bent over the table, punching his massive fists into the rubbery white mass before him, a wisp of dark hair slid from beneath his chef's hat and fell over his eye. He impatiently poked it back, leaving a little smear of flour on his forehead.

At that moment, he lifted his head and his hooded eyes fell on me. I was so surprised by the sudden eye contact I automatically lifted my hand in greeting. The baker's eyes shifted to my raised hand for a split second as if he'd never seen anything quite like it before in his life. Then his eyes shifted back to my face. That's when I noticed how blue his eyes were. Beautifully blue. Stunningly blue. Dark hair and blue eyes. How yummy is that?

Unfortunately, his eyes were also icy. The tip of a pink tongue came out to lick away another smear of flour from his lip, and Jesus God, wasn't *that* mesmerizing Unfortunately, he was looking at the same time like he wouldn't mind throwing *me* on the table and sprinkling *me* with flour and pounding *me* to a rubbery pulp, then tossing *my* ass into the fucking oven for staring at him. And except for the oven part, I think maybe I wouldn't have put up much of a fight if he had. Just getting those heavenly hands on me might make it all worthwhile.

Was I smitten, or what?

Just as I was about to offer the hunky baker my very best smile (I have several I drag out for certain social occasions), the baker turned his attention back to the bread dough in front of him, discarding me like I'd never been in his line of sight at all. I supposed it was a good thing. At least he wouldn't see the thirteen shades of red I had turned having those smoking hot eyes aimed in my direction.

Someone tapped me on the shoulder, and I jumped two feet straight up into the air. Just before I came back down to earth, I saw the faintest hint of a smile cross the baker's face. He was laughing at me. I added three more shades of red to my collection, but there wasn't much I could do about it.

I turned to find Mr. Burger smiling a benign smile and stuffing the rest of his jellied croissant in his mouth with a long index finger. "Didn't mean to scare you there, son. You must be Harlie. Sylvia told me to expect you."

I stuck out my hand. "Uh—hi. Sir."

Mr. Burger glowered like the baker and gave me a perfunctory handshake. "Don't call me sir. Makes me feel older than I already am. Call me Tom. Or better yet, just call me Burger."

"Oh. Sorry, sir. I mean, Mr. Burger. I mean, Tom. I mean, Burger."

Burger gave me the look of a man who feels himself settling into a mud hole all the way up to his hairline and knowing there's not a damn thing he can do about it. Rather like a Mensa member trying to carry on a conversation with a nitwit and knowing the possibility for stimulating chitchat is just a fucking pipe dream, he molded his face into a parody of patience, which didn't fool me at all. In truth, he was simply bored. Now, apparently, Julie and I were *both* barnacles on his ass.

He gulped down the last of his croissant. "When can you start?" he asked.

That was a surprise. "You mean I got the job?"

Burger shrugged. "If Sylvia says you're okay, you must be okay. No contagious diseases, right?"

"Uh, right."

"You're not lazy, are you?"

"Uh, nope."

"You wash your hands after you go to the bathroom, don't you?"

"Every time."

"Then you're better than half the employees I have now. How's nine bucks an hour?"

"Gee, that's great."

"Then that's the interview. You're hired. Start tomorrow. Seeya." And he turned and walked away.

I seriously considered doing a little jig before departing the premises, but decided not to. I satisfied myself with giving the baker one last worshipful glance before leaving the kitchen to give Sylvia the good news.

To my surprise, the baker was curling a finger in my direction, beckoning me toward him.

Holy shit. With my heart thundering in my throat, I weaved my way through the kitchen workers and stepped into the baker's little world of ovens and flour and bread dough and pie pans. When I got there he didn't bother sticking out his hand to introduce himself or say hello. He simply said, "You'll be my assistant. Pop already arranged it with me."

"P-pop?" I stammered. Up close the baker was even more gorgeous than he was from thirty feet away. He towered over me. I don't know if I ever mentioned it before, but I love men who tower over me. And who the hell doesn't? Aside from the towering thing, he also had a cute little dimple in his chin, a hint of a five o'clock shadow that was truly sexy, and the most beautiful hands I had ever seen in my life, even covered with flour. Tearing my eyes from those hands and trying not to imagine how they would feel on my body, I stood mesmerized by the shadow of two dark nipples peeking through the fabric of his sweaty T-shirt. Holy Mother of God.

It took me a second to find my voice. "Who's Pop?"

But I knew before he ever told me. I could tell because the baker gave me the same Mensa/nitwit look Mr. Burger had given me thirty seconds earlier. Snarky genetics in action.

"Oh." I said. "Mr. Burger's your dad. But I thought he was...." I let my words trail away, not sure I wanted to go there.

"You thought he was *what*, exactly?"

"Nothing. Nothing at all."

"Brilliant," the baker said. "Maybe you shouldn't talk unless you have to. Be here at 6:00 a.m. I'll whip you into shape then."

I gave him a military salute, clicked my heels together, and stopped myself on the very brink of throwing my hand in the air and spouting a *Heil, Hitler!* I offered up my very best smile instead. Smile #6, I think it was. The one I always use when I'm turned on and feeling kind of stupid and don't know what else to do.

If the baker found me amusing, he covered it well. In fact, all he did was turn away to grab a huge wooden spatula-looking thing that was four feet long and flat on one end. Opening an oven door, he slid the paddle into the fiery furnace and scooped out a gigantic tray of biscuits.

When he turned back, he blinked as if surprised I was still there. I watched him slide the pan of biscuits onto the counter before sticking out my hand. "My name is Harlie."

He ignored the hand. "I know."

"What's yours?"

He looked like he was giving up state secrets when he said, "Milan."

"Nice name," I said, and meant it. I immediately wondered if I could work it into a book.

"Oh," Milan said, "I almost forgot." He reached under the table he had been kneading the dough on and pulled out a stack of white shirts and pants. Baker's clothes. There was even a little chef's hat like the one he was wearing perched on top the pile. He flapped the clothes against his leg and a cloud of flour dust damn near obliterated us both. "You might want to wash these before you wear them to work tomorrow. If they don't fit, don't worry about it. We're not too fashion conscious around here."

I gaped at the clothes he thrust into my hands and knew immediately I would look like a first-class twit wearing them.

Before I could argue, he said, "Six o'clock. In the *morning*," and turned away for the final time. What a charmer.

I took the hint and left, not quite sure if I was all *squee* with excitement because I'd be working with the hunky baker, or scared crapless because the hunky baker seemed like a grouchy hard-ass, or simply depressed as hell because I'd never get in the baker's pants looking like the Pillsbury doughboy.

I was so stunned by the way things had turned out, I forgot to say good-bye to Sylvia when I left. To make matters worse, I was halfway back to the Belladonna Arms before it dawned on me that working with the baker, I wouldn't be getting any tips.

Well, poop.

DIGGING THROUGH my closet I hauled out all my dirty clothes. Since they had been stuffed in the trunk of my car in a garbage bag for the last four months, they didn't smell so nice. (I hadn't exactly spent a lot of time packing when Dan threw me out of his life, the prick.) I gathered everything up, along with my new work uniforms, which I hadn't even tried on yet but hated already, and set off in search of the laundry room.

I found the place where I thought it might be. In the basement. And it was exactly what I expected. A mess. The washers and dryers were rusty and coated with lint. The laundry room floor was awash with dust bunnies the size of rats. And only one 40-watt bulb hanging from a string in the middle of the room illuminated the place, if you wanted to call it illumination.

There was nowhere to sit while I waited for my clothes to wash, so I snatched up a bucket I found in the corner and, tipping it over, plopped my ass down on it. After a few minutes of listening to the washers thumping and rattling and filling up with water and watching the dust bunnies meander here and there around my feet like a flock of hamsters, I was so mind-numbingly bored I set about cleaning up the place.

Someone had left a stray sock on top of a dryer, so I gave it a shake, stuck my hand in it, and used it as a dust rag to wipe the lint and grime from the top of all the washers and dryers. Then I noticed a tiny door off to the right, and sure enough, it turned out to be a broom closet. It even had a broom in it. The broom was in pristine condition. I don't think it had ever been used in its life. In my imagination, the broom was surprised as hell when I came along and actually picked it up. I could almost swear I heard it gasp.

Writers. We imagine all kinds of weird shit.

I went to work cleaning the floor and herding all the rat-sized dust bunnies into a pile in the corner where I employed my stray sock again to pick them up and deposit them in a wastebasket that looked like it hadn't been emptied since sometime around the Civil War. I grabbed up the overflowing wastebasket when I was finished and headed for the trash room down the hall.

I continued to work, straightening the place up until my washers had finished cycling. Then I tossed my two loads of clean laundry into one gigantic rust bucket of a dryer, which had to be older than I was, and stuffed in a couple of quarters to bring it to life. The dryer sounded like a dump truck stacked with scrap metal bouncing along a street paved with bowling balls, but at least it was putting out some heat. While my clothes dried, I snatched up an old string mop standing in the broom closet and ran some water over it in the utility sink to remove the mushrooms growing in amongst the strings, and boy was that disgusting. I then proceeded to mop up the residue from all the slaughtered dust bunnies I had disposed of earlier.

I was finishing up when a tall, skinny guy with freckles and screaming red hair that stuck straight up off the top of his head like a frazzled pencil eraser came humming through the laundry room door with a basket of clothes under his arm. Right behind him trailed a plump little guy with a hairless, chubby face like a cherub. The little guy wore a fringed suede shirt like Daniel Boone and the lower half of his body was stuffed into crisp new Levi's jeans, so stiff and blue and tight I wondered how he could breathe.

They were the most mismatched pair of humans I had ever seen in my life. In fact, they didn't really *appear* human. They appeared more like—Muppets! Of course. That's who they reminded me of. Beaker and Dr. Bunsen Honeydew of the Muppets. One tall and geeky and red, the other short, pale, smooth, and round. As soon as I figured that out, I realized they weren't mismatched at all. They were made for each other!

They stopped in the doorway and gaped around as if they couldn't believe their eyes. Beaker wore a blossom of acne on either cheek and his skin was as pale as typing paper, except for the freckles. He was wearing an I'm With Stupid T-shirt. Bunsen wore a baseball cap that read Don't Believe Everything You Read on the front of it, which seemed apropos, if questionable.

"Am I in the wrong place?" the redhead asked—me, presumably. Although he didn't look at me. He was still too busy taking in the spotless washer tops and the sparkling tile floor, still wet from the mop.

"Nope," I said. "You're in the right place. You guys new to the building too?"

They shot me a tandem look of surprise, like two puppets held by the strings of the same puppeteer. Jim Henson, no doubt. "Hardly," Dr. Honeydew piped up, tugging at the waistband of his brand new Levi's as if they were cutting off his oxygen, which they undoubtedly were. Not to mention killing a few sperm cells. "Why would you think that?" he asked. Snippy.

"Well," I said, a teeny bit irked at his attitude but still trying to be friendly. "You're holding a basket of laundry and you just asked if you were in the wrong place. What was I supposed to think? Either you're lost or you've never done laundry before."

That last line was meant to be funny, but once I said it, I was rather sorry I had because truthfully neither one of them looked all that spotless, if you know what I mean. I was afraid maybe my sarcasm might have struck a little too close to home. Wars have started that way.

They seemed to think so too. Bunsen coughed up a pointed "Harrumph!" while Beaker screwed his face up like he was concentrating on trying to analyze what I had said so as to parse it down to see if it turned out to be an insult. They both gave me a long, absorbing perusal like they were sifting through my thoughts telepathically so as to gather up the catty ones and throw them back in my face, since they maybe weren't quick enough to think up any on their own. Which proved to be the case when Beaker said, "You writing a book?"

"Well, actually, yeah," I began, trying to hide a grin since his rejoinder had been so fifth grade. "I am writing a book, but it has nothing to do with—"

"I've lived here for three years, I'll have you know," Beaker said. He hooked a thumb at his partner. "PJ has been here almost a year. We just never saw the laundry room clean is all. What the hell happened?"

"Me," I said. "I happened."

The redhead swooped his eyeballs over the place again, finally centering his attention on the tile floor. It was beginning to dry now, and it looked pretty good if I said so myself. "The floor is yellow," he said. "I never knew the floor was yellow."

"Me either," the cherub echoed. "I thought it was gray."

I stepped forward and stuck out my hand, still trying to be neighborly although I was getting a little tired of having to work so damn hard at it. "I'm Harlie Rose. I just moved in. Glad to meet you both."

The redhead juggled his laundry around in his arms until he came up with a free hand, which he reluctantly poked in my direction. We shook.

"Charlie," he said. "From 3A." He dropped my hand and snagged his partner by the arm to drag him close. "This is my boyfriend, PJ. We're kleptomaniacs."

That was certainly a conversational stop sign. Stopped *me* cold, at any rate. "What," I stammered, "*both* of you?"

I don't know why I said that. It just popped out. I tried to strike a more conciliatory tone, groping around for a positive comment. It took me a minute. Positive comments seemed to be in short supply all of a sudden.

"It must be nice to have common interests," I finally offered, lame but sincere. *Yeah,* I thought. *Common interests. Like grand larceny and petty theft.*

The redhead had the good grace to shuffle his feet and look uncomfortable. He blushed so deeply the acne on his cheeks looked like bubbling pools of lava in the mouth of a volcano. "We're not kleptos *all* the time, of course. Only when we forget to take our meds. Arthur told us we had to tell the new tenants about it in case anything turns up missing. That way they'll know where to go to get their belongings back. If we haven't sold them first."

"Oh," I said, suddenly fairly uncomfortable myself. "Ummm, glad you let me know. Apartment 3A. I'll jot that down." Since I didn't know what else to say, I smiled in a "sorry you're sick" sort of way, which probably didn't look any more sincere than it felt. "It must be hard for you."

"No shit," Charlie grumped. "I hate taking those fucking meds."

"Meds suck," PJ echoed. "Shoplifting's cool, though."

Charlie grinned. "Totally cool."

PJ's eyes came to rest on my bottle of laundry soap sitting on one of the washers. Suddenly, without turning his head, he pointed the opposite direction toward the door leading out to the hall and exclaimed, "Holy shit! Was that a ghost?"

I jumped. Spinning around to look where he was pointing, I didn't see a thing. When I looked back, my laundry soap was in Charlie's basket.

"Excuse me," I said. "That soap is mine."

All three of us gazed down at the bottle nestled in among their dirty clothes. Bizarrely, they both had the good grace (and unmitigated gall) to appear surprised. I guessed they hadn't taken their medicine today.

"How odd," Charlie said, plucking it out of his basket and placing it back on the washer where it was before. "It must have fallen in."

"Yeah." PJ grinned. "It must have fallen in."

Fallen in, my ass, I thought, trying to remember if I had locked my apartment door before I came downstairs. I sure as hell hoped so.

"Welp," I said with forced good cheer, "I'll just grab my clothes out of the dryer and be on my merry way." *Before one of you twits swipe the fillings out of my teeth.*

Two minutes later, with all my possessions securely in hand, I was hustling up the basement stairs and wondering what other surprises the Belladonna Arms held in store.

Behind me I heard Charlie mutter to his boyfriend, "He seemed nice. Maybe we'll ask him over for dinner."

PJ grunted. "Yeah, let's. I liked his watch."

THAT EVENING, I was stretched out on my couch digesting dinner, and Gizmo was sprawled across my stomach digesting his. I was pondering whether or not to invest in a few cans of honest-to-God cat food or simply continue to feed the old reprobate from my stock of people tuna. While I was pondering and weighing the ramifications of both and trying to tell myself I wasn't being cheap about it, just frugal, there came a knock on my door.

Gizmo grumbled and growled when I scooted him off my chest and headed for the door. Of course, by the time I got there he was already snoring again. Apparently his snit was all for show. He was too lazy to drag it out into a full-fledged tantrum.

If I had owned a peephole I might not have been quite so shocked when I pulled the damn door open. As it was, I had no prep time whatsoever.

Arthur stood on my doorstep decked out in full queenly regalia. And a big queen he was too. He already stood a head taller than me, but with a massive red wig arranged in an intricate pile of curls and twirls and swoops and dips, he stood *two* heads taller than me. And the wig was only the beginning.

Plopped in among the wig's rolling terrain there perched a nelly little cowgirl hat that couldn't have been more out of place if it had been sitting on top of a water heater. A teeny satin string hung down from either side of the hat and hooked under Arthur's chin (well, *one* of his chins) to hold the hat securely in place, assuming it could have pried itself loose from all the hairspray anyway.

Arthur wore enough makeup to paint a house, and his false eyelashes were so long and lush and poked so far out from under the brim of his hat they looked like two whisk brooms flapping around on either side of his nose. The sweeping lashes were also coated with glitter, and every time he blinked, a little shower of what looked like radioactive snow drifted down to pepper his cheeks. I wondered if Arthur had held a stencil over his mouth to get his cherry red lipstick to look the way it did, all bee-stungy and permanently puckered up. From either earlobe hung dangly rhinestone earrings in the shape of two more cowgirl hats. They must have been from the Jesus-What-The-Hell-Was-I-Thinking Collection by Avon.

And all that was just Arthur from the neck up.

From the neck down, Arthur was a true extravaganza. He was so overdone, he made all other drag queens who'd passed this way before him look like a bunch of rag-laden Carmelite nuns who had gotten a little carried away with their vows of poverty.

Arthur wore a glittery, knee-length square-dance dress that stood almost straight out to either side of his broad hips because of the countless petticoats he had strapped on underneath. The dress was bright red and several sizes too small. From the waist up it had been stretched around Arthur's massive torso like a pig intestine enclosing a humongous bratwurst. I had no idea how he squeezed himself into it, but when he did it pushed everything up and caused an overflow in the chest department that would have sent Jayne Mansfield, had she been alive to see it, into the clutches of a massive inferiority complex, which would likely have been a new experience for her.

But as for Arthur, square dancing was out of the question, I'm afraid. One do-si-do and there would have been man tits flying everywhere. Unfortunately there was also a fair crop of chest hair on Arthur's bosom and on his massive bare shoulders. His cleavage was so deep and dark and bottomless I kept expecting to see a groundhog poke his head out to look for six more weeks of winter. Arthur had somehow managed to squeeze into a miniscule pair of tap shoes with gold bows on the toes. They had so much ankle flesh rolling over the sides they looked like muffins. Once again, as I had the first time I'd spotted Arthur in drag—when he was hauling trash out to the curb in stiletto house slippers in the middle of a monsoon—I wondered how the hell the man could walk at all.

To top off the ensemble, Arthur held a cupcake in his hand with a lighted candle poking up from the middle of it, burning merrily.

He stood proudly before me, as motionless as the Statue of Liberty. I scoped him out from head to toe, which must have taken upward of a minute. There was a lot to scope out. When I was finished, he coyly batted his long eyelashes, causing me to grab the doorsill so I wouldn't be swept away in the downdraft.

Beaming, he thrust the cupcake at me. "This is to celebrate your new job, sweetums. Congratulations!"

I blinked, not so much from the cupcake or the sentiment or the "sweetums," but from the endless yards of red taffeta. My God, the man was shiny.

I dragged a smile up from somewhere and retrieved the cupcake.

"Well, golly, Arthur. Thank you."

Arthur's smile stretched itself out as wide as it could go.

I still stood there, staring. Somehow I couldn't pull my eyes away. You know how car wrecks are fascinating? Well, this was worse.

Seeing my stunned expression, Arthur apparently chose to interpret it as a compliment.

"You like?" he sang out happily. "I did what you said, see?"

"A-and what was that?" I asked, trying desperately to remember. "What the hell did I say?"

Arthur gave me a jovial slap on the chest which almost knocked me over. "Oh, *you!*" he squealed. "Such a kidder. You told me to dress western." He took a step backward and did a dainty turn, which made his petticoats flare out even wider, exposing a pair of really chunky thighs underneath, thick and well-forested like a couple of moss-coated tree trunks. "See? I dressed western. Didn't I do good? What do you think? Come on, tell me the truth. What do you think?"

I couldn't. Think, I mean. There wasn't a single thought in my head. Well, okay, wait a minute. Maybe there was one.

"I told you to dress like a cow*boy!* Not—not—"

"Let's not nitpick," Arthur quipped. "Cowboy, cowgirl. What's the difference?"

"There's a *lot* of difference, and just who the hell are you supposed to be, anyway?"

Arthur gave me a teeny pout, which was a truly bizarre thing to watch what with the fiery red cheeks and bee-stung lips and those goddamn glittery whisk brooms flapping around in front of his face.

"I'm Dale Evans, silly! The *queen* of westerns!" He peeked over my shoulder and apparently spotted Gizmo snoring away on my couch, grunting and slobbering in his sleep. He gave the cat a little finger waggle of greeting with his three-inch press-on nails. "Hi, Matilda!"

"Matilda?" I asked. "She has balls, Arthur!"

Arthur laughed. "I know! A nervy little thing, isn't she?"

"That's not what I mea—"

He glanced down at the cupcake in my hand, then reached in and blew out the candle himself. I guess he thought I would set fire to myself if he didn't, although I rather suspected *he* was the one decked out in combustibles, not me.

He gave my cheeks a maternal pat with both hands, then squeezed them together with his fat fingers until my lips were puckered out, my teeth were grinding together, and I felt like a guppy.

He gave my head a little shake. "Good luck with your new job, honey. Now I'm off to the movies. I have a date."

"You're kidding," I said, before I could stop myself.

He wasn't listening. He released me and did a couple of pirouettes to show off the petticoats—there must have been nine or ten under there—then he shot me the same merry wave of good cheer he had given Gizmo. When he stopped spinning and his petticoats swayed to a standstill around him, he gave me a wink.

"It's my first date with the man. Wish me luck."

"Uh, good luck." I wondered if Arthur's date was at this very moment saying the same thing to someone else, and I wondered if later he would revisit that moment right before he shot himself in the head.

I dug deep to find a smidgeon of courtesy. "Well, good luck, then!" I called out as Arthur flounced off, clattering and gleaming and sparkling his way toward the stairs like a big round ball of red tinsel. "Have fun. Thanks for the cupcake. Enjoy the movie. Be home by ten!"

"Oh, you silly!" Arthur flapped a twenty-pound hand in my direction and tittered as he disappeared down the stairwell, giggling and glittering and tip-tapping along the way.

I softly closed the door behind him, took a moment to soak it all in, then stuffed the cupcake in my mouth.

Dale Evans?

AN HOUR later I was slugging back a beer and standing in front of the bathroom mirror, staring at myself in horror. The white work uniform I had been given was a disaster. The pants were so big I had to hold them under my armpits and roll them up at the ankles like a nine-year-old. The white baker's shirt that went with the pants was even bigger. I could walk three steps in any direction and never rustle the fabric of either one of them. When I plopped the stupid white chef's hat on my head, it fell over my eyes and almost swallowed my head completely.

I looked like a cast member of *Honey, I Shrunk the Kids*.

Crossing the apartment to fetch another beer (that's how appalled I was), I felt like a big fluffy cumulus cloud scudding across the sky.

Milan was a sex god in his baker's suit. Why couldn't I be a sex god too?

That thought had barely entered my head when I heard rustling outside my apartment door.

Still holding my pants up under my chin I yanked the door open, prepared to kill anyone who said one derogatory word about my ensemble. What I found on my doorstep stopped me cold.

It was Arthur again. He was still dressed in his cowgirl drag, only now the happy light had left his face and he looked merely… heartbroken. Trails of tear-laden mascara had smudged his cheeks and his chins were quivering as if he were fighting back a sob. He was holding a tray of cupcakes. The same sort of cupcakes as the one he had brought me earlier.

"How was your date, Arthur? You're back awfully early."

He sucked in a great, tremulous gout of air and a new spurt of tears overflowed his eyes. He thrust the tray of cupcakes closer to me, so I took them. As soon as I did, he plucked a lace handkerchief from his overflowing bodice. He dabbed at his eyes and blew his nose with a loud honk.

"He laughed at me," Arthur said, plucking the false eyelashes from his eyelids and folding them into the hanky. "He took one look and laughed. And then he turned around and walked away. Still laughing."

I reached out and took Arthur's hand. "Oh lord, Arthur. I'm so sorry." I tugged him across my living room and deposited him on the couch, causing his skirts and petticoats to rise up around him, almost swallowing him whole. When Gizmo opened his eyes and saw this huge glittering creature sitting next to him, his hair stood on end and his tail suddenly puffed up like a blowfish. The poor cat took off like a shot, propelling himself through the front door, not to be seen again for two days.

Heading for the fridge, I grabbed a couple of beers. I twisted them open and plopped myself down on the couch at Arthur's side, offering him one. He accepted it with a gentle smile, and said, "Thanks, sweetie." Then he hiccupped and the tears started anew.

Between hiccups and sobs, he told me why he'd come.

"I'm starting a real diet tomorrow. That's why I brought you the rest of the cupcakes. I had to get them out of my kitchen." He cast sad, longing eyes at the cupcakes, which were sitting on the coffee table in front of us, as if even now he was tempted to change his mind. Then he resolutely turned to me. "No more drag, Harlie. First thing tomorrow I'm going shopping for real clothes. From now on it'll be lumberjacky butch stuff for me. Nothing else."

I patted his knee. At least I hope it was his knee. There were so many petticoats in the way I couldn't be sure. "Well, that's probably for the best, don't you think? Although you're a lovely drag, you really are. But still—"

He purred through his bee-stung lips, "Still what?"

I sighed. "Still I think you'll be happier the other way. You know. Being butch."

He reached into his neckline and pulled out two bags of dry navy beans, and here I thought it had all been tits. Shows how wrong you can be, huh?

"You'll be my style guru from now on, Harlie. I swear. Whatever you tell me to wear, I'll wear. Tonight was just too *mortifying* to ever go through again. From now on I'll be a *real* cowboy."

"Well, you don't have to be a *cowboy*, Arthur. You can just dress normal."

"Normal?"

I should have known that word would be unfamiliar to him.

"Yes. Normal. Like a truck driver or a shoe salesman or the guy who delivers Sparklett's Water. You know. Normal."

He sagely nodded his head—the head still topped with a massive red wig and a cowgirl hat. "I think I see what you mean. Normal. Yes. It's a stretch but I can do that. I'm sure I can."

I wondered.

I tried to lighten the mood. "Thanks for the cupcakes. Are you feeling better now?"

He nodded. "Thank you, Harlie. You're a sweet boy." Then his eyes opened a little wider. He took in my outfit as if now was the first time he had noticed it.

"What the hell are you wearing?"

I blushed. I could feel the blood surging into my ears. "Tomorrow I start working as a baker's assistant."

Arthur's chin quivered. "Oh. You poor thing. You know that uniform doesn't fit, don't you?"

I narrowed my eyes, sarcastic as hell. "I suspected as much."

"Then take it off."

I narrowed my eyes ever further. "Say *what*?"

Arthur cackled. "Oh, don't get all virginal on me, precious. Give me that uniform and all the others you have, and I'll alter them before you start work tomorrow."

"So I won't look like a cloud?"

"Yes, honey. So you won't look like a cloud. And give me a pair of your regular jeans and a shirt to measure the uniforms by."

"Can you do that?" I asked.

He spread his arms wide and twirled his skirts. "If I can make this, I can make anything."

"Gee," I said, honestly impressed. "I guess you can."

I was out of the baker's suit in less than ten seconds, standing in front of Arthur in my tighty-whities and shoving the rest of the uniforms into his hands. Half-naked I gathered up a shirt and pair of jeans from the bedroom and hustled back, thrusting those into Arthur's arms as well. "Oh, thank you thank you thank you, Arthur." Then I tugged the huge white hat off my head. "Can you fix this too?"

He gave me a sad smile, and why wouldn't he? Could I *be* any more pathetic?

"I'll try," he said, biting back a grin.

He reached for a cupcake, then thought better of it. Heaving a massive sigh, he clutched the lump of clothes to his chest, snatched the two bags of dried beans off the coffee table, and headed for the door. His tap shoes clicked across my hardwood floor like castanets.

"I have a pass key," he said. "I'll return these before morning. I'll try not to wake you. It may take a few hours."

"Thank you, Arthur. You're a real friend." And before I knew what I was doing, I stepped into the man's arms, rested my cheek on his bulging bust line, and gave him a long hug.

He gave a sniff and hugged me back. When I felt a fat finger slide beneath the waistband of my underwear, I gently pushed him away. He merely chuckled.

At the door, he looked back one more time. "Thank you, Harlie."

"Thank *you*, Arthur."

He quietly closed the door behind him, giving me one last lingering ogle as I stood there in my BVDs.

"Luscious," he muttered as the door clicked closed between us. Although in all fairness, I'm not absolutely sure whether he was referring to me or the platter of cupcakes.

Chapter 5

I WOKE up to find my work uniforms neatly folded and stacked inside my front door. Leery, I tried one on, and wonder of wonders, it fit perfectly! Even a tiny tuck had been sewn into the back of the chef's hat so it wouldn't slip over my eyes and make me look like a doofus.

Arthur might be a strange, strange man with questionable cross-dressing instincts, but there was no arguing the fact he knew his way around a needle and thread. I must admit I was a little surprised he hadn't got carried away and sewn on any sparklies or feathers while he was at it.

Standing in front of my bathroom mirror all decked out for work and happily not looking like a moron, well, not a *complete* one, made me want to do something nice for Arthur. Something special. Something like quite possibly setting him up with my new boss, Mr. Burger. They were both of an age. They were both lonely, or so it seemed to me. I wasn't sure about Mr. Burger liking Arthur, but I was fairly certain Arthur would fall head over heels for Mr. Burger. After all Burger was tall, financially solvent, and he owned a deli. Arthur too was tall and financially solvent. At least I assumed he was well off since he owned the Belladonna Arms. That must be worth a substantial chunk of change. And as for Mr. Burger owning a deli, well, one look at Arthur's waistline would tend to suggest Arthur might find access to a deli somewhat of a dream come true. No?

But Arthur wasn't the only one I was seeing hope for on this fine morning, I thought, still standing there admiring myself in the bathroom mirror in my perfectly tailored baker suit. The fact that I no longer looked like a big fat squishy marshmallow in an ill-fitting work uniform gave me a little hope I might even be able to do something nice for *me*.

Something concerning a certain baker, maybe. If he wasn't straight. And if he wasn't already in a relationship. And if I didn't make a complete jackass of myself at work. I wasn't exactly a dunce when it came to flirting, after all. I'd been around the block a few times. I knew how to entice a man. I might not know how to *keep* one, but I could certainly get one interested. Don't get me wrong. I'm not as slutty as ChiChi. But slutty is highly overrated anyway. Sometimes what is called for is a goodly portion of finesse with a *teeny* dash of sluttiness thrown in to add a little spice to the enterprise.

I turned and craned my neck around to check out my ass in the mirror. After Arthur's tailoring coup, the old caboose was now nicely outlined in the seat of my white pants and no longer lost to view in folds and folds of fabric. I'm not a conceited sort of guy, honest to God, but I know my strengths and I know my weaknesses. And my ass is definitely not a weakness.

I tipped my chef's hat to a debonair angle, gave myself a wink, and before I could have second thoughts, I stalked through the apartment toward the front door, snatched up the house keys along the way, and stuffed them in my pocket. Ten seconds later, after hanging a thank-you note on Arthur's door, I was out on the street strolling jauntily toward my first day of work at Broadway Deli and feeling like a million bucks.

By the time I got there, my jauntiness was a thing of the past and my million-dollar feeling had depreciated to a nickel and three pennies. I was a nervous wreck. I hate the first days of *anything*.

It was 6:00 a.m., and the deli didn't open until seven. Since the door was locked, I tapped on the window and sang out, "Yoo hoo!" A moment later, with a jangle of keys and the throwing of a bolt, the door swung open, and I found myself face to face with Milan.

Once again he was decked out in white and looking gorgeous. He was so tall and so *solid*. His broad chest hovered directly in front of my face as we awkwardly greeted each other. I stood close enough that I could smell the clean scent of Sea Breeze on his skin. Maybe he used it as an aftershave. I gazed up into those bottomless blue eyes I remembered so well from yesterday and said, "Good morning."

He coolly nodded and relocked the door after ushering me inside.

The place was unlit and empty, totally different from yesterday. I eyed his wide shoulders and long legs as he strode between the empty booths to the kitchen. The kitchen was as brightly lit as an operating room, but again, aside from the two of us, there wasn't a soul around.

When he turned, he must have seen the surprise on my face.

"We're bakers. We start earlier than everyone else."

I nodded. "Of course." I clapped my hands together and tried to look eager. "So where do I start, boss? What do I do first?"

"First you don't call me boss."

"Then can I call you Milan?"

"Yes."

"Good. It's a really great name."

His stunning blue eyes disappeared for a second as he blinked in surprise. "Is it?" His lips didn't twist up to show pleasure but they didn't turn down and sneer and snap and snarl at me either. He merely seemed curious as to where I was going with all this.

I gave him my best smile. "You bet. Milan is a *great* name. I'm sure your wife or girlfriend has told you that a bazillion times."

He cocked his head to the side and studied me like I was a new breed of fish he had never encountered before—a new breed of fish with deplorable social skills. "I don't have a wife or girlfriend," he stated flatly.

My heart gave a happy little thump inside my chest (good God, maybe he *was* gay) even while I aimed a sympathetic pout in his direction. "I can't imagine why."

This time he simply shook his head and turned away. He pointed to the wall behind us. "Ovens," he said. Then he pointed to a door off to the right. "Storage." And finally, he made a little walking motion with his fingers between the two areas. "Your job is to fetch me what I need when I need it. If you don't take all day about it, and if you're still here a couple of weeks from now, maybe then I'll begin to teach you how to bake some of the simpler items."

"So I'll be your gofer."

"Yes. For now. Is that too much of an offense to your highbrow sensibilities?"

I laughed. "No."

"Good."

"How come you don't have a girlfriend or a wife?"

This time I could have sworn I spotted the merest hint of a grin on his handsome face, but if I did, he managed to snuff it out before anything came of it. "Are you always this annoying?"

"Am I annoying?" I said it for show, of course. Hell, even I know how annoying I can be.

For the first time, he seemed to notice something different about me. He let his eyes travel from the tip of my chef's hat, perched jauntily atop my head, to the fitted top and streamlined trousers of my perfectly altered baker's uniform. The only part of me that was less than stellar was the beat-up old running shoes I wore on my feet. I wasn't about to ruin new shoes traipsing back and forth in the gunk on a deli floor. I've worked in restaurants before.

At long last, Milan's smile made a cameo appearance, if just for a moment. I caught the briefest glimpse of snowy teeth and the tip of a pink, pink tongue behind them. "You're the first person yet who ever fit into that uniform."

"Thank you." I did a slow turn to show off the rear view (I wasn't born yesterday), and I'm pretty sure I caught his eyes lingering for a second on my ass. That *really* got my heart thumping harder.

"A friend of mine altered them last night. Hope that's okay."

He shrugged. "Sure. I don't mind at all." He seemed to weigh his next words carefully as his eyes travelled up and down my body yet again. "You look nice. Maybe I can get your friend to alter my uniforms too."

"Certainly," I said with a sneaky grin and far too much hope in the inflection. I held out my hand. "Just slip them off, and I'll run them over there right now."

The smile that met that request was a little broader, but it had a short shelf life. "Maybe I'll get back to you on that one."

"I sure hope so," I said.

This time he definitely smiled. It was a nice one, too, even if he did roll his eyes while he did it. "Let's get to work. We'll be opening soon."

"Golly," I said. "*There* it is."

"There what is?"

"Your smile."

He finally let it go. A laugh, I mean. He actually laughed. "Are you trying to schmooze the boss?"

"Couldn't hoit."

He arched an eyebrow and gave me a Snidely Whiplash sneer. He let his eyes range over my five-foot-six frame. Then he gazed down at his own six feet four. "Couldn't hurt? That's what you think."

"I like the sound of that." I did, too.

"Maybe some other time," he said.

"You promise?"

"I never promise anything."

"Darn," I muttered under my breath as he led me toward the storage room. If he heard, he chose not to mention it. And I was too engrossed in watching his ass and long legs and wondering what kind of pain he was talking about to worry too much about the words coming out of his mouth.

Never knowing when to shut up, I dug my grave a little deeper. "Why were you glowering?"

He didn't bother turning around but kept on walking. "When?"

"Yesterday."

A touch of frost iced his voice. "I wasn't."

"Yes, you were."

"Okay, I was. Happy?"

"So why were you? Glowering, I mean."

"It's private."

"Ah, come on, you can—"

Milan stopped in his tracks and whirled on me. "If you want to keep this job, you'll shut up right now." His eyes were as hard as diamonds.

Gulp. "I'm sorry. I didn't mean to pry."

"Yes, you did. But don't do it again."

You win, I thought, flinching away from the glare in those steely blue eyes. It took me a second, but I found my voice. "I won't do it again. I need this job. I'll try to be good."

"See that you do," he said, and turning away once again, he led me to the storage room, and my first day as a baker's assistant began in earnest.

Not another relaxed word crossed either of our lips the whole day long. If there was ever to be a friendship between Milan and me, I figured I had already pretty well blown it out of the water on my very first try.

Jeez, I'm such an idiot.

I DRAGGED my poor pathetic body through the front door of apartment 2A in a little cloud of flour dust. I had never been so tired in my life. Milan had worn me out. "Fetch this." "Fetch that." "Clean up this mess." "Scrub out that oven." I'm not built for working under the thumb of a man I find sexy and intriguing but who lacks even a trace of the social graces and who wouldn't know or acknowledge a compliment if it snuck up and bit him on the ass—a task, by the way, which I would have been more than happy to take on myself. Biting his ass, I mean. If you could see Milan's ass you would understand why. Christ, the warmest thing he had said to me all day was "Don't drop that tray."

Just before I dropped it.

To make matters worse, I had spent the entire day with the man, and even now I couldn't say with any certainty if he was gay, straight, bi, or neutered, but I was leaning toward straight. After all, his father was gay, so what were the odds of him being gay as well? Pretty slim, I'd say.

Milan might have shown a trace of good humor when I had coyly asked him to remove his uniform so I could take it to be altered, but that didn't really tell me much. And in the same vein, the looks he gave *my* body might have simply been his way of checking out how professionally my uniform was altered. The only absolute truth I had gleaned from spending the day with Milan Burger was that he didn't like people snooping into his private affairs. As I had done. Asking if he was married, asking if he had a girlfriend. I was still banging myself in the head for that. But he had paid me back. Oh, yes indeedy.

The man had worked me to the bone.

My back ached, the pristine white uniform Arthur had so painstakingly altered for me looked like it had been trampled to rags in a cattle stampede, and I had either burns, blisters, or cuts on seven of my ten fingers. I wouldn't be able to comfortably beat off for a week, and after a day of sniffing around Milan like a dog in heat, that was the one thing I really wanted to do.

Good lord, the man was sexy.

Trying not to sob I was so goddamn tired, I headed straight for the bathroom, shedding clothes along the way. I filled the tub with steamy water after throwing in half a bottle of bubble bath (I can't be butch *all* the time), and when it was sufficiently frothy and had the entire apartment smelling of apples, I sank into it up to my nose and closed my eyes in bliss.

At that moment, my cell phone rang. I ignored it.

The hot bath felt like heaven. I could actually feel it sucking the pain from my muscles. The apple-scented suds bobbing around my chin filled my thoughts with pleasant memories of strolling through an apple orchard one day a couple of years back with Dan at my side. It was on a trip we had taken to Napa Valley. We had been happy then. At least I had. Who knows how long Dan had been happy. With me. With us. Maybe never. Who knows?

The phone fell silent. A couple of minutes later, it rang again. This time I knew—I absolutely *knew*—it was Dan on the other end. What could he possibly be calling about? Was he having second thoughts? After four months apart, did he suddenly want me back?

Again I let the phone ring down to silence without trying to pick it up. It was at that moment—that *precise* moment—I knew I was over Dan. Even if he wanted me back, I wouldn't go. I would never be able to trust him. That was a given. And did I really want to live like that?

The answer to that question was a resounding no. Unh-uh. Never again.

So when the phone rang a third time, my mind was made up. Suddenly I was eager to tell Dan exactly where he could stick his feeble attempt at reconciliation. Suddenly I was eager to tell him I had moved on, and in no uncertain terms. Suddenly I was eager to tell him to fuck off. Gaily and with great enthusiasm. *Golly,* I thought. *Maybe I've finally grown a pair of balls.*

I leaned over the edge of the tub and plucked the phone from the pocket of my filthy baker's pants, which were still lying in a heap on the bathroom floor. I wiped my hand dry on a dirty pant leg before hitting Receive because, hell, I don't know. I'm not an electrician. Maybe you can electrocute your ass grabbing a cell phone when you're lying in two feet of soapy water.

I felt in full control as I calmly stated, "Harlie Rose speaking. How may I help you?"

It took me exactly one heartbeat to realize it wasn't Dan at all. It was Sylvia.

"Oh, Harlie!" she wailed into the phone. "I had no idea they were going to stick you in the kitchen. I thought you'd take *my* job."

I tutted her to silence. "Don't worry. It's not so bad. Milan was nice." *For a serial killer.* "And I'll get used to working the ovens." *Just like they did in Dachau.*

Sylvia was still wailing. "But you'll be working twice as hard as the servers, and you won't get any tips! I'll talk to Mr. Burger first thing tomorrow. I promise I will."

I felt my stubborn streak kick in. "No, Sylvia. Don't. It's not so bad. Really. If it gets to the point where I can't take it anymore, I'll talk to Mr. Burger myself."

"Are you sure?"

"Yes, I'm sure. So stop worrying. The worst that can happen is I'll learn a trade."

"You already have a trade. You're a writer."

I groaned. I'd almost forgotten about the new book. I had to work on *that* tonight. I *had* to.

"Look, Sylvia, I'm in the tub, and I'm starting to prune. Don't worry, please. I've had worse jobs, and at least I have Milan's ass to stare at all day. It's a fine ass, in case you hadn't noticed. Uh, by the way—what's his story? Is he like a homophobic Baptist or something? I figure he must be straight, at least. Right? Is he straight?"

I could almost feel Sylvia's grin coming through the phone. "No, honey. He's not straight. Him and his dad are both gay. Milan has a lover. They've been together for more than a year, I think. Why? Didn't he tell you that?"

"He didn't tell me anything except 'Move your ass,' and he didn't say *that* in the fun way, if you know what I mean."

Sylvia tittered. "I think I can figure it out."

"Is he always so grouchy?"

"Why?" she asked. "Was he grouchy? How grouchy was he?"

"Well, did you ever see a rattlesnake trapped in a metal mailbox on a hot day while somebody pounded on the mailbox with a baseball bat for three hours?"

"Uh, no."

"Well, picture it, then."

"That bad, huh?"

"Yes. That bad."

"Want me to talk to him?"

"No," I said. "Then I'll just seem like the whiny new baker's assistant who went running to the transsexual behind the cash register because I was too chicken to stand up for myself."

She giggled. "Yes, I guess you would. Tell you what, Harlie. I have two more days to work before I'm out of there. I'll ask around. Maybe somebody knows what's up with Milan. He has always been sort of quiet, but I've never known him to be a poophead before."

"Poophead? Try asshole." I slapped a mound of bubbles and froth flew all the way across the bathroom and splattered the wall. "I think he hates me."

If Sylvia had been in the room, she would have patted my cheek. I know she would. "Oh, Harlie, don't be silly. Who could hate you?"

"You've never met my ex."

"Hmm. Okay. You've got me there. But maybe your ex had a reason."

"Thanks a lot."

"Oh, hush. You know what I think?"

"What do you think, oh wise one?"

She giggled again. "I think you like Milan. I think you'd like to get to know him. I think you'd like to get to know him in a *nonculinary* sort of way, if you catch my drift."

"Oh, I caught it."

"And?"

"Well, hell, Sylvia! Who wouldn't? The man is gorgeous. But I don't mess with people who are in relationships. It's my one big rule." As an afterthought, I added, "What's yours?"

"What's what? My one big rule?"

"Yes, Sylvia. What's your one big rule? What's the rule you live by above all others?"

She didn't hesitate, and by that simple fact, I knew she was telling the truth. "My one big rule is to help my friends every chance I get."

I felt a tear leak out of eye. "Then I guess we're both a couple of saps."

"Yes, Harlie. The best kind of saps."

"Maybe," I grudgingly admitted.

Sylvia let a comfortable silence slip into the conversation. Then she abruptly ended it. "So don't worry, Harlie. I'll try to find out what's up with Milan, and I'll do it on the sly. He'll never know. All right?"

"All right."

"Pete will be home soon. Have a nice evening, Harlie. Get some rest. Tomorrow is another day."

"Don't remind me."

She tutted with sympathy and ended the call.

I tossed the phone onto the pile of filthy work clothes, pinched my nose, and ducked my head under the froth to shut out the world entirely.

When I came up for air, sweeping the soap from my eyes and gasping for air, I didn't feel much better than I had before. In fact, when my phone beeped again and I quickly snatched it off the floor thinking it was Sylvia, I found myself feeling considerably worse all of a sudden when I realized who was calling.

"This is Ramon. How was your little jog in the park the other day?"

Uh-oh.

"ChiChi tells me you followed him there."

"ChiChi said *what*?"

"Listen, *pendejo*, if you want a boyfriend, go find one of your own. Don't try to steal mine."

"I didn't follow ChiChi into the park," I snapped. "He followed me!"

"Why would he do that?"

"You figure it out!"

"ChiChi wouldn't do that!"

"Oh, no?"

"No. He loves me."

I listened to Ramon's furious breathing over the phone. From the living room, I heard scratching at my front door. Probably Gizmo stopping by for a snack. The bathwater I was soaking in was turning cool, and I was getting depressed as hell.

He loves me, Ramon had said. *He loves me.*

Suddenly I didn't have the heart to burst that innocent bubble. There was too much hope in the way Ramon had spoken the words. Too much *certainty.*

I coughed up a long stuttering sigh and rolled my eyes so far up into my head I almost passed out. "I'm sorry, Ramon. It won't happen again."

Ramon couldn't seem to believe what he had just heard. "Say what?"

"I said it won't happen again. And make sure you tell ChiChi I said so, okay?"

The silence lasted so long, I thought perhaps the call had been terminated and I hadn't noticed.

Then Ramon spoke softly. Almost too softly. "Thank you, Harlie. I—I know what ChiChi is like. I know he probably made the first move on you. Not the other way around. Thank you for twisting everything around and trying to take the blame. But I know the truth. Okay? I'm sorry I yelled at you. I was just saving face, I guess. Trying to maintain a little dignity."

"I know, Ramon. I figured that out. If it's any consolation, I think ChiChi is a putz for making you feel that way."

Sadly, in a voice that barely carried to my ear, Ramon said, "So do I." And after a brief flurry of staticky silence, he added, "Good night," and hung up the phone.

Suddenly I was exhausted. And it wasn't all from work either. I was exhausted in the heart.

A flurry of thumping on my front door dragged me out of it. The thumping was considerably more insistent than it was a few minutes ago. Somebody was getting pissed. *Oh, good,* I thought, dragging my weary, dripping ass out of the bathtub and snatching a towel off the rack to dry off, *there's a friend at the door. Impatient and grumpy, but still a friend. And I don't have too many of those, do I?*

Naked and still dripping, I wrapped the towel around my waist, padded through the apartment on wet feet, and yanked open the door.

Gizmo's motor immediately kicked in, and he stepped across the threshold purring like he owned the place. And me. He bumped his forehead against my shin to say hello, and I scooped him off the floor to hold him close. It was kind of nice feeling owned.

Together we headed for the kitchen and a little communal dining. Me and the cat. That would put me in a better mood, right? *Right?*

WORK IN PROGRESS   75

Chapter 6

As IT turned out, I didn't have to wait for Sylvia to get the dirt on Milan to find out why he was being such a shit. I got the dirt from the horse's mouth instead. Or I should say the horse's *father's* mouth.

Mr. Burger came to me on my lunch hour during my third day of working at the deli. Since my first day of employment, when Milan and I had sparred briefly and I had taken a feeble shot at flirting with the hunky baker, we hadn't shared another twelve words together—if you discounted direct orders, which he periodically lobbed at me like lawn darts.

I was perched on a garbage can in the back alley gnawing on a foot-long pastrami and cheese and sucking on a Diet Coke large enough to drown a Rottweiler in. Mr. Burger gave me a jovial wave and came over to perch himself on an adjoining trash can like we were old friends.

The first thing he said was "You didn't have to pay for that sandwich, son. You get free meals when you're working here. Didn't Milan tell you that?"

"Nope."

He gave me a weary nod, as if he'd expected as much. "Before you go home today, I'll get your money back and stuff it in your locker. Okay?"

"Thank you, sir. I appreciate it."

He settled in, wiggling his skinny ass around on the garbage can to get a little more comfortable. He clenched his fists in a cozy manner and let them dangle down between his long legs as he swayed his feet back and forth like a kid perched on the edge of a porch swing.

"So, how do you like working here, Harlie? Not too rough for you working in the kitchen, I hope. I imagine you would have rather been serving."

I was touched by his friendly manner. Truth be told, I hadn't encountered much warmth since I'd come to work there, other than the fucking screaming heat shooting out at me every time I opened one of the oven doors.

"The job's just fine, sir. It isn't easy, but that's okay. No job is."

"Just call me Burger, son. Not sir. I feel old enough as it is. Every time somebody calls me 'sir,' I feel like I'm ready for the slag heap."

I gave him an understanding smile. "Sorry. I'll try not to do it again. I thought—uh—more mature men liked to be called sir."

Burger spat up a gurgly chuckle. "Think again."

We let a companionable silence settle around us as I continued to gnaw at my sandwich and slurp my way through my giant-ass Diet Coke.

Finally, Burger broke the silence with a question out of the blue, which I immediately suspected was the main reason he came over to talk with me to begin with.

"And how are you getting along with Milan? I don't seem to see you two smiling much as you're back there working the ovens and sweating like a couple of cretins. It's a hot job, working the ovens. I did it myself for several years."

"Did you?" I asked.

"Yeah. But that's about a century ago. Let's talk about now. So— you and Milan. How are you getting along? You can tell me anything, you know. I won't make a big deal out of it. If something's not cooking on all the burners, I'll just casually do what I can to set it right. So let me have it, son. How are you and my boy getting along?"

I sucked in a deep breath, let it out, then sucked in another one. Then I decided, fuck it, and said what I wanted to say.

"He hates my guts. I think maybe you should just let me go and find him somebody he can get along with. I'll find another job. Although I admit I'd miss your pastrami."

Burger's face was creased with two very attractive dimples for an old man to put on display. "It is good, isn't it." It wasn't a question. It was a statement of fact, just as it should have been. Burger's pastrami really was the best I'd ever eaten.

But he didn't stay focused on the pastrami for long. He gave me a hurt look and clucked his tongue like a cowboy urging on a stubborn palomino. "He doesn't hate you, son. Milan's just going through some personal problems right now." Burger tore his eyes from my face and stared out over the length of the alley to the street outside and all the traffic sliding back and forth on Ninth Avenue. "A lot of us are."

I knew I was taking a big risk, but I couldn't seem to stop myself. I reached out and laid my hand on Burger's arm. "I'm sorry you lost your lover," I said softly. "It must be really hard to lose someone like that."

He didn't seem startled by my words as much as he was by the touch of my hand on his arm. When he lifted his eyes from my hand to center them on my face, there was a mist blurring his pupils and his dimples were gone. Burger almost seemed relieved to have somebody bring the subject up rather than himself. He studied my expression of concern for the longest moment, then offered me a sad little smile.

"It's the hardest thing I've ever endured, son. Someday, if it ever happens to you, and I pray it won't, you'll understand what I mean."

"Yes, sir," I said softly. "I mean Burger. I'm sorry you're going through it."

If he was surprised I knew his story, he didn't show it. I supposed he realized that secrets among employees in a place like this would be few and far between. I'll give him credit, though. It didn't seem to bother him.

Burger gazed soulfully at me and pushed his dark hair back off his forehead. Now I looked closely, I realized he only had the merest trace of gray at the temples. The rest of his hair was lush and wavy and black. I suspected Milan's hair would look just like that, although so far I had yet to see him without his chef's hat.

Burger cleared his throat and blinked the mist from his eyes, as if it was time to get back to business. And when I thought about it later, I realized that was exactly what he was doing.

"Harlie, I don't want you to go blabbing about any of this to anybody, but I feel I should tell you something. Can you promise me you won't say anything?"

"Yes."

He nodded matter-of-factly, as if he expected nothing less.

"Like I said, Harlie, Milan is going through some personal problems right now too. I think maybe that's why he's being so hard on you. I don't want you to hate him for it, okay? I'm sure he'll lighten up on you as soon as he gets his head out of his ass and realizes he's not the only one in the world with problems."

Another silence settled around us. My half-eaten sandwich lay forgotten in my hand.

Burger cleared his throat. "Son, I know you're gay, so I know you'll understand what I'm about to tell you."

"How do you know I'm gay?" I interrupted.

He gave me a world-weary smile. "Let's just say it takes one to know one."

I felt a blush rising to the back of my neck. After all, I'm not exactly lumberjack material. I should have seen that coming. "Okay," I said. Urging him on, I prodded, "And Milan?"

"Milan is gay too. I'm not sure you knew that. Did you?"

Sylvia had told me Milan was gay, but I didn't want Mr. Burger to think Sylvia was gossiping about his son. So I merely said, "Well...."

Burger gave me a knowing smile. "I guess the old 'takes one to know one' line applies to other people than me. Anyhoo, Milan lost his lover too. That's what's bothering him. That's why he's acting the way he is."

"Did his lover die like yours did?"

Even now Burger seemed surprised to hear it spoken so matter-of-factly that his lover had actually died, and according to Sylvia that had happened almost a year ago. At my words, Burger's breath caught in his throat. But he quickly recovered.

"No, Harlie. They broke up. I'm not sure who left who. I just know it happened. I'm afraid Milan is about as talkative to me right now as he is to you."

"I'm sorry."

This time it was Burger's turn to snake his long skinny hand out and rest it on my arm. "Thank you, Harlie. You're a good boy."

He went back to watching the traffic at the end of the alley for a moment. "I guess what I'm asking you, son, is to give Milan a little space until he can get his head wrapped around everything that's happening to him. He won't be this way forever. Milan is a good man. And a kind one. Not a—not a—"

"Morose asshole?" The words were out of my mouth before I could stop them.

Burger stared at me for a good three seconds, then threw his head back and howled with laughter. "Damn, son. I couldn't have expressed it better myself. You have a way with words. You should be a writer."

"Actually, I am."

And Burger laughed even louder. He sniffed up a little snot, and added, "Well, there you go, then."

He scooted his skinny ass off the garbage can and gave me a wink. "Finish your lunch and get back in there before Milan sics the dogs after you. And remember, from now on your food is free. Don't even ask. Just serve yourself and let it go at that. Okay?"

"Yes, sir. Thank you."

He offered up a warm smile that was really quite charming. He dusted off the seat of his pants before wagging a long finger in my face. "And that's the last 'sir' you get. All right?"

"All right."

"Good. I'm glad you're with us, Harlie. You're a good worker. And someday I'd like to read something you wrote. Deal?"

"Deal."

With that, he was gone. I watched him walk through the deli's back door, and as the door hung open for a moment on its slow hinge, I spotted Milan back by the ovens. He was leaning against the wall, staring off into space with empty, emotionless eyes as if he didn't have a care in the world.

Now, of course, I knew better. He had cares, all right. He had bunches. He had so many cares, in fact, they were tearing him apart. But what I didn't know was what I could do to cheer him up. Should I try to be a friend, whether he wanted a friend or not? Or should I leave him alone and let him battle his own demons in his own sweet time? And if I did that, how much more abuse would I have to take from the guy before he stopped riding *my* ass? (And when I say riding *my* ass, I mean not in a good way.)

It was two days later I realized I wouldn't have to do anything. Milan would do it for me.

THE BRAIDED challah bread was one of Milan's specialties, and as I pulled a long tray of it out of the oven with my oversized mitts and my face squinted up against the heat, I had to admit it was nothing short of a work of art—golden brown, as soft as cotton, and with a fragrance that made your salivary glands open up like spigots.

As I arranged the loaves on a cooling rack, carefully because they were hotter than hell, Milan came up beside me and watched me work.

It looked like he was about to chew me out for some infraction or another, but instead, he leaned in and spoke quietly into my ear. "Pop says you're a nice guy."

I stopped what I was doing and stared at him, wondering if I would see sarcasm on his face because there didn't seem to be any in his voice.

Was I hallucinating? He couldn't be saying something pleasant, could he? "What? What did you say?"

"I said Pop likes you."

That had me blinking back my surprise. Not at what he'd told me, but at the fact he had told me at all.

I eyed him warily. It was sort of like petting a rattlesnake. You never know if you're going to get bitten or not. "I like your dad too. He's a nice guy."

Milan shuffled his feet and looked uncomfortable. Maybe even more uncomfortable than me. Then he raised his head and spoke again. This time when he spoke, his eyes were welded to mine, as if it wasn't easy for him either, yet he was determined to hold on until he got his point across.

"I was talking to Sylvia too. She told me you broke up with your lover a few months ago. She said you're just now getting over it."

This time I took a moment to consider his words. I wasn't sure what he was getting at, but I thought maybe I should let him finish getting it out, whatever it was.

"I didn't break up with him," I said. "He broke up with me."

"Why?"

The question was so abrupt and so surprisingly rude that all I could do was stare at him for a minute. Then I realized if I was going to answer, I might as well answer with the truth. After four days of putting up with the guy's shit, I didn't much care if I made him mad or not. Oddly enough, being on the verge of hating Milan Burger gave me a certain amount of freedom to say what I wanted to say without worrying about how it came out. "I don't know why he left me. He never explained it. He just left. One day he loved me, the next day he didn't. And that's all there was to it. Anything else you want to know? Want to hear about me crying myself to sleep the first couple of months? Want to hear about me wondering for weeks on end if he was with somebody else? Maybe that would make you feel better."

Milan looked like I had slapped him. "N-no. I don't want to know anything like that."

"Oh," I said, acting all nonchalant, when what I really wanted to do was slap him in the puss with a loaf of bread. "Okay, then."

Milan's cheeks flushed. God, he was handsome, and God, I was being a prick.

Maybe just so he wouldn't have to look at me, he eyed the challah bread cooling on the racks. He wiped a dribble of sweat from the side of his neck. I wasn't sure if it was from heat or nerves, and I didn't much give a shit.

"I figure hell is a bakery," he said with an odd little smile. "Let's go outside for a few minutes and cool off. I'll grab us a couple of Cokes along the way. You like Diet, right?"

"R-right."

I watched him swing open the door to the huge walk-in cooler in the corner. When he came out, he was carrying two cans of soda and two ice-cream sandwiches. He wasn't smiling, but he didn't look pissed off either, for a change. He hooked his finger at me and led me through the back door.

He pointed to a trash can. "Pull up a seat."

So I did. If I'd been mad before, I was over it now. The cool air on my skin and the cold soda in my hand was enough to knock the mad out of my system. I was never very good at staying mad anyway. Maybe I'm attention deficient.

We both popped our soda cans open and took a long pull. Sighing contentedly, we then tore the wrappers from our ice-cream sandwiches and bit off a couple of chunks of heaven.

When Milan spoke, his voice was kind. It was a tone I had never heard him use before—with me or with anyone else—and it snagged my attention like a fishhook.

"I'm sorry I've been so hard on you, Harlie. I had no right to do that."

Even perched side by side on trash cans, as his father and I had been a few days earlier, Milan was so tall and broad shouldered he of sort loomed over me like a tree. I felt tiny sitting next to him.

My eyes were continually drawn to his strong, elegant hands. They were so beautiful, with their backs sprinkled with dark hair, and I was intrigued by the way that hair swirled into a little forest at the man's wrists. Milan's forearms were corded with muscle, and the dark forest of hair continued all the way up to his heavy, rounded biceps. At that point, his skin paled, the hair sloughed away, and all that was left was a velvety expanse of smooth, smooth skin that coated those rolling biceps like a silken sheathe. I so wanted to lay my lips to those rolling mounds of muscle, to feel the heat of them, and maybe taste them too, and the very moment that thought entered my head, I felt my dick give an eager tug, shaking itself awake.

I shuddered at the unexpected surge of lust and groped around for something to say or do to camouflage it.

I shifted my ass around on the garbage can. What else was I supposed to do? At least it gave my dick a little relief. "I thought you just didn't like me," I said. *Brilliant.*

Milan stopped gnawing at his ice-cream sandwich and turned inquisitive eyes in my direction. He nibbled at his lower lip for a second before he spoke. I could tell he was carefully considering what he was about to say. A look of such sweetness came over his face that I froze like an ice sculpture, staring at it. His words were so sincerely uttered, I felt the melting ice-cream sandwich begin to dribble down my forearm, and I didn't even care.

"It wasn't you, Harlie. It was me. See—my lover just left me too. A few weeks ago. I—I'm not sure, but I think for some reason I've been taking it out on you. I'm sorry. I've been a real dick. I hope you'll forgive me."

Dick. He said dick. Trying not to concentrate too hard on that development, I licked the ice cream off the back of my hand, stalling for time. I wondered if his father had spoken to him.

"S'okay."

He leaned in closer. "What? I couldn't quite hear you."

I cleared my throat and wondered when my dick would explode since it was now at critical mass. My God, the man was overpowering to be around. "I said it's okay. That you've been a dick. Maybe I deserved it."

At that he grunted a mellow chuckle. "Maybe you did. What with being a prying little shit and all."

I straightened my back and poked my chin out, trying to look indignant. "I wasn't prying! I was attempting to get to know you. That's all it was. Jesus!"

Milan laughed. "You were snooping and you know it. You were fishing around trying to figure out if I was gay."

"I already knew you were gay."

"You did not."

"Well, I *wanted* you to be!"

That little statement stopped us both in our tracks since neither one of us saw it coming.

"I didn't mean to say that," I mumbled.

Milan's face exploded into a rosy blush like a burning Christmas tree. "So you're finally being truthful. That's a nice change of pace."

I downed the last of my ice-cream sandwich and took a long pull of Coke before I found the courage to speak. When I did finally get the words out, I found myself reverting to a fourth-grade vocabulary. "Oh, blow me."

Milan studied me for a couple of heartbeats, and then he said, "Maybe later." And without another word, he picked up his Coke can and empty ice-cream wrapper and toddled off toward the deli door. I could only see the back of his head, but somehow I knew he was smiling.

I guess I knew it because I was smiling too.

Once he got to the door, he stood there holding it open for me. He stooped to give me a little salami-salami-baloney bow, and said, "Come on, kid. Back to work."

I didn't budge from where I sat. My hard-on wouldn't let me. "I'll be in in a minute."

Milan got a knowing look on his face as if he knew exactly why I was stalling for time. But at least he had the decency to allow me that little bit of dignity.

"Well, don't be long," he said with a teeny grin playing at his lips. "It's time for the biscotti."

I nodded and turned away, praying to God my face didn't look as red as it felt.

Milan chuckled to himself and let the door swing closed between us.

Chapter 7

AND SUDDENLY, just like *that*, life became fun again.

With the passing of a little time, I found myself truly over Dan. From a thousand kernels of imagination, my new book began to take shape. I had carefully gleaned a tiny coterie of friends from among my new neighbors at the Belladonna Arms—Arthur, Sylvia and Pete, Stanley and Roger—and that was a blessing since I have never been one to make friends easily. I'm afraid I made it somewhat of a point to avoid ChiChi and Ramon, ChiChi because I still didn't trust him and Ramon because I still felt guilty, although the fact that his lover made a pass at me was sure as hell no fault of my own. I had also grown to appreciate Gizmo's periodic visits and actually missed him when he was off bumming food and abusing the hospitality of someone else.

While I wouldn't call my easing of tensions with Milan anything other than *détente*, which was basically all it was, there was also a *thrum* of something going on in the background every time he came within two feet of me during the course of our workdays together. Call it what you will. Animal magnetism best defined it for me. It was the same desire to be near the man that I had sensed the first moment I met him. But there was also a longing there—a *pull*—that strangely transcended sex. It was a craving I began to feel even when I was nowhere near Milan. Gradually, as my days at the deli stretched into a week, then two, then three, I began to feel a sort of comfort when Milan was near. It was such an odd feeling that I no longer flirted with him at all. Somehow it seemed wrong to do so. We had both been through enough with our past relationships that perhaps we needed nothing more right now. At least until we were ready.

After our initial chat in the alley, Milan no longer spoke of his ex. Nor was he cold in his dealings with me. While he might not be particularly effusive, he was always polite and friendly. And if I sometimes spotted him lost in thought, at least he wouldn't appear annoyed I had caught him at it. He would simply give me a little self-deprecating shrug and get back to work.

Mr. Burger, too, became somewhat of a comfort to have around. For one thing, he was the kindest man I had ever worked for. I began to understand why Sylvia and all the other employees at the deli were so protective of him. We would see each other all day at work, of course, but even then, every time our physical paths converged, he would reach out and give me a friendly pat on the shoulder, or a simple brushing of fingertips across my back. In a quiet voice, he would take the time to ask me how I was, ask me how my day was going. It was an acknowledgment I was there, nothing more. He was not making a pass, he was not making inappropriate gestures, he was simply being a good boss and maybe even a little bit of a friend.

It was odd how the three of us, Burger, Milan, and I, were in the same boat as far as our personal lives were concerned. Each of us was in the process of recovering from loss, and somehow that realization of a shared hurt made us closer. Made us more aware of each other's feelings. Made us a little more understanding. We were each of us a work in progress, and we were each of us dealing with it in our own way.

That feeling of a common goal, a common healing, added respect to our friendships. We respected each other now. Or I imagined we did. We were war buddies who had all fought a battle of sorts and were now in the process of recovering from it. It was like the deli was a trauma ward, and after a long tough rehab, we were finally on the mend. We were transitioning. Each in his own way.

And speaking of works in progress....

Sylvia's surgery was quickly approaching, and one day out of the blue, she asked me to a dinner party at her apartment. I knew Sylvia by now. I knew she couldn't cook anything but Toll House cookies. So when I asked her who was preparing the dinner, she laughed.

"I'm having it catered. So stop worrying."

Since that waylaid my fears nicely, I happily accepted the invitation.

How was I supposed to know nature would have a couple of tricks up its sleeve, huh? Not to mention Sylvia. She was a tricky little minx as well, I would soon learn.

Two days before the dinner party, I went knocking on Arthur's door with the intent of making headway on one more work in progress: Arthur's transformation. And I thought Sylvia's dinner party would be the perfect place to foist a brand-new, butch Arthur onto an unsuspecting world.

He answered the door in the periwinkle blue dressing gown I had seen him wear back on the first day we met. Perhaps his marabou-feathered, stiletto-heeled mules had not survived that rainy day after all, for now beneath the hem of his voluminous dressing gown, he was wearing a butt-ugly pair of men's house slippers made of some sort of god-awful chopped up carpeting material. At least he was wig and makeup free. That was a step in the right direction.

"Get dressed," I said. "We're going shopping."

He was holding a gigantic turkey leg in his fist, like Henry the VIII. Or maybe it was an ostrich leg. God knows it was big enough. "We are?" he asked in surprise.

"Yes. We're going to debut your new butch wardrobe at Sylvia's party. You'll be the hit of the evening. But before we can debut it, we have to buy it."

He looked like I had just strangled his mother. "But I was going to wear my new culottes and a faux mink jacket I found in the Goodwill Store up the street. It's to die for! I even have a new wig with the most darling pigtails in the ba—"

"Nope. You're going butch. Now get dressed. Let's go shopping."

"I have a nice housedress I could slip into, I suppose. Sort of a June Cleaver sort of thing. A little more sedate. Would *that* be all right?"

"No. You'll wear pants."

"Pants? As in—plain old fucking pants?"

"Yes. And a shirt and men's shoes. I assume you *have* men's shoes lying around."

He looked doubtful. "Well, of course—at least I—well, sure, Harlie. I mean I *must* have a pair of men's shoes *somewhere*."

I plucked the turkey leg out of his hand. It must have weighed two pounds. "And you're supposed to be on a diet, remember? Now go get dressed. And bring a credit card." *A big one.*

He wandered off, shaking his head and mumbling something about pushy tenants. Ten minutes later he was back. He was wearing a black suit so tight across his paunch if he ever got it buttoned they would have to use the Jaws of Life to get him back out of it again.

I wasn't impressed. "Don't you have anything casual?"

"No!" he snapped. "And where's my turkey leg?"

I burped and looked guilty. Then I presented him with the empty turkey bone I was hiding behind my back. He immediately gave me that "you strangled my mother" look again.

I stared at his black suit. "You look like you're going to a funeral."

"And why wouldn't I?" he huffed. "That's what this suit is for. To be buried in. Unfortunately it's the only butch thing I have lying around. So it's either I go in this or I go in drag or we don't go at all."

He shot me a look of rebellious superiority but I squashed it like a bug. "Fine. Wear the suit. Let's go."

Four hours later, Arthur and I were no longer speaking to each other, but at least he had his new clothes, although I swore I would never go shopping with him again for the rest of my life. Ever. And I meant fucking *ever.*

LIKE A proper guest, I arrived on the doorstep of 4B at precisely the requested time. It was a casual dinner, so I was decked out in my best blue jeans (commando style since I was shooting for comfort) and a new black T-shirt with my least scuffed white tennies on my feet. To me, clean tennies and a black T-shirt is damn near formal attire. Get over it.

Since it was once again raining like a motherfucker, it was rather nice not to have to battle the elements to get where I was going. Even from the fourth floor landing, I could hear the storm battering at the old neon sign perched atop the Belladonna Arms, shaking it this way and that and eliciting a series of truly unnerving squeaks and rattles, as if the whole contraption was about to unscrew itself from its foundations and come crashing to the ground.

Sylvia and Pete met me at the door with wide grins. Sylvia wore a cute little retro skirt with a slit up the side and a huge safety pin the size of an ear of corn holding the flap together. It was topped off by a simple white blouse with red piping. Gold hoop earrings dangled from Sylvia's ears. Standing beside her at the door, Pete was wearing blue jeans, sort of like my own except his were ironed. He also wore a berry-colored polo shirt that showed off his long lean torso beautifully. I wouldn't exactly call Pete handsome, but there was something about him when he was in the presence of Sylvia that made him sexy as hell. Even the large elfish ears that poked out from either side of his head like a kid's couldn't detract from that sexiness. Seeing the two of them together was always tantamount to suddenly understanding what love was all about, and it floored me every time.

Together, Pete and Sylvia scooped me into their arms, Sylvia kissing one cheek and Pete pecking the other. Then I was ushered through the door to greet the rest of the guests.

Since it was a small gathering, everyone but Arthur and the caterers were already there. Knowing Arthur as I did, I suspected he was waiting for the proper moment to make a fashionably late entrance. I just hoped when he did, he would be wearing the new *manly* clothes we had spent four horrific hours shopping for two days earlier. If he came in drag I was going to wring his neck.

Stanley and Roger were sipping wine by the window, staring out at the storm. They too came over and gave me a warm hug when I waved hello.

ChiChi and Ramon were sitting cross-legged on the floor by the coffee table, tearing through a plate of Toll House cookies. Ramon gave me a friendly enough hello, but ChiChi simply leered and winked, making a point of staring at my crotch while he did it. I nodded to Ramon and ignored ChiChi completely. With the proper motivation, I can be a bitch too.

Charlie the kleptomaniac was standing by a bookcase holding a terra cotta figurine upside down as if he were a collector checking out the maker's mark. The foot-high statue seemed to be a rendition of some sort of ancient Indian god. Probably from Pier One. I doubted if

Sylvia and Pete had a collection of pre-Columbian artifacts scattered around the house.

Stanley, a student at Beaumont, the college just down the hill from the apartment building, was in his last year of studies to become an archeologist. When he saw what Charlie was looking at, he quickly crossed the room to pluck it from his hand and place it back on the shelf.

"That's the Aztec earth goddess, Toci. But it's a Tijuana knockoff, Charlie. Don't waste your time. Steal a cookie instead."

Charlie clutched his chest and made a point of looking mortally offended. "I wasn't going to swipe it. I took my klepto pills. I did. Ask Bruce."

Bruce, Charlie's chubby lover with the cherubic face and the penchant for swiping everything that wasn't nailed down, was sitting at Charlie's feet leafing through an original copy of *Winnie the Pooh*, which Sylvia had once told me was her most prized possession. She had been presented with it on her fourth birthday by the same parents who would later turn their backs on her when they learned their little boy better identified with being a little girl, and wasn't *that* a kick in the head for a couple of God-fearing parents. The fucking twits.

It was Roger who came to the rescue this time, snatching *Winnie the Pooh* from Bruce's fingers and carefully tucking it back on the shelf where it belonged, safe and sound. Bruce looked as hurt as Charlie had.

"We *both* took our pills, you know," Bruce whispered, casting surreptitious eyes in Sylvia's direction, obviously embarrassed. "You don't have to watch us like a hawk. Besides, we wouldn't steal from Sylvia. What kind of dicks do you think we are?"

Roger patted Bruce on the head like a poodle. "Sorry, Bruce. I apologize," he said. He didn't sound thoroughly convinced by Bruce's plea for fairness but he was being nice about it. Roger was not only gorgeous, he was also astonishingly kind. *Lucky Stanley*, I thought for the gazillionth time.

Gazing around, I realized Sylvia had played to her strengths as far as hors d'oeuvres went. Several platters of Toll House cookies were placed strategically around the room. The cookies were neatly sliced into bite-sized chunks. Some of them had a Rolo nailed on top with a bright shiny toothpick, while others were sprinkled with Raisinets held in place with a smear of chocolate frosting. I scooped up a fistful of the ones covered in Raisinets and worked my way around the room, gobbling them down as I went, trying all the while to be sociable and wondering when my sugar level would peak.

When Sylvia's weird hors d'oeuvres had taken the edge off my hunger, I snagged a beer from the fridge where Pete directed me. Although the evening had barely begun, I noticed ChiChi seemed already to be a little drunk. He and Ramon were whispering fiercely to each other from their spot on the living room floor. Sylvia casually passed them by, ruffling their hair as she went in what was probably an attempt to ease the tension, but it didn't quiet them down much. I wondered if I was the reason for the argument, but since I couldn't do anything about it if I was, I decided to ignore the situation altogether.

I cornered Pete. "So," I said, beaming like a nitwit and hoping I had sucked all the chocolate off my front teeth so I wouldn't look like an idiot. "It won't be long now before the little woman will really be the little woman."

Pete blushed so hard I thought his ears were going to catch fire. "Her decision completely," he said proudly. "I told her she didn't have to change a thing for me, but well, this has always been her dream. I'm just happy I could help her see it done."

I patted Pete's cheek and he blushed even redder. But he looked pleased too. "You're a lucky guy, Pete." I grinned. "And Sylvia's lucky to have you. If you ever get tired of her, come look me up, okay?"

He laughed. "Like *that's* gonna happen."

"I know."

He gazed across the room at Sylvia, where she was speaking softly to Charlie and Bruce. A lump formed in my throat at the look of love that lit up Pete's face. *I want that,* I thought. *That's the kind of look I want to see in my eyes when I look in a mirror.*

The doorbell rang, and the lump in my throat got even bigger. This time it was a lump of nervous anticipation. *Holy shit, it must be Arthur. The moment of truth is at hand.*

It was Pete who answered the door, and even if I hadn't been watching, I would have known something momentous was taking place by the pall of shocked silence that suddenly oozed over the room like a truckload of wet cement.

Sure enough, it was Arthur. And sure enough, he was dressed as a man in the clothes we had bought together.

As soon as he stepped into the room, all sound fell dead with an almost audible *thud*. Everyone froze in place. A goodly portion of the room's oxygen seemed to get sucked through the open door behind him, leaving a vacuum in its place. I wasn't sure, but I thought I felt my ears pop.

Poor Arthur looked exquisitely uncomfortable in his new ensemble of western jeans, plaid work shirt, and leather vest. Unbeknownst to me, Arthur had made a further excursion for accessories. And as one might guess, Arthur's talent for accessorizing was a little over the top.

A bronze belt buckle the size of a minipizza held up his pants and caught the light like a laser show. On his feet he wore shiny new Tony Lamas with hand-stitched cacti and a couple of lizards on the sides that must have set him back three or four hundred bucks. Lord knows what he had done with the simple, manly work boots I had chosen for him to compliment the jeans.

His face was bright red. That was because he had cinched the belt with its big-ass buckle so tightly around his waist he had rolls of fat protruding from both above and below, sort of like a massive ball of Play-Doh someone had dumped in the street and ran over with a car. All he needed was tread marks on his belly. The western-cut jeans he had on were so new and stiff and unforgiving, I wondered if he would be able to bend his knees when he walked. The fly of his jeans cut so deeply into his crotch I figured it was a good thing Arthur was as gay as a cotillion since all his little swimmers must be down there clutching their throats and dying of asphyxiation anyway.

A black Stetson sat perched on Arthur's head with a huge mirrored hatband encircling it and catching even more light. The Stetson had been my idea. The mirrored hatband hadn't. Another example of over-the-top accessorizing if ever I saw one.

At least Arthur's face was scrubbed clean of every smidgeon of makeup, and he had even let a five o'clock shadow appear, assuming, I supposed, that it would enhance his butch factor. And by God, it did.

The man was positively awash in masculinity. All three hundred pounds of him.

When he stepped into the room, I could hear him grunt with the effort of trying to bend his pant legs at every step.

While everyone stood around, mute with shock, Arthur's eyes sought me out, and the second they found me they narrowed to mean little slits.

"You miserable fuck," he muttered through clenched teeth.

I raised my hand in a phony gesture of goodwill, hoping not to get my head bitten off, but expecting it just the same. "Hi, Arthur. So good to see you. You look great!" Privately, I wished he had rethought the accessories. The hatband and belt buckle were certainly too much. And in hindsight, 4X pants would certainly have been a better choice than 3X, but it was a little late to worry about it now.

"Are you going to be able to eat?" I whispered in his ear. "Your pants look a little tight."

"This is worse than a girdle," he hissed back. "I'm dying here."

I clucked in sympathy, then slung my arm over his shoulder. It was quite a stretch, by the way.

"Take your hat off and stay awhile," I said. "And if it's any consolation, you look butcher than hell. Quite the hunk of masculinity, yesiree."

"You think so?" His eyes weren't quite so slitty and mean now. He was hanging on to my compliment like Gizmo hanging on to a meatball. "You really think I look butch?"

Sylvia and Pete, and then Stanley and Roger, all swooped in to circle Arthur. Everybody spoke at once.

"You look *great*, Arthur!"

"Much better than taffeta!"

"Love your boots!"

"Your diet is working too, darling. You're absolutely wasting away. I'm so jealous!" That was Sylvia, who probably weighed less than Arthur's belt buckle even when she was soaking wet. For sheer creative complimenting, nobody could ever top Sylvia. She could sift around and find the good in a bad situation every single time. I rather admired her for that.

Arthur began to look a little perkier, what with all the praise being tossed his way. He even began to swagger a bit, rather like a thespian who has finally unearthed the crux of his role and nailed exactly what it needs to really make it tick. Being a drag queen requires a certain amount of attitude. And so does trying to pass one's self off as butch. Especially among a group of friends who know better than to believe it for a minute. To Arthur, I suspected this was just another form of drag, and once he got his head around that fact, he began to enjoy his performance.

Not that anyone believed his butchness for a minute. They knew Arthur too well for that.

But happily the man who walked in the door next, didn't.

A CLATTER of pans outside the apartment door heralded the arrival of the caterers.

Before Pete could hustle off to the door to let them in, Sylvia sidled up to me and whispered in my ear. "This is for you, Harlie. I've been imagining you two pussyfooting around and sidestepping each other like a couple of wary boxers for the past month. It's time to move along to the next level."

I didn't know what she was talking about. "Sidestep *who* exactly? And the next level of *what*?"

She batted her eyes at me and smiled. "You can thank me later."

"I—I—"

She slipped her arm through mine and held me in place like she was afraid I might try to bolt as together we turned to watch Pete usher in the caterers. "Just watch," she breathed, so only I would hear.

So I watched.

The first person through the door was Mr. Burger. The second person through the door was Milan. It was the first time I had ever seen him away from work and not in his white baker's outfit, and my God, the man was stunning! Like I didn't know that already. But somehow away from the massive kitchen down at the deli and suddenly flung into the narrow confines of Pete and Sylvia's tiny Belladonna Arms apartment, Milan became a giant. And a pretty one too. Needless to say, since the room was filled with gays from one end to the other, every eye was drawn to him immediately. And why the hell wouldn't they be?

Milan was dressed in black slacks and a white dress shirt with the top three buttons undone, showing just enough skin to set my heart to fluttering. His long sleeves were rolled up, displaying a tantalizing stretch of dark-haired forearms. A gold watch, a little too big, flopped around on one wrist. His chocolate brown hair, so chocolate as to be almost black, was unhindered by the chef's toque he always wore at work. Now, in its newfound freedom, his hair showed itself to be thick and wavy and a little too long. Lord, it sat there on his head begging for someone to run their fingers through it. In a moment of sheer horny desperation and questionable faith, I offered up a silent promise to God that if only he'd let me get my hands in that luscious head of hair just once, I'd give up the last three years of my life as a sort of door prize for St. Peter. It's not like I'd be giving up much, I reasoned. I'd probably be old and useless by then anyway.

Later, after the way the evening turned out, I would remember that promise and wonder if I had actually shortened my life. But frankly, by then I would figure it was totally worth it, so I didn't much care either way.

I stood there staring at Milan with my mouth hanging open, salivating like a bloodhound. It was then Sylvia leaned in and whispered, "You're welcome."

She left me and went to welcome Burger and Milan, and together, she and Pete showed them the kitchen where they could unload everything they had brought with them. After that, she placed a beer in each of their hands and scooted them back into the living room, where they could join the party as guests, not caterers.

"We can serve ourselves," I heard her say to Burger. "Your work is over. I'll set the buffet up. For now I want the two of you to come and meet our friends."

While introductions were being made all around the room, my eyes never once left Milan's face, although I tried not to be creepy about it. Sylvia seemed to be enjoying my torture because she waited until she had introduced him and his father to everyone present before she tugged Milan in my direction.

"And of course you know Harlie. Harlie, come say hello to Milan."

I was stunned to see a flash of relief in Milan's eyes. Only then did I realize he was shy, and meeting everybody in the room had been somewhat of an ordeal for him. How could anyone who looked like him be shy, I asked myself. And why was I blushing? *Why the hell am I blushing?*

Milan's deep, resonant voice had a smile in it when he said, "Hi Harlie." His dimples flashed as he took me in from head to toe. My blush deepened. I'm pretty sure it did, anyway.

When Milan's beer came out to clink against my own, I thought I might pass out. And when he came to stand beside me and rested his hand on my shoulder as he turned to survey the room, I thought I might have some sort of coronary infarction going on. With Milan standing this close, his dimpled chin was level with the top of my head. I breathed in his heat and damn near passed out again.

Like spectators, we watched the room. I wasn't surprised to see ChiChi staring at us with a hungry look in his eyes. And Ramon, standing next to ChiChi, didn't seem particularly surprised by his lover's reaction. Nor did he seem to enjoy it. He was hissing something that didn't sound like the Lord's Prayer in ChiChi's ear, but ChiChi just continued to stare at Milan, ignoring Ramon completely. Ignoring me now too, since his interest was now centered on Milan. Once again, my heart went out to Ramon.

Stanley and Roger and Charlie and Bruce were giggling in a corner about something or other, and Sylvia had dragged Pete into the kitchen where they were banging pots and pans around and setting up the buffet. When they had it the way they liked it, Sylvia pulled Pete into a corner and stood on tiptoe to plant a kiss on his chin. Apparently that wasn't enough for Pete, who wrapped his arms around Sylvia and lifted her a foot off the ground so he could kiss her back. And wasn't that like the sweetest thing ever!

I forgot about Pete and Sylvia when Milan's broad, warm hand came up to cradle the back of my neck. It settled in there like it had found a home, and I was so happy about that I actually had to close my eyes to better savor his touch. He leaned in to whisper in my ear. "I'm glad you're here. I'm not very good in crowds."

I swiveled my head to look at him, and his sweet breath rustled my lashes. This close, I noticed specks of gold in his blue eyes. His mouth was so soft and lush and sexy, I was tempted to take a taste. But of course I didn't. I wasn't ChiChi, after all.

I cleared my throat so I could talk since my voice box seemed to have been suddenly stripped down and sold for parts. Or maybe it was just nerves, what do you think? "I'm glad you're here too, Milan. I had no idea you were coming."

"Sylvia and Pop set it up. Don't ask me why." He gazed out at his father, who was still milling around, meeting everyone. "It's good to see Pop getting out for a change. Sylvia's no dummy. I'm sure that was the reason she asked us here. I'm just along for the ride, I think. Sort of like a pack mule to lug all the food around."

I knew better. Sylvia had told me so. But I saw no reason to tell Milan and make him more uncomfortable than he already was. Besides, I didn't want to do anything that might make him want to remove his hand from the back of my neck. I liked that hand there. I would have Krazy Glued it in place if I thought he wouldn't notice.

Trying not to appear completely slutty, but probably failing miserably, I scooted in a little closer to the towering man beside me. When I did, Milan's hold tightened almost imperceptibly on my neck. I felt his fingers slip into my hair and sort of nestle in. Our eyes came together again.

"Your hand feels good," I managed to say without squeaking.

"So does your hair," he said softly.

His bottomless blue eyes, with those beautiful flecks of gold scattered in their midst, burrowed into mine. His fingers moved in my hair, and I tilted my head back and closed my eyes at his touch. I had idea the man could be so gentle.

When I forced my eyes open, he was gazing around the room. "Look at that," he said.

So I looked.

Mr. Burger was sitting on the sofa. Beside him sat Arthur. Arthur had removed his cowboy hat, thank God, so he looked a little less like a geriatric version of an overgrown Village People (Village Person?) on steroids. Arthur and Burger were laughing about something or other and looking like they were having a real good time together.

"Good grief," Milan said.

"What?" I hoped it didn't have anything to do with him wanting to take his fingers out of my hair.

"That man Pop's talking to. What was his name? Arthur? He sort of looks like Pop's ex. The one who died. Isn't that funny?"

I studied Burger and Arthur a little more closely. They were not touching. They were doing absolutely nothing which could be construed as intimate. Yet they were both completely at ease in each other's company. They looked as if they had known each other for years. Burger was jabbering about something or other, and Arthur had tears of laughter coursing down his cheeks.

"Holy shit," Milan said when his father reached out and brushed one of those happy tears from Arthur's cheek. In all fairness, Arthur looked considerably shocked by the touch as well. He paused in his laughter for a moment to study Burger's face. The two men made eye contact for one silent moment. Then Burger started jabbering again, and Arthur once more burst into laughter.

"Love pollen," I muttered, lost in the beauty of that silent moment of connection I had seen the two older men make.

Milan's fingers were still at the back of my neck. His breath brushed my face as he whispered close to my ear, "What did you say about pollen?"

I jumped. "Nothing. Just thinking out loud."

By this time I couldn't help noticing a few interested stares coming at us from various partygoers. Most notably ChiChi, if not Ramon. Roger and Stanley also seemed to find Milan and me intriguing.

"You ready for another beer?" Milan asked, pulling his hand away at last.

I nodded. "Sure," I agreed, missing his touch already.

Two spots of color rose to his cheeks. "I assume you'll still be here when I get back."

"You couldn't push me away with a bulldozer."

"Good," he said, leaving me to wonder what the hell he meant by *that*—hoping I knew but not really feeling cocky enough to believe it for a minute.

When he walked away, heading for the kitchen to fetch the beers, all six feet four of him, I sucked in some oxygen like I hadn't had a good breath of air for about five minutes. My hands were sweating, and the back of my neck was tingling, still missing the heat and pressure of his fingers at my nape.

Roger and Stanley swooped in like pigeons the second Milan was gone. "You look shell-shocked," Stanley grinned.

I blinked. "Do I?"

"Just a little," Roger said. "He's something of a dish, isn't he? Sylvia told us you two work together?"

"Yeah," I said. "I'm afraid to turn around. Is he coming back yet?"

They both nodded. "Yeah, he is."

"Then go away," I hissed. "Please!" Nothing pushy or desperate about me.

Stanley shot me a salute, and he and Roger took off, heading for the buffet. I made a mental note to thank them later.

Milan walked into my space as if he had never left. He handed me a beer, and the moment he did, his bottle-cool fingers once again found the back of my neck.

"I like having you close," he said. "I hope you don't mind. I get a little uncomfortable at parties."

"So do I," I lied. However my second sentence wasn't a lie at all. "I'm glad you're here with me too."

Milan's dad and Arthur had wandered off to the buffet line and were now standing in the kitchen, speaking softly to Pete and Sylvia. Probably about her upcoming surgery. I took a moment out of my own revelations to offer up a silent prayer that everything would go okay for her.

"Look at Pop and Arthur," Milan said.

Burger was standing next to Arthur with his hand at Arthur's back. If Arthur knew it was there, he didn't let on. I was a little surprised to think Arthur could be so cool under pressure. Jesus, maybe there was more common sense to Arthur than I thought.

"They look cozy," I said with a smile. "Maybe they'll end up friends."

I turned to see what Milan thought of that and found him staring so deeply into my eyes I drew back a little bit.

"What?" I asked. "What did I say?"

Milan gave his head a tiny shake. "No. I was just wondering the same thing about us. If maybe—you know—we'll end up friends."

I swallowed hard. "Were you really thinking that?"

"Well, yeah. Is that okay?"

I could have orated for the next two hours on the subject. Given a little time, I could have produced pie charts and a PowerPoint presentation. But for the sake of brevity, I narrowed it down to one word. "Yes."

"Really?"

Was that hope I saw in Milan's eyes? Did his fingertips actually stop simply resting at the back of my neck and begin stroking me there instead? Was I imagining that? Or was it really happening?

I couldn't stop myself. I had to say the words. "You do know how beautiful you are, don't you?"

He stared across the room at the window, taking in the storm outside and maybe sifting through the thoughts in his head to figure out what he wanted to say. When he turned back to me, I knew he had made a decision. And it would change the dynamic completely when he said it.

"I know how beautiful *you* are," he answered. "I know I'd like to get to know you away from work. I know I'd like us to maybe go on a date and get to know each other better. Do you think that might be something you'd consider doing too? I mean with me. Would you go out on a date with me, Harlie? You know, if I ever got up the courage to ask you?"

"Yes," I said. "And I think you already did." I turned toward him and stared at the hollow of his throat since it was right there at the level of my eyes. When I was physically capable of tearing my eyes from that wonder, I lifted my chin to focus on his face instead. He was so handsome it almost took my breath away. "I can't believe you're asking me out."

Milan laid a hand to his own chest as if stilling the heart beneath. "If I had my way, I'd do more than that."

Breathless and stunned and a little bit scared, I asked, "What? *What* would you do?"

"This," he whispered, and leaning in, he laid his lips gently over mine. I thought maybe I heard a tomblike silence suddenly fall across the room, but I was too lost in the kiss to worry about it much. Milan's lips tasted of beer. They were also cool from the bottle he had been sipping from. His breath smelled of honey and gentle hunger—a delicious combination of flavors if there ever was one. When I stepped closer, melting into his kiss, I felt Milan's heart hammering against my chest. But only for a moment. He suddenly seemed to realize we were in the middle of a room full of people and probably sticking out like a couple of sore thumbs.

"Wow," he breathed after lifting his lips from mine. "I liked that."

I stammered back, "Ditto."

"You taste great."

"So do you."

"Not that I want a relationship or anything."

My heart gave a lunge inside my chest. What the hell was it doing? Somersaults? "Neither do I," I intoned.

"I don't want to be—you know—*involved* with anyone right now."

"Unh-uh. Me either. Not that. Not *involved.*"

"I'm not ready for that."

"Oh, God no. Neither am I."

"I'm just not ready."

"Me either. Not ready by a long shot. So far away from being ready I couldn't get any less ready if I *tried* to be ready." *Brilliant. Nice sentence structure.*

"Still, Harlie. I'd really like to see you away from work. Just casually, of course."

"Sure. You bet. No problem at all. Casual's good."

Casual, my ass. I was lying through my teeth. I didn't want anything casual with Milan. I wanted him and me to be humping like monkeys. I wouldn't call that casual, would you? I wondered how casual I'd appear if I reached into his fly and pulled his dick out. Jeez, the man was hot. And God, I was a slut.

Milan studied his feet, thinking things over, maybe, and then he once again raised his eyes to my face. He stared at me like he was memorizing the terrain. I prayed to God I didn't have anything unfortunate hanging out of my nose. My mouth was still moist from his kiss, however, and that took my mind off the worrying. I slid my tongue out and tentatively dragged it over my lips in the hope of tasting him again. He smiled when I did it, as if he knew what I was doing. For a moment I thought he was going to lay a gentle fingertip to my mouth and test it himself, but he didn't.

"I have a confession to make," he said.

For one horrible moment, I imagined him saying it was just a practical joke. That he wasn't interested in me at all. Not casually or any other way. But he didn't. Not by a long shot.

"I knew you would be here tonight. Sylvia told me you would."

"Did she?"

"Yeah. That's because one day when we were chatting on the phone, I told her I'd like to get to know you better, but I didn't know how to go about it. I don't like getting involved with people at work. It's—difficult."

"So I'm fired, right?"

He grinned. "Gee, now why didn't *I* think of that? It would have simplified things considerably. But then I wouldn't have been able to see your butt every day in that perfectly tailored baker's uniform." He blinked in surprise. "I don't believe I said that."

Neither did I, but I sure liked hearing it. I caught my reflection in a mirror on Pete's living room wall. I was beaming like a spotlight. I couldn't have pried the smile off my face with anything short of a crowbar and maybe two or three ounces of plastic explosive. *Jesus,* I thought. *Gloat much?*

I reached up and plucked a loose eyelash from Milan's cheek. "Work is looking up."

"No shit," Milan said, matching my smile with one of his own. He tousled my hair like he might a six-year-old's; then he painstakingly tried to put it back in place, apologizing profusely.

I rested my forehead on his chest and giggled. "Stop apologizing. You can mess up my hair any time you want."

"Okay. Uh, thanks."

I reared back far enough to look at him without going cross-eyed. My mouth disengaged from my brain and set off to forge its own path through the minefield of our conversation. Even when I heard the words I started spewing, I couldn't quite believe I was the one saying them.

"Did you really like it when you kissed me?"

Milan's face softened and his heavenly blue eyes grew dreamy and warm. "You know I did."

"Then would you mind doing it again? I was caught off guard last time. You didn't give me any warning at all. No heads up. Nothing. I didn't know it was coming, see. This time I'd like to know what's happening so I can analyze your kiss a little more carefully."

"Jesus, what is this? A third-grade pop quiz?"

"More like a wine taster judging an intriguing vintage."

"An intriguing vintage, huh? I like the sound of that."

"I thought you would," I said. "I *think* you're a good year, but I need to taste you one more time to be sure."

"You're flirting," he said.

"You think?"

Milan's face softened even more. He smiled and his dimples popped into view. He cocked his head to the side a split second before gripping my shoulders and pulling me into him. This time when he covered my mouth with his, he did it like he meant it. His tongue squirmed into my mouth and set up camp. I squeezed my eyes shut as my own tongue wiggled past his and reconnoitered the opposing campground. My toes curled in my shoes and my dick woke up with a yelp.

This time our kiss lasted forever, or seemed to. When we finally separated, Milan held my gaze with his for a good ten seconds while our faces hovered only inches apart. Then reality began to creep in, and we both realized where we were again. We looked around the room and saw everyone staring at us, jaws agape. And why the hell wouldn't they be?

The only sound in the room, other than my own heartbeat thudding in my ears, was Arthur whispering to Milan's dad. "That's my stylist," Arthur was saying. "Picks out all my clothes, don't you know. Couldn't live without him. He seems to have a thing for your son. Had you noticed?"

Burger nodded, obviously not caring one little bit that everybody was soaking up every word they said. "Oh, yeah. I noticed. You should see them at work, avoiding each other and tap dancing around each other. They seem to have finally ironed out *that* problem. Not much avoiding or tap dancing going on at the moment, wouldn't you agree?"

"I most certainly would," Arthur smiled, edging closer to Burger until their shoulders were brushing.

Burger eyed Arthur and chuckled. "Let's have another beer and leave the young ones be. I think maybe we should get to know each other a little better."

"Nothing could make me happier." Then, as if remembering what he was wearing, Arthur added, "Pardner."

And both men grinned.

The sound level slowly went back to normal as everyone returned to what they were doing before Milan and I had unintentionally grabbed their attention. I turned to find Milan once again staring at me.

He ran a finger around the neck of my T-shirt, and my knees almost buckled.

"You drive me crazy, you know," he said.

"I do?" I couldn't believe what I was hearing. In fact, I couldn't believe anything that was happening. I wondered if my hard-on was blatantly obvious, but I was afraid to draw attention to it by looking down to see.

Milan's finger came up and lifted my chin. I thought another kiss was on the way, but he fooled me this time. He merely left his fingertip tucked beneath my chin while he stroked my cheek with his thumb.

"Yes, Harlie. You do. You drive me fucking nuts."

I rummaged through my mind, but there was nothing there. As empty as a vacant house. "I'm sorry, I seem to have forgotten the question."

"You asked if you really drive me crazy. I'm telling you the answer is yes."

"Good to know." How lame was that for a response?

A dribble of cold sweat slid down my ribcage and made me shiver.

Milan smiled again. This time there was such hunger in it, I thought I might swoon. "I felt that," he said. "You shivered."

"It's not what you think."

"Yes, it is."

I didn't argue because I knew he was right.

A crash of thunder outside the living room window made everybody jump. And as soon as everyone had finished laughing at themselves for being startled, the lights went out—

—startling them again.

Chapter 8

IT WAS Arthur who squealed like a little piggy. There was no mistaking his screeching falsetto. So much for his cowboy drag. And while he was squealing, somebody's hands came out of the dark and pulled me into the middle of two really nice arms. No kidding. They were burly as all get out with big rolling biceps that felt hard and soft and warm and cool and comforting and scary all at the same time. I wasn't sure they were Milan's arms until his mouth found mine and he stuck his tongue down my throat. Then I was sure.

"I can recognize his kiss in the dark," a little voice screamed inside my head. "I know what the man tastes like now. How cool is that?"

Milan mumbled words around our kiss. "What are you thinking?"

With his lips still on mine, I mumbled words right back. "I'm thinking I never want the lights to go on."

Pete lit a candle, and suddenly the room wasn't dark any longer. "Well, shit," the little voice in my head chimed in again.

"Sorry, folks," Pete announced, holding the candle high. "Looks like a power outage. But not to worry. Sylvia and I have tons of candles."

Great.

Soon there were lighted candles everywhere. Milan and I pried ourselves apart, not because we wanted to but because we thought we should. We wandered into the kitchen hand in hand and piled a couple of plates high with lasagna and antipasto (it was an Italian buffet) before plopping ourselves down in a corner of the living room floor out of everyone's way, where we quietly began stuffing ourselves. Not once as we ate did we not touch each other in some manner or other. The bumping of a knee, the brushing of a shoulder, the reaching out of a hand.

The storm outside gathered strength. The neon sign on top of the building rattled somewhere in the stratosphere far above our heads. And nearer at hand, another storm appeared to be brewing. It was the storm between Ramon and ChiChi. Their voices were getting louder, and they were becoming harder and harder to ignore.

I glanced over to where they were sitting, still by the coffee table as they had been all evening. The moment I glanced in their direction, I saw ChiChi snort a line of powder from the back of his hand. It was obviously either meth or coke, and Ramon was looking extremely unhappy about what his lover was doing, as well he should have been.

"Don't do that here!" Ramon hissed.

But ChiChi waved him off. "Shut the fuck up. Leave me alone." ChiChi's words were slurred. Not only was he snorting drugs, but he was drunk on top of it. Not the ideal dinner guest by a long shot.

Pete seemed to agree with me. Always a gentle person, he knelt behind the two with a hand on each of their shoulders and whispered quiet words into their ears. An expectant hush settled over the room.

ChiChi wore a leer on his face as he listened to Pete's whispered words, while Ramon merely appeared embarrassed.

He grew even more embarrassed when ChiChi shrugged Pete's hand away and stumbled to his feet. "I thought this was supposed to be a party!" he railed, dragging Ramon to his feet as well. Pete took a step back as if not sure what ChiChi was going to do. I wasn't worried, however. ChiChi was a little guy, and Pete was as tall as Milan. If a fight ensued, I figured ChiChi would find himself on the losing side of the battle.

Ramon reached out for ChiChi's arm to calm him down, but ChiChi pushed him away.

"I'm leaving," ChiChi snarled at his lover. "You coming?"

Ramon appeared mortified. "Yes," he muttered, nodding his head to Pete. "Maybe we'd better go."

"Fuckers!" ChiChi spat, as sort of an all-around good-bye to every staring face in the room. When he turned to me and sputtered, "Asshole," I ignored him the best I could. As did Milan, who, still sitting on the floor next to me, laid a protective hand on my leg. At first

I didn't understand why ChiChi had turned his venom on me. Then my mind cleared, and I began to understand a few things. Such as the weird conversation in my kitchen on that first day I met the two lovers. And later, the little scene in the park with ChiChi when he was trying to get me into the bushes. Maybe what it all boiled down to was ChiChi simply didn't like not getting everything he wanted, and apparently I was one of those things he wanted.

While I was pondering all this, Arthur stepped forward and scooped ChiChi up by the back of his shirt like a mother cat picking up a marauding kitten.

"Go home and sleep it off," Arthur growled, dragging ChiChi toward the door. "And next time you go to someone's house for dinner, don't be such an ass." At the door, he spun a seething ChiChi around to face him. There was no humor in Arthur's face. None whatsoever. It was the first time I had even seen him mad. "And ChiChi, the next time I see you with drugs in my apartment building, you'll have thirty days to get out. You and Ramon both. Do you understand? It may not be the Ritz, but the Belladonna Arms is my home." Arthur waved his hand, encompassing everybody in the room. "It's home to all of us. So if you want to keep calling it your home too, you'll knock off the drugs. Got it?"

ChiChi looked like he was ready to fight back, but Ramon grabbed his arm and pulled him through the door and out into the hall.

I could see Ramon fighting back tears. "We understand, Arthur. I'm sorry. I promise it won't happen again." And as Ramon and ChiChi stood there in the flickering candlelight, Arthur quietly, but firmly, closed the door in their faces. Just before he disappeared from view, Ramon's eyes opened wide in shame, and he cried out, "Sylvia, I'm sorry!"

Sylvia looked almost as horrified as Ramon had. She walked into Pete's arms, and he held her close in a comforting embrace. "Don't worry, babe," Pete whispered with his lips in her hair. "Ramon will straighten him out."

"Poor Ramon," Sylvia whispered back and buried her face in Pete's chest.

Arthur awkwardly patted them both like puppies. "Don't let it ruin your evening, sweeties. Come on. I haven't seen either of you eat yet. Let's fix you both a plate. That'll cheer you up." He patted his bronze belt buckle. "I could use some cheering up too. Throwing people out of parties builds up quite an appetite."

"I'm with you," Milan's dad laughed, taking Arthur's arm. "I feel like I could eat a horse!"

"Neigh!" Arthur said, grinning lewdly.

Sylvia and Pete followed the two older men into the kitchen, while Milan and I went back to our dinner.

This was turning out to be one of the damnedest dinner parties I had ever attended.

THE POWER was still off, so after we had satisfied our hunger (at least for food), Milan and I sat quietly in our little corner of the room watching the party play out before us in candlelight. The glitch in the evening due to ChiChi's stupid outburst seemed to have been forgotten, or at least determinedly pushed into the past. Sylvia and Pete were standing at the window watching the storm outside and chatting with Charlie and Bruce. Over by the sofa, Stanley and Roger were laughing and joking with Arthur and Mr. Burger. The four of them seemed to be having a real good time. My boss and my landlord in particular seemed to be enjoying each other's company. My plan to get the two of them together had been successfully implemented, and I hadn't even been the one to do it. It had been Sylvia who accomplished it.

I had to admit she was one hell of a woman. Or would be after the surgery.

Milan's fingers lay laced through mine. We were sipping fresh beers, too stuffed to move. Sylvia had soft music playing in the background, and my thoughts were once again turning to the feel of Milan's hand in mine.

"Your hand is warm," I said.

"Guess that means I'm alive. Phew! You never know when that might stop."

"Very funny. So what are you thinking?"

The angles of Milan's face were muted by the candlelight, rather like a painting of riotous colors photographed in black and white. All the beauty and the symmetry of the art was still evident, but the passion in it was dimmed.

It took Milan so long to answer my question I was beginning to think he hadn't heard me. I should have known better.

"I was thinking I'm glad I came tonight. I almost didn't."

"Why was that?"

He gazed down at his huge hand cradling my smaller one—at our feet touching as we sat there against the wall with our legs stretched out in front of us. "I'm not much on parties. Not very sociable, I guess."

"I'm glad you came too," I said.

He smiled and studied my face in the flickering light. "Are you?"

"Yes."

I let the silence embrace us for a minute. I could hear my pulse beating inside my head. Again, I felt a rush of desire surge through me. I was glad it was dark, so he couldn't see me get all red and flustered. "Do you still miss your lover?"

His eyes found mine and held me in his stare. Had I said the wrong thing? Had I just fucked up the evening completely? Apparently not.

He answered slowly, as if really thinking about what he wanted to say. "No. I've been too preoccupied with other things lately to think about him."

"Well, that's good, isn't it?"

He nodded. "Yes. It's very good."

"What were you preoccupied with?" I asked. "Work?"

He pushed his mop of dark, wavy hair back out of his eyes and gazed around the room for a second before answering. Then his eyes meandered back to mine. "You, Harlie. I was preoccupied with you."

Once again I was grateful for the darkness. "Ah, yes," I droned. "The idiot trainee. Yeah, I'm sure that kept you busy as hell, trying to turn a moron into a baker."

"No," he smiled. "Not the trainee part. And not the moron part either. Just you. Just having you there with me every day. Day in and day out. Having you there and wishing I could just, you know, be more relaxed with you. Get to know you. Maybe even become friends. Like normal people do."

"We are friends," I said. "We're normal too. At least I think we are. Sort of."

He nodded almost imperceptibly. His dimples made a brief appearance, then disappeared again. "Now we are. After tonight we are."

"Normal?"

"No. Friends."

I nodded. "That's because Sylvia set us up."

Milan looked surprised. "She did?"

"Yes. Just like she set your dad up with Arthur."

Milan stared across the room at the two older men happily chatting together, and a dreamy expression settled on his face. "Oh," he said softly. His expression calmed, as if only now was he beginning to understand.

I brought his hand to my face and held it to my lips while I spoke. "I didn't realize until you walked into this room tonight that you are shy. Isn't that right? Is that one reason you had such a hard time loosening up around me?"

Milan chuckled. "That and the fact that we didn't get off to a very good start. You can be a wiseass. I didn't want to get in the line of fire of your acerbic wit. You do know you're a wiseass, right?"

I shrugged, still holding his hand to my lips, enjoying the hardness of his knuckles pressed to my mouth as I breathed in the scent of his skin and felt the scrape of the hair on the back of his hand tickle my nose. "That's what I do when I'm nervous. I go all sarcastic. But not you. You apparently just clam up when you're nervous. So are you nervous now?"

"No. And I like the way your mouth feels on my skin."

The way he said those words made a dozen scenarios pop into my head—delicious scenarios with delicious expanses of naked skin in every one of them. My skin. Milan's skin. My tongue lapping at the terrain like a kid with an ice-cream cone.

I laid our clasped hands in Milan's lap and we both jumped. Holy crap, he had a hard-on! Needless to say, two seconds later I had one too. I hated to do it, but I slid our two hands a little to the left so they wouldn't be pressing on his dick. Seemed the courteous thing to do. Disappointing, but courteous.

"Oops," I said.

He laughed. "It's you, Harlie. Half the time I'm around you, I'm hard."

"Even at work?"

"Yeah. Even at work."

"I wish I'd known. I might have done something about it." Put an oven mitt on it maybe. Kept it away from the hot trays. Blown him on the trash can out back in the alley.

When he didn't say anything, I once again wondered if I had said too much. At least he couldn't read my mind. Thank God for that. Then he opened his mouth, and I realized he wasn't thinking about what I'd said at all.

"You asked me, Harlie, so now I'm asking you. Do you still miss *your* lover?"

I didn't hesitate. And I didn't lie. I was too turned on thinking about Milan sitting next to me with a hard-on to do either. Hell, I could barely talk at all. So I simply said, "No."

He seemed surprised. "Just—*no*?"

I gulped in some air and tried to explain myself better. "Don't get me wrong. I spent plenty of time missing Dan. Miserable fucking months of it. But then one day I just got mad. After that, I was okay. Plus, by then I had someone else to focus all my attention on."

Milan's face twisted into a tease. His fingers tightened around mine. He leaned in close and gave me a sexy leer. "Please tell me it was me, you little shit."

I tapped my forehead against his and held it there with my eyes closed. "Yes. It was you. Hope that's okay."

Milan's voice was hushed. "It's more than okay. Jeez, Harlie, one would think you might have figured that out by now."

"I'm sorry," I said. "I'm still trying to wrap my head around the fact that you're sitting there with a hard-on." *Howzabout I wrap something else around it. Like my lips. Huh, Milan? How would that work out for you?*

Milan smiled and reached up to stroke a thumb gently across my lips. His eyes were so centered on mine I felt like a squirming butterfly pinned to a piece of cotton. "I wish I knew what you were thinking," he said. "Or maybe I do." His fingers once again tightened around mine and he shifted our clenched hands back to the hardness in his lap. "God, Harlie. I wish you wanted me as badly as I'm wanting you."

"What makes you think I don't?" I took over steerage of our clenched hands and laid his on *my* lap for a change. When his eyes popped open a little bit wider, I knew he had felt what I had put his hand there to feel.

At that moment, the lights came back on. We hardly noticed at all.

A sexy smile splayed Milan's mouth wide, and he snuggled closer. The pepperoni on his breath smelled delicious. We were sitting propped against the wall with our legs sticking straight out in front of us. I had slipped off my shoes earlier, and now my toes, which came to about midshin on Milan, went exploring under his pant cuff. Even through my sock I could feel the raspy roughness of Milan's leg hair, and suddenly all those imaginings I had imagined earlier came roaring back to life inside my head.

The back of his hand shifted in my lap, and my dick began singing the "Hallelujah Chorus." I love when it does that.

Then suddenly a shadow fell over the two of us, and we both jumped in surprise, accidently banging our heads against the wall when we did.

The shadow was Milan's dad, and he looked like he was trying not to laugh. He squatted down to our level and winked. "You boys nervous about something?"

Milan did not drop my hand, but he did scoot it a few inches west, off of my crotch and onto my leg. "What's up, Pop?" Milan's cheeks and ears looked cherry red in the bright new light, and I realized he was blushing. I didn't worry about my face, because I had been blushing for about an hour now. Or maybe it was just a really long hot flash. Having Milan's hand on one's crotch would do that to anybody.

Now it was Mr. Burger's turn to look uncomfortable. I saw him cast a furtive glance across the room at Arthur, who was watching the three of us like a hawk. I was pretty sure I knew what was happening, but I waited for Mr. Burger to lay it out in all its gory abandon.

"Milan, I'm going to be leaving. Arthur and I are going out for a drink."

"In this weather?" Milan asked.

Then Mr. Burger appeared even *more* uncomfortable than he had before. "Well, uh... okay, Son. You caught me. We're going down to Arthur's apartment for that drink. We have some... uh... business to attend to."

Milan stared across the room at Arthur, and we both grinned when the cowboy gave Milan a little finger wave. "I see," Milan said. He gathered up a fistful of his father's shirt and pulled him close. "Is this the sort of business that requires protection? Want to borrow a condom?"

"Asshole," Burger grunted as he pulled away and unrolled his long frame to stand over us again. He looked down at Milan and cleared his throat. "It might not be a bad idea for you not to drive either after all the beers I've seen you slurp down tonight." He glanced at me, then gazed back at his son with a devilish light in his eyes. "Maybe even *you* can find a place to wait out the storm."

"I know just the place," I blurted out, surprising even myself.

Milan whipped his eyes at me. "Really?"

"Yeah."

Mr. Burger looked pleased. "Good. Then it's all settled." He reached down to tousle the hair on both our heads. "You kids have fun."

Milan studied Arthur from across the room. Arthur had his cowboy hat on and was obviously eager to leave. He was chewing his nails and staring at the back of Burger's head as if wondering how things were going to pan out. Poor Arthur.

"Your date looks anxious, Pop. Best not keep him waiting."

Mr. Burger gazed back over his shoulder and puffed himself up in pride. "Ain't he something?" He said it more to himself than either of us.

But Milan responded anyway. "He most certainly is. For a cowpoke."

"Arthur's a great guy," I threw into the mix, not because I felt I had to, but because I believed it. "Just so you know, that's not the way he usually dresses." No point going into detail, right?

After Burger and Arthur gave Pete and Sylvia a warm hug and made their exit (hand in hand, I couldn't fail to notice), a general exodus ensued. Before we knew it, the party was over, and after giving our host and hostess a hug and a kiss of our own and wishing Sylvia the best of luck with her upcoming surgery, Milan and I found ourselves out in the hall. Arthur and Burger were still there, leaning against a wall and speaking softly.

After a quick smooch from each of them (Arthur to me and Burger to Milan), the two older men wished us good night, and with a "Yeehaw!" from Arthur and a chuckle from Burger, they tripped off down the stairs like a couple of kids. I had never seen Arthur navigate the stairs so eagerly.

I stuffed my feet back into my shoes and took Milan's hand, smiling up at him. "I'm on two," I informed him, "Come on."

And with my heart in my throat, I jogged down the stairs to my apartment door with Milan close behind.

Chapter 9

I LOOKED around the apartment and envisioned it through Milan's eyes. "Kind of a dump, huh?"

Milan scoped out the battered furniture, the books everywhere, the scuffed-up tile on the kitchen floor off to the right. Shyly returning his eyes to me, he said, "I think it's wonderful."

He took it upon himself to close the apartment door behind us. Flicking the lock as if he was on a first name basis with it, he then connected the security chain as if he owned the place. He was a man taking control of the situation and looking hunky as hell while he did it. I liked that. I liked that a lot.

When he turned back to me, Milan took me in from head to toe as if he had never seen me before. It was such an odd thing for him to do, I said, "Having second thoughts?"

He frowned. "No way." He stepped closer until he loomed over me. With a soft smile, he rested the palm of his hand on my cheek. His thumb slid through my hair and over my ear. His voice was as soft as his smile. "Can I ask you something, Harlie?"

It took all my willpower not to walk into his arms and start ripping off his clothes. "I guess so. What is it?"

He took a moment to listen to the storm howling outside the building. He seemed to enjoy the sound of it. Actually, so did I. The roaring wind and peppering raindrops tapping at the window wrapped us in a comforting cocoon of sound that made the night even more intimate than it already was. And considering the hard-on I still had poking down my pant leg, I figured it was pretty darned intimate already.

Milan's eyes never left my face as he twiddled my ear between his thumb and forefinger. "Don't you think it's kind of funny the way we cut through the bullshit tonight and opened up with each other? Don't you think it's... *strange?*"

When I twisted my head and laid my lips to the palm of his hand, his eyes lit with a fire I had never seen there before. With the scent of his skin filling my head like potpourri, I said, "No. I think it just took us this long to figure out how we wanted to handle it."

"Do you really have it figured out?" he asked.

"I think so," I said.

I brought my hand up and rested two fingertips against the hollow in Milan's throat at the place where his shirt collar lay open. It was the spot where I could see his pulse tapping out the rhythm of his heartbeat beneath his skin. I had been watching that little flurry of pulse all evening, every time an opportunity presented itself. I held my breath now until I was finally able to feel the movement of it beneath my fingertips.

When he realized what I was doing, he laid his broad hand atop my chest and closed his eyes, all the better to feel *my* heartbeat. Only the storm outside the building interrupted our silent quests. A moment later, Milan's blue eyes opened wide. "I feel it," he said. "I feel your heart."

He edged closer and, as he had at the party, lightly pressed his other hand against the back of my neck as if daring me to try to escape.

"You're so gentle," I said, my eyelids fluttering as I soaked in the heat of his hand on my skin. "A gentle giant. That's what you are."

He smiled. "You think I'm a giant?"

"Compared to me you are."

He stooped to brush his lips over mine. When his hand circled my back and he pulled me into him, I felt his hard cock press against my stomach. I trembled and pressed my own erection against him so he'd know it was there. His mouth smiled over mine.

"You feel good," he whispered. His breath fell hot upon my face. "You feel *better* than good."

I couldn't stand it another minute. With trembling fingers I wormed my hands between the crush of our bodies and went to work on his shirt buttons. I was almost down to his navel when he apparently decided I was going too slow. He took a step back and tore his shirt away, flinging it across the room. Then he yanked my T-shirt over my head and tossed it over his shoulder, damn near scraping my nose off in the process.

He pulled me back into his arms, and the incredible sensation of our two naked chests making contact for the very first time took my breath away. I pressed my mouth to his throat and inhaled his scent. He cupped his hand to the back of my head again, holding me there against him. I closed my eyes and let the overpowering nearness of him sweep me away. I reached up to caress his back. I clutched the silky smooth heat of that broad expanse of flesh and felt the muscles beneath the surface of it ripple across my fingertips. With my head tucked comfortably under his chin, I slid my mouth away from his throat and explored the expanse of his rising chest, tasting and kissing and lapping at his skin as I traversed every inch of it. When I found a nipple, hairless and firm, I sucked it into my mouth. He gave a gasp, and I felt a tiny shudder run through his body.

His voice was a gentle rumble inside his chest. "You know what you're doing, don't you?"

"Maybe," I breathed.

His hands were on my own back now, massaging, rubbing my fevered skin. Then they headed south, and the next thing I knew he was kneading my ass through my jeans and periodically dipping a fingertip or two beneath my waistband, as if further reconnoitering was called for and he was damn well going to do it whether I wanted him to or not. Needless to say, it was okay with me. I had no issue with reconnoitering.

I found his belt buckle and tore it open just as he pushed my jeans down over my hips without even unbuttoning them in the front.

"I think your pants are too big," he mumbled into my hair. "And don't think I don't appreciate it."

"Double negative," I grunted. That was the best I could do because at that precise moment, my jeans slid completely off my hips, whispered down my legs, and finally came to rest in a crumpled pool around my ankles. The moment they did, my cock sprang up and tucked itself into the crotch of Milan's slacks like a rabbit diving into a hole.

That's when I decided his pants had to go. And I meant *now*. I fumbled with the snap until it popped open, slid down the zipper, and finally, with trembling hands, pushed his trousers down to the floor and out of the way.

Enter the second cock of the evening.

Milan's dick boinged into mine, and for a minute I thought they were going to start dueling. Milan wrapped his arms around my naked ass and picked me straight up off the floor. He tried to walk me toward the bedroom, but we were both hobbled with our legs wrapped around each other and our trousers bunched around our ankles.

Except for our peckers dancing about like divining rods and whapping each other in the head, we couldn't move. I started giggling. Milan said, "Wait a minute. Something's wrong here." Then he started giggling too.

"Maybe we can take better stock of the situation if we step away from each other," I suggested.

"Nope," he said. "No stock's going to be taken here. You feel too good. That's the last thing I want to do, waste time by stepping away and taking stock."

"Okay," I said. "If that's the way you feel about it." I buried my face in his chest and went for his nipple again.

That got him moving. "Only one way out of this predicament," he grinned. And without asking permission or sending me a heads-up e-mail or anything, he picked me up like a sack of potatoes and flung me over his shoulder.

While I hung there with his arm between my legs and his hand splayed over the crack of my naked ass to hold me in position, he balanced himself like a high-wire artist and, first on one foot, then on the other, he toed off his shoes. Then he kicked and kicked and tap-danced around until the trousers that were hobbling his feet finally went flying across the room in the same direction his shirt had gone.

I hung down his back like a side of beef while my dick stabbed into his shoulder. I figured I could reach his ass with my one free hand, so I did. It looked too delectable not to *try*, all fuzzy and firm and waiting for a little attention down there two feet below where my head was hanging.

So while I groped his ass and kissed his back, still hanging there upside down, Milan went to work prying off my shoes, ripping off my socks, and finally peeling my blue jeans down over my feet and tossing them aside.

He kissed my hip. "Ah. That's better. Where's the bedroom?"

"Thataway," I said, my voice all husky and breathless. I pointed with my foot to the door leading off the living room to the left.

He took a firmer grip on my ass and strode through the bedroom door, flipping the light switch on as he went. I continued to hang down his back like a throw rug draped over a windowsill. With the overhead light burning cheerily, the room was as bright as day, but that didn't seem to bother either one of us very much. The next thing I knew we were falling, but apparently it was a controlled fall. In other words, Milan knew where he was going with it. I guess it comes in handy to be as tall as a tree and as strong as an ox.

We hit my mattress, bounced two times, then came to rest in each other's arms.

He found my mouth with his, and I felt the velvet heat of his long naked body cover every inch of mine.

"You're overdressed," I gasped, trying to talk around the two tongues currently thrashing around inside my mouth.

"Sorry," he gasped back, and without breaking our kiss, he lifted first one leg and then the other and pulled off his socks, dropping them over the side of the bed. "Better?"

"Mm-hmm."

He gently eased me away, sat up beside me, and stared down at me laid out before him like a pupu platter. His gaze travelled from my head to my feet and back again. His blue eyes were smoldering, and I mean smoldering in a *good* way. He brushed his hand along my flank, then laid his other hand across my chest.

"Oh, man," I mumbled, loving the feel of his big hands on me.

I lay beneath his gaze, completely exposed, my cock as hard as granite and begging for a little attention. But even that wasn't foremost on my mind at the moment. All I could really think about was Milan. How handsome he was. How beautiful.

His chest was broad and deep and hairless. Because of the weather lately, neither one of us was very tanned. His nipples lay like mahogany discs atop his pale skin. He sat cross-legged on the bed beside me with one of his knees pressed against my leg and the other against my side. His legs were long and hairy and sexy as hell. I could see the bulge of his sharply outlined calf muscles even as he sat there. I reached out a hand and played my fingers along one of them, just to explore the crisp, clean lines of it. His legs looked strong. Far stronger than mine.

"You run," I said, since only a runner's legs look like that.

He nodded and ran his fingertips over my thighs, tracing the indention of my quads with his fingertips. "So do you, I think."

And I nodded back.

Between Milan's folded legs, his cock stood upright, as stiff as mine only bigger. He was uncut. I was not. His corona, fat and filled with blood, peered through the sheath of skin surrounding it. A splash of precome had spilled from his urethra. It lay there glistening like a rope of silver. With a grunt I pushed myself up to rest on my elbows, and while he watched with widening eyes, I rolled into his lap and gently pushed his foreskin back. Bending in close, I licked the precome away with a flick of my tongue.

Not doing anything more, I sat up beside him and crossed my legs as he was doing. I licked my lips. "Delicious," I said in a voice weak with desire.

Milan leaned into me, once again covering my mouth with his. While we closed our eyes and let our kiss once again carry us away, we eased ourselves back down onto the bed. Wrapped in Milan's arms, I pressed my face into the hard bicep I had longed to touch since the very first day I met him. The skin there was just as I imagined it would be. Soft and firm at the same time. It was also scented with his heavenly musk. When he moved I could feel that ball of muscle, ripe and alive, flex against my face, and I swear it was one of the most erotic experiences of my life. It was as if all my nerve endings were at DEFCON 4, buzzing and twanging below my skin, waiting for the battle to finally begin. God knows I was ready to leap into the fray, and I had a pretty good hunch Milan was ready too.

"You're incredible," he whispered. "I've wanted to see you like this for so long. I was beginning to go a little crazy thinking about you all the time and never doing anything about it."

"Really?"

"Yes, really."

We lay on our sides facing each other. I pushed his arm up over his head and slid my lips through the hair in his armpit, breathing in the heady scent of him and smiling as the soft hair tickled my face.

"I love this," I muttered, lapping at his skin like a kitten with a bowl of milk.

I felt him nod his head, but he didn't speak. He watched me, rapt, his lips slightly parted. His breath gave a hitch when I went exploring again, ducking away from his armpit and sliding my lips over the wales of his ribcage as I gently eased him onto his back. When my mouth found his stomach, smooth and firm and delicious, I laid my free hand on his leg and gently massaged his firm, fuzzy thigh with my fingertips. Sliding my lips downward and moving my hand simultaneously upward, I cupped his heavy balls in the palm of my hand and brushed my lips over the head of his cock, once again sipping away the fresh smear of precome I found there.

A tremor ran through Milan's body as I slowly eased his plump cock into my mouth, deliberately savoring it as I went, dragging out the sensation for the both of us as long as I could. More precome seeped from his urethra and my heart fluttered inside my chest at the sweet saltiness of it. Milan arched his back into the movements of my mouth as I took him in deeper, hungry for another taste of him, skimming his slit with my tongue, urging, coaxing, pleading for one more drop of precome. One more sip of nectar.

"Slide around," he whispered. "Face the other way."

Without waiting for me to respond, he gripped my legs and twisted me around on the bed. My knee struck the headboard, and he scooted us closer to the foot of the bed so we had room to stretch out. His mouth then headed for parts unknown. They didn't remain unknown for long.

"Oh, God," I heard him say, and the next thing I knew I was doing the same thing he had done seconds before. I was straining upward and arching my back when the heat of his mouth circled my cock. He took me all the way in, and I cried out. Milan's hot mouth worked on me until my heart was banging away like a jackhammer. Taking a fistful of his hair, I tried to hold his head still so he would stop or at least slow down. I didn't want to come yet. Not yet. But I couldn't postpone it long if he kept *that* up.

To take my mind off what he was doing, I pulled his fat cock deep into my mouth again and played my fingertips over his balls. They were plump and firm and so tight against his body I felt sure he wasn't far from coming either. His precome was flowing on a regular basis now. I guess his O-ring was shot. I had never been with anyone who dripped like that. It was such a turn-on, I could barely contain myself. In fact, I couldn't.

"Come for me," I begged around his cock. "Please, Milan. Come for me. I want to taste you. I want to feel you fill my mouth."

If he wasn't in the mood for an orgasm, he failed to mention it. Instead, he pulled back, cupped my balls in his hand and muttered, "You da boss." Then his mouth descended on my cock once again and he went to work on it with a vengeance, leaving me breathless and trembling. I could feel my come building up inside me, roiling in my balls, pleading for release. So to take my mind off what he was doing *again*, I did everything to him he was doing to me, which really didn't take my mind off *anything*, as you can imagine.

While I slavered away at his beautiful cock, Milan suddenly made a little noise in his throat and his hips lifted off the bed at the same time, driving his cock deeper into my throat. Somehow I knew the time had come.

I released his cock from my mouth and pressed my lips to the base of his shaft. With his balls on my chin, I slid a fingertip between his legs and rubbed it against his hot opening. At that, his hips came even farther off the bed, but I rode him, never taking my mouth from the base of his shaft.

"I want to watch," I muttered, pulling back just enough to improve my view. "I have to see."

When he reached down and clutched my hair, I knew we were at the point of no return. I watched, breathless, as his come welled out of him as if in slow motion. Instead of shooting skyward as my own come does, his oozed lazily from him in a massive gout, thick and hot. It flowed from his cock like lava spilling slowly over the lip of a volcano until it all but covered his shaft completely with warm, fragrant cream.

When his flow was almost spent and his ass had collapsed back onto the bed, I licked at his cock like a cat with a bowl of milk, lapping away the thick come and swallowing it as I went. It tasted like heaven. As I dipped his come-slathered dick into my mouth one more time to clean it off good and proper, Milan once again began a frenzy of shuddering, and to my surprise and utter delight, one more freshet of hot come erupted from him to fill my mouth.

With my hands all over him, I took everything I could get. And as his cock began to soften in my mouth, he sat up, still trembling, and scooped me into his arms. He laid his hungry mouth over my come-moistened lips and licked away whatever drops of his own come I had missed.

When he was satisfied I was clean, he laid me gently back on the bed and with a sexy, gentle smile on his face, he muttered, "My turn."

Poke-assing along with his tongue like he had all the time in the world, he traced snail trails of saliva across my skin from my shoulders to my feet. He took his sweet time exploring every valley and plain he ran across. His hot mouth played at my balls until I was shivering like a cold puppy. And finally, when he decided he was finished driving me crazy, he got to the heart of the matter and stuffed my dick once again into his velvety hot mouth and started working at it as if it were an all-day sucker.

By this time I was so turned on I didn't even try to be subtle. I wrapped my legs around his head, and before I could count to three, my dick took control of the situation once and for all.

Milan apparently did not expect me to shoot so quickly. He was still piddling around, licking and nibbling at my corona, trying to be clever and thinking he was giving me a treat, when in reality, by this time he didn't have to do anything. He could have lain there like a fallen sycamore and I would have come all over him anyway. Before he had a chance to figure that out, my fuse ran out and my goddamn dick exploded in his mouth.

My come erupted with such force that it sprayed his face, shot up his nose, damn near blinded him in one eye, and soaked his hair from his hairline to the crown of his head.

By the time he got control of the gusher and had managed to direct my stiff-as-iron dick back into his mouth before the entire harvest was lost, Milan was giggling and laughing and trying not to choke on the come still shooting down his throat.

I was so out of control I was flopping around like a fish out of water, and it was all Milan could do to hang on. Still laughing, he held me down with one arm over my heaving chest and the other over my trembling legs as he continued to suck and slurp and drain me of every last drop of come still gurgling forth.

By the time my thrashing began to calm and my heart began to feel like maybe it wasn't going to disintegrate after all from all the abuse it was taking, Milan pressed his mouth to my stomach and just lay there giggling while he waited for me to get hold of myself.

I looked down at him hovering over me. His face and hair were drenched with my juices. I grinned when he caught my eye.

"You're a mess," I said. "Sorry about that." My heart was still beating like a tom-tom.

He stared back at me with a devilish smile. I thought I had never seen a sexier smile ever.

"And that was only our first try," he said, licking away another string of come he had spotted splattered across my stomach. I didn't know if it was his or mine, and at this point in the proceedings, I figured it didn't much matter. "Imagine what we can accomplish after we practice a few times."

I liked the sound of that. "Does that mean you might want to take another stab at it one of these days?"

"Try to stop me," he said, and once more he pressed his face into my stomach. I gave another shudder when he dipped his tongue into my belly button and left it there for a while.

I curled up around his head, holding his face to my gut and tracing my fingers along the furrows of his muscled back. He kissed his way up my torso until his mouth found mine.

As he tasted me yet again, and I tasted him, we pulled each other close. We lay there in each other's arms and listened to the storm rage around us as the rain tapped at the windows, and the wind shook the old rattletrap sign far above our heads. I found myself melting into him, letting the delicious heat of his skin and the memory of everything we had just done calm me to the point of sleep.

"Tall men really are worth the climb," I muttered into his ear.

His snowy teeth found my earlobe and took a gentle nip. "And little guys come like Super Soakers."

Our heartbeats slowed as we lay there in the brightly lit room on the disheveled bed and listened to our voices mist away to memory as they melded with the thrumming of the storm outside my bedroom window. A lazy contentment settled in as I thought back over everything we had done and said through the course of our first long evening together. I dozed at some point, but when I woke I found Milan's arms still wrapped around me, holding me tight. The scent and feel of him carried me through the hours, and I realized I had never once in my life felt as safe and protected as I did that night.

I woke to the dim light of early morning with Milan's strong, heavenly arm still draped across me. As he snored softly into my shoulder, I listened to a bird chirrup and chatter sweetly outside my bedroom window. It took me a minute before I realized what the gaily chattering bird signified.

Holy crap. The storm was over.

The flutter of eyelashes against my skin and the feel of warm fingers skidding across my stomach made me turn my attention once again to the man in bed beside me.

"Good morning," I mumbled into his hair.

Milan nestled closer. His mouth found my neck. When he said, "G'morning," his voice was a sleepy, sexy grumble.

Then he tensed. "What time is it?"

I scrunched down into the bed until we were head to head. Burrowing closer, I found his lips with mine. I took a minute to give those heavenly lips the attention they deserved. Then I whispered, "Don't worry. It's Sunday. You don't have to work today."

His responding kiss was yummy, but he didn't speak. Uh-oh.

"*Do* you? *Do* you have to work today?"

He pulled back far enough to focus on my face. "Yeah, actually I do. Me and Pop have a morning catering job. A wedding at the Westgate Hotel. I have to get the van back to the restaurant and get things ready."

"Oh."

His eyes were sexy and heavy with sleep. He gazed past me and squinted at the morning light shining through the window. "Holy shit, Harlie. What time *is* it?"

"I don't know. Sixish?"

"Oh crap!" He gave me a quick kiss and threw the covers aside.

I ached with longing at the day's first sight of his naked body. Broad back, strong ass and legs shadowed with hair, head of wavy dark-chocolate hair sticking straight up off the top of his head. Then I ached a little more remembering the night we had just shared. The things we had done. My heart gave a sad little lurch inside my chest when I lay there in my suddenly empty bed and watched Milan hustle his naked body to the bathroom and duck through it, dragging his clothes along behind him.

Two minutes later, the door opened and he came out fully dressed. I had never seen anything so depressing in my life. His hair was combed and the only thing that hinted of the night we'd shared was the still-sleepy droop of his eyelids over his electrifying blue eyes.

He leaned over the bed and kissed me on the nose. "I'm sorry, Harlie. I really have to go. I'll talk to you later, okay?"

And before I could answer, he was gone. The fucker.

I leaped from the bed and threw a pillow across the room just so God would know how pissed off I was. Then I heard my front door reopen and footsteps race back across the apartment.

The next thing I knew Milan was there, scooping me into his arms and holding me a foot off the floor while he covered my mouth with his. He pulled back far enough to be able to speak without clacking our teeth together.

"Thank you for last night," he whispered. "Can I see you tonight?"

I thrashed around for something to say that wouldn't make me sound like a heartsick twit caught in the middle of a snippy-ass snit. "Glutton for punishment, huh?"

"You bet," he said, flashing his pearly whites and aiming his dimples at me at the very same time, a deadly combination of artillery if there ever was one. He stared back at the door he'd just come through. "Did I hear a pillow hit the door?"

"I dropped it," I said.

"All the way across the room?"

"Maybe."

He stared at me with narrowing eyes while his dimples stayed behind to man the fort. "You're a terrible liar. You were mad that I left."

He was still holding me in the air like a rag doll. "Aren't you getting tired holding me up?"

"Never," he smiled.

And needless to say, that's all it took. I wasn't pissed off anymore. In fact, I was now the opposite of pissed off, whatever that might be. Breathless, I wrapped my bare legs around his waist and flung my arms around his neck. My dick, still stiff and hungry, felt so good pressed against the front of his shirt I thought I might swoon. While his palms cradled my naked ass and a finger or two settled directly over my sphincter, which was fodder for a whole new raft of imaginings, I buried my face in the crook of his neck to get another whiff of the man.

I nodded my head and squirmed my ass around in his hands. "What was that question you asked me?"

He laughed. "I asked if I can see you again tonight."

"You really want to?"

He beetled his brows and gave me a stern look, which didn't really pan out very well, because his dimples were *still* showing. "You know I do," he said. "I want it more than anything."

"And you won't forget?"

"No, Harlie. I won't forget," he said with a grin. "How could I?" And once again he pressed his warm mouth to mine. His kiss was gentle and not so gentle at the same time. My favorite kind of kiss.

Thirty seconds later he plucked his lips from mine and eased me down onto the edge of the bed. Before turning away, he let his fingers trail across the head of my dick, making me shiver. "I'll take care of that later," he said with a smile.

I couldn't seem to find my voice. "Okay," I rasped.

This time when he closed the apartment door behind him, I didn't throw anything. Or call him a fucker. Or get all homicidal or hurt or crazy. In lieu of all that, I simply leaped to my feet, hard-on and all, and executed a little Irish jig across the bedroom floor.

Nothing bipolar about me. Nosiree.

Chapter 10

IT WAS the longest morning of my life.

I tried to work on my book but somehow couldn't concentrate. I scrambled up a bunch of eggs for breakfast, then sat at the kitchen table picking at them like a spoiled kid. I finally gave up and set the plate aside for Gizmo, since he would probably be popping in any minute as he wended his weary way around the building, glomming handouts from all the easily bamboozled tenants.

I replayed over and over in my mind every minute of my night with Milan. By simply closing my eyes I could relive the feel of his body against mine. By standing still for a minute, I could once again taste his kiss. And by clutching my heart so I wouldn't go into cardiac arrest, I could remember the moment his come billowed out of his cock and reexperience the glorious heat and scent and taste of it as I lapped it away while Milan's long luscious body bucked and trembled beneath me, and boy, wasn't *that* the Cadillac of all memories. Milan sprawled out naked beneath me was a wonder. Milan in the middle of an orgasm, arching his back, thrusting his hips, and shaking like a fucking leaf was a gift from God. And not just any old gift either. It was like the best gift *ever*.

At one point in the morning I did my perv thing and buried my face in the sheets on Milan's side of the bed, just to smell his scent again. I should probably have changed the sheets after everything we had done in that bed the night before, but I couldn't bear to. What if he didn't come back like he said he would? What if I threw those damn sheets in the laundry and washed his smell away and he didn't come back at all? His smell would be lost. What would I do then?

As soon as I sat back and analyzed my thoughts rationally, I knew I was begging for trouble. Milan and I had shared a wonderful night together, it was true. But maybe that was all it was to him—a wonderful night. Maybe he didn't see anything more in it than that. Maybe he was simply being polite when he asked if he could come back. He was still my boss, after all. And he was still kind of a mystery to me as well. Quiet people usually are. After all, I wasn't psychic. How was I supposed to know what was going on inside his head? Maybe he slept with *all* the help at the restaurant. Maybe I was just this month's Catch of the Day. Or maybe he came at the drop of a hat for anybody who seemed the least bit interested. And wouldn't that be a fucking bummer.

At eleven o'clock I heard a soft scraping at my front door. I opened it expecting to find Gizmo tapping his foot impatiently and desperately demanding a can of tuna, but what I found was Arthur standing there holding Gizmo in his arms, allergies notwithstanding, and darned if *both* of them didn't look desperate.

"Can we come in?" Arthur shyly asked. He was back in his Belladonna Arms drag. This morning he wore a chenille housecoat with bunny slippers and a snood wrapped around his bowling-ball-sized head. The snood was made of lace and sprinkled with red sequins that sparkled in the light. Lucy Ricardo would have loved it. To add a little more bling, which was the last thing Arthur needed, he wore clip-on faux ruby earrings that dangled off his earlobes and caught so much light in their multifaceted red surfaces it was like staring into a furnace. Between the sequins and the rubies, I could barely stand to look at him.

I squinted into the glare. "My God, Arthur, your earrings are *blinding*."

Arthur is a glass-half-full kind of guy. "Oh, thanks, honey. If you like them so much maybe I'll let you borrow them sometime."

"Uh, thanks."

Gizmo leaped down from Arthur's arms and flounced off to the kitchen. Never one to stand on ceremony, he sailed onto the counter with a grunt (he really needed to go on a diet) and immediately began scarfing up the plate of scrambled eggs I had left there earlier. Gizmo seemed to know the eggs were for him, although to be honest, I'm pretty sure he would have eaten them anyway.

Arthur still stood at the door peeking around the jamb. "Is Tom's son still here?"

It took me a moment to remember who Tom was. Oh. Mr. Burger. "No, Arthur. Milan is gone. He had to go to work."

Arthur smiled and patted his snood, a la Mae West. He sauntered through the door and headed for the kitchen like Gizmo had a minute earlier. He snagged my arm in passing and towed me along behind him. "Tom went to work too. Can we talk, honey? I really need to talk."

"Certainly, Arthur. Sit down. I'll get us some coffee."

I did my domestic, hostessy bit, pouring two cups of coffee and placing a box of donuts on the table while Arthur watched my every move. Only when I sat down across from him and plucked a donut out of the box did he speak. Since he didn't reach for a donut himself, I knew what he was about to say must be of the utmost importance. In fact, Arthur ignoring a box of donuts was enough to scare the pants off me completely.

"What's wrong?" I asked, all the while wondering why Arthur would take the trouble to don his Lucy Ricardo drag and still not bother to shave the stubble off his face.

I'll give Arthur credit. He may not know when to shave, but he also isn't one to beat around the bush. He leaned across the table and took a death grip on my hand. It was only then I noticed he was wearing press-on nails. Two inches long, blood red, and sharp as knives. They were also sprinkled with glitter. Just what he needed. *More* bling. "I'm in love," he stated flatly.

"With who? Mr. Burger?"

He stared blankly. "Who's Mr. Burger?"

"Tom," I said. "Tom is Mr. Burger. The man you left the party with last night."

"Oh. Mr. Burger. Of course." His press-on talons clamped down harder. "Oh lord, Harlie. The man was wonderful. So sexy. So giving. So fucking *nice!* And I think he liked me, Harlie, I really do."

I tried to pry my hand free. He was cutting off the circulation and his press-on nails felt like thumbtacks poking into my skin. "Well, of course, he liked you, Arthur. What's not to—"

"He told me he *liked* a man with meat on his bones. That's what he said! Can you imagine?"

"No, I—"

"And he wants to see me again!"

"Did he say that?"

Arthur frowned, but not for long. "Yes! Of course he said it. You think I'd make it up? He's coming over this evening! And he spent the night, Harlie. The entire night! We had the most amazing sex. At one point in the night when he was slavering away at my ass with his head buried all the way up to his clavicles—"

I flew out of the chair and clapped my hands to my ears. My donut sailed across the room and landed in the sink, where Gizmo immediately pounced on it. "Lalalalalala! Too much information, Arthur! Too much information!"

Arthur had the good grace to blush, but I could see he still wanted to impart every nanosecond of his evening with the incomparable Mr. Burger. And secretly, I had to admit, if the father was anything like the son, then maybe Arthur had good reason to crow. But still, I didn't want to hear the details. I mean I *really* didn't want to hear the details.

Arthur assumed a pensive look. Don't think *that* wasn't bizarre considering his glistening snood and his ruby earrings and his unshaven face. "If only he wasn't so old."

"What are you talking about, Arthur? Mr. Burger's probably the same age as you. He might even be a little younger."

Arthur cast a suspicious gaze around the kitchen as if he thought the NSA had agents hiding under the sink. "Well, don't spread it around, Harlie." He gave his snood another pat, leaving it crooked. "A lady has to have a few secrets."

I dragged my hand over my face like Moe Howard. Sometimes doing that just feels right.

"Look, Arthur, I'm glad you had a wonderful night. I really am. And I had a wonderful night too, thanks for asking, which you didn't. But I have some work to do, and I sort of have a date later too, so maybe you can get to the point of your visit."

"Huh?"

I sighed. "What is it you wanted?" I asked, trying not to roll my eyes. I snagged another donut, determined to hold on to this one no matter what outlandish piece of information Arthur shot across my bow.

Arthur hemmed and hawed and sipped his coffee and chewed on his press-on nails and said, "Excuse you," to the cat when Gizmo, still sitting in the kitchen sink, burped up a mouthful of donut. (And here I'd thought the man never beat around the bush.) Finally Arthur came to the point.

"I think Tom is ready to see me as I really am."

"Meaning?"

"I was miserable dressed up like a cowboy last night. It wasn't me, Harlie. It wasn't me at all." He flung his arms wide, melodramatic as hell. "I couldn't breathe! I couldn't effervesce! I think I should let my true light shine through tonight when Tom comes over. I think I'll bless him with my true essence."

"Your true essence. As in thirty yards of taffeta, a six-pound wig, and a quart and a half of makeup applied with a trowel. *That* sort of essence?"

"Well—yeah. You think I shouldn't?"

After one date? Two years wouldn't be enough prep time for that.

"Geez, Arthur, *I* don't know," I said, opting for a more diplomatic response. Drag queens are so sensitive. "I just think you're getting awfully worked up over one date."

Arthur drummed his two-inch scarlet fingernails on my kitchen table and glared at me like I had pooped in his coffee. "Have you looked in a mirror this morning, Harlie? You might be interested to know you are positively *aglow.* I haven't seen you this happy since you moved in. And I suspect all your rosiness is due to the fact that *you* had fun last night too. Am I wrong?"

"Well, no, but—"

Arthur waggled a finger in my face. "I watched you two at Sylvia's party. Smooching and hanging all over each other. Tom told me how the two of you were dancing around each other at work and how he knew his son wanted to get to know you but maybe didn't quite know how to go about it. That's why Tom coerced Milan into working Sylvia's party with him. Tom knew you'd be there. I'll bet you weren't aware of *that, were* you?"

"No, I—"

"So don't sit there telling *me* not to get my hopes up when you're sitting across from me positively *flushed* with memories of last night."

Here he leaned in closer and winked. "Not that I don't understand, mind you. My God, Tom's son is a gorgeous hunk of manhood!"

I grinned. "Ain't he though?"

"And if he's hung anything like his daddy—"

"Lalalalalala!"

Arthur slapped my hands away from my ears and then seemed to realize his tirade had drifted astray. He straightened his back, not to mention his snood, and declared firmly, "So don't go telling me not to get my hopes up, Harlie Rose. You should be a little more understanding since it seems to me we're both in the same pickle. What do you say to that?"

I stared at him for a good five seconds. "My God, Arthur. You don't really think I've fallen in love with Milan in one night, do you? I'm not *that* flaky."

Arthur tsked. Twice. "Well, I'm sorry to hear that, Harlie, because as far as me and Mr. Burger go, I most certainly *am* head over heels in love with the man. If that's being flaky, so be it. And frankly, son, it feels so good I hope I *stay* flaky."

"I'm sorry, Arthur, but people just don't fall in love overnight."

He pulled his housecoat tight and adjusted an earring. "Oh, shut up."

I felt a smile drift across my face. "You do look happy, Arthur. And you're right. I'm happy too. But as for you springing the Queen of the Belladonna Arms on poor Mr. Burger, I'm not so sure."

Arthur's face fell. "Those straight clothes kill me, dammit. Nothing moves. Nothing gives. Nothing *flows*."

"It's not supposed to flow, Arthur. It's just supposed to—be. It's supposed to make you look masculine. And sane."

Arthur shot me a derisive squint. "This from a guy whose fashion statements run to blue jeans and T-shirts and who sticks his tongue down people's throats at parties."

I pouted. "That hurt."

As if his mind was made up, no thanks to me, Arthur slammed his massive hands down on the table, and I jumped two feet into the air. Even Gizmo, from the top of the fridge, where he had gone to digest his eggs and donut, peeled open one sleeping eye to see what all the racket was about.

Arthur stuck an upright finger in my face and left it there for a minute quivering in indignation. "Fine!" he growled. "One more night in those butch clothes you picked out from the Wrangler Iron Maiden Collection. But if Tom and I have a *third* date, he's going to find the real me waiting for him at the door. The softer me. The more delicate me. And yes, Harlie Rose, I don't mind saying, the *true* me."

Not waiting for me to respond, although in truth I didn't have the vaguest idea what to say anyway, Arthur threw his nose in the air and huffed off in a snit. Only at the door did he finally turn and give me a wink. "Thanks, honey. You're probably right. I should introduce the real me to Tom in easy dollops. Don't want to scare him away. A man can only take so much woman, after all." He held his hands two feet apart. "And a woman can only take so much dick."

"Lalalalalalalalalalala!"

He laughed, blew me a kiss, and eased himself out the door.

THE PHONE rang at three. The moment I realized it was Milan, my heart scudded into hyperdrive.

He skipped the greetings and went right to the meat of the matter (a wee joke). "Do you like prime rib?" he merrily asked.

"Uh, yes."

"Had dinner?"

"No."

"I have six pounds of leftover prime rib and a platter of scalloped potatoes. Interested?"

I was finally getting my heart under control. My mouth was another problem altogether. "Only if you come with it," I said.

His voice slid into wily mode. Wily and sexy as hell. "I wouldn't want to interrupt your writing."

"What?" I giggled. "A man with that much meat isn't an interruption. He's a gift from God."

I could sense Milan's smile over the phone. At least I thought I could. His voice softened. "I've thought about you all day, Harlie. Have you thought about me?"

"No," I said. "Who is this anyway? Is this a wrong number?"

"Very funny. I enjoyed last night. Did you enjoy last night?"

"If I say yes, will I get a raise?"

"Maybe. Are you saying yes?"

"Yes. You bet. Absolutely. Best night of my life. How much of a raise do I get?"

"Best night of my life too," Milan cooed without a trace of humor, and I almost dropped the phone.

I lowered my voice accordingly. I can coo too when it's called for. "Why aren't you here yet?"

"Thought I'd go home and shower first."

"Shower here."

In the ensuing silence, I heard the grumbling roar of the work van through the phone, and I realized Milan was already on the road. The silence lasted for a good ten seconds.

Finally he said softly, "I could do that."

"And don't forget your meat."

"Is that like a *homosexual double entendre*?"

"You bet."

"Can I spend the night?"

"You bet."

"Can we do everything we did last night and more?"

"You bet. Uh, by 'more,' you don't mean—"

"We'll figure it out when I get there."

Now *there* was food for thought. "O-o-kay. And when will that be exactly?"

"Two minutes."

I jumped off the couch. "What! I haven't showered yet either!"

"Oh, good," he said, his voice getting all purry and sexy again. "We'll shower together."

"It's a small tub."

"All the better."

"Will you really be here in two minutes?"

"Nope. One. I'm pulling up to the Belladonna Arms right now. I'm afraid I have a confession to make."

"What is it?"

"I was going to come over whether you wanted me to or not. Is that pushy?"

"Not pushy enough. If you were really pushy you'd have been here by now."

I heard a car door bang shut. "Buzz me in," he said.

"There's no buzzer," I scoffed. "What do you think this is, the Ritz? We're lucky we have a porch and a front door."

"Hope I don't run into my dad."

"Is he coming too?"

"Not with me. He's coming to see Arthur."

"I think Arthur's already in love." The words were out of my mouth before I could stop them. Apparently Milan didn't mind.

"Just between you and me, I think Pop is too."

I felt a smile of wonder creep across my face. "Well, ain't that something."

"Let me in," Milan said. There was a smidgeon of pleading in the words that really turned me on.

"I told you, we don't have a buzzer."

"No, you fool. I'm at your door. Let me in."

"Oh."

I raced to the apartment door, flung it open, and there was Milan, balancing in one hand a stainless steel pan filled with scalloped potatoes, on top of which perched a second pan stacked with slices of prime rib. He was pressing his cell phone to his ear with the other hand. He wore black slacks, a white shirt, and a red vest. Catering drag.

"Baby," he said.

And my heart puddled at my feet.

I ushered Milan in, told him I'd be right back, and raced down the stairs to Arthur's apartment. He answered in a black cocktail dress with a Gloria Swanson turban stuck on his head and a martini glass in his hand. The hat had one long egret feather sticking up on the side and the martini glass contained three olives on a stick and what looked to be about a quart of gin. It was a really big glass. A school of guppies could have lived in there for a year. If you drained the gin, of course.

He also had a big fat cigar stuck in his mouth, and the reek of it almost knocked me flat.

"Arthur," I hissed. "Get out of drag! Mr. Burger is on his way over."

"Who?"

"*Tom.*"

He made a face that was hard to read, but it was somewhere between "Holy fuck, I'm in trouble now!" and "Ooh, my man is on the way!" Personally I would have been focusing on the "Holy fuck" part if I'd been standing there looking like he did.

"I guess I'd better change, then," he pouted. "I just got dressed too. Brand-new Big Mama panty hose and everything. About to relax with a drinky poo."

"Butch," I said, rolling my eyes.

"Thanks," he responded, preening. Then he eyed me askance. "Oh, wait. You're being sarcastic."

I tugged him and his thirty yards of taffeta to me and gave him a peck on the cheek. "Good luck, Arthur. I've got my own man upstairs. Gotta run."

"Toodles, sweetcakes. Thanks."

"You're welcome, Arthur, and please don't say toodles or drinky poo while Burger's here. And don't mention panty hose either. You're shooting for masculine. Remember? Try to be a hunk. And for Christ's sake, get rid of that cigar!"

He gave himself a whack on the side of his turban that would have killed Gloria Swanson dead if she had been the one wearing it, and if she wasn't dead already.

"Yes. Hunkalicious. Masculine. Big-ass butch motherfucker. No cigar. That's me. I'll do it."

Yeah, right.

Without further ado, I raced back up the stairs, my conscience clear. Arthur's hopeful transformation from raging queen to "Aging and Overweight Stud of the Month" was forgotten before I ever got back to my door. I took a deep breath and slipped into my apartment. The minute I did, Milan pulled me into his arms.

Arthur was *really* forgotten then.

MILAN AND I sat opposite each other in the old claw-footed bathtub. I figured even the rust stains in it were older than I was. Our knees poked up through the suds because frankly there wasn't enough room for both of us to be in there at the same time, but we were happily making do.

Milan looked bemused. "I've never taken a bubble bath before."

"Don't worry," I said. "I won't tell anybody at work."

He grinned and stretched his long hairy legs out to either side of me and propped his feet on the edge of the tub. I rested my head between his feet and closed my eyes. My left leg rested in his lap. Somewhere under the water Milan's cock poked my ankle. He was as hard as a hammer handle. Like I wasn't. And all this served to make my left leg really happy. In fact, the left leg was so happy the *right* leg, which was shunted off to the side of the tub and relegated to merely brushing Milan's hip, was seriously considering suicide.

He interrupted my insane mental ramblings by saying, "Sylvia's so nice."

I opened my eyes and studied his face. "You like her."

His face reddened. It reddened even more when I caressed his strong calves and kissed the instep of his foot. "I like her and Pete both," Milan said, flexing his toes like maybe I was tickling him with my lips, although judging by the lurch of his dick against my ankle, I don't think his being tickled was really the problem. "Sylvia is the most loving and generous person I know. I want nothing but the best for her. When you get to know her better, you'll feel the same way."

"I *already* know her better, and I *do* feel the same way," I said.

I stroked the soapy hair on his legs and watched his toes flex again. I assumed that meant he enjoyed what I was doing. "Whenever she finally goes in for her surgery," I said, "we should go visit her at the hospital. Maybe Stanley and Roger will go with us."

Milan smiled. "And Arthur and Pop. We'll all go together. We'll take her flowers. She loves flowers." And as an afterthought, he added, "Plus some of my croissants. She loves those too."

I was crazy about Sylvia. I really was. But somehow I couldn't get past the rush of knowing Milan was lounging naked in my bathwater with me tucked comfortably between his legs. "I'm glad you came over," I said, resting a hand on each of his knees and once again pressing my lips to his foot.

"Then come here," he said. He reached across the tub and pulled me to him, sloshing about three gallons of water over the edge of the tub and onto the bathroom floor. Like I cared.

He slid me around in the tub until my back was to him; then he tucked me against his chest and wrapped his arms around me to hold me close. He slid his hands through my soaked hair and combed it away from my face with his fingers. When I snuggled my head under his chin and relaxed against him, I shivered at the delicious feel of his stiff dick pressed against my back. When his hand slid down my stomach and gently grasped *my* dick, I shivered a little more. We lay like that for the longest time, while the bathwater grew tepid around us.

My voice sounded lazy and content when I heard it with my own ears. One would almost think I wasn't turned on at all. "So your dad liked Arthur, huh?"

Milan's mouth found my neck. It felt so good I leaned in to his kiss. While his one hand still softly cradled my cock under the water and his other hand splayed across my chest, I played my hands along his thighs, loving the feel of his bristling wet leg hair against my palms. I wished I would never have to move again because I knew wherever I ended up in life, it would never be as perfect as the place I was in right then.

Milan's voice was warm and velvety. He sounded as comfortable as I felt. "He did," he said. "Pop liked him a lot."

As much as I loved Arthur, I still couldn't believe what I was hearing. I wondered vaguely if that made me a bad person.

"Aside from being about the same age," I said, "they don't really have that much in common, do they? I'd hate to see Arthur get hurt."

Milan tugged me a little bit closer, his bulging bicep tucked neatly under my chin, his breath hot on my ear. I closed my eyes and ate it up. Every second, every sensation. I had always been a sucker for cuddling, and I was quickly learning Milan was a master at it.

"Pop's last lover was a character too. And he was a big guy like Arthur. You know, when Pop and I were prepping the wedding this morning, he was in a really good mood. I don't remember the last time he was so... *bouncy*. I don't know what he and Arthur did last night, but whatever it was, I think he enjoyed the hell out of it."

I remembered what Arthur said about Mr. Burger burrowing into his ass all the way up to his clavicles and I knew immediately that was a piece of trivia I should probably not impart to Mr. Burger's son. Hell, I was still sorry Arthur had imparted it to me. Not only was tact called for at the moment, but I thought a few complimentary Arthur testimonials would be prudently appropriate as well.

"Your dad will never find a man as loyal and funny and *special* as Arthur. He's a sweetheart. He's a little odd at times, but sometimes odd is good. *Eccentric* is good. Don't you think? Don't you think your dad would like an eccentric boyfriend?"

"He's never had one that wasn't."

I thought that boded well for Arthur.

"Arthur's well off too. He owns this apartment building, and that must be worth a pretty penny. They are both business owners, him and your dad. Don't you think that's serendipitous?"

"Good word choice," Milan said, smiling against my neck. "You Arthur's agent or something?"

"Just a friend," I said, wondering if I was lying. I *was* sort of his agent after all.

Gizmo lay sprawled on the hamper, flicking his tail and staring at us.

Milan said, "Your cat is certainly voluptuous. A few sit-ups wouldn't kill him."

"It's not my cat."

"Whose cat is it?"

"Nobody knows."

I twisted my head around as far as I could and kissed Milan on the chin. His warm, soapy hand held my head in that position long enough for his mouth to find mine. As we kissed, his fingers circled the head of my dick under the water and his thumb slid luxuriously across my slit, eliciting my first hip thrust of the evening. God, he had a marvelous touch.

"I love the way you feel," he said, nibbling at my ear.

"Which part of me?"

"The whole package."

"Will you spend the night again?"

He considered that for a moment. "Do you want me to?"

"What do you think?"

He considered *that* for a moment. "I think I *want* you to want me to."

"Then I do."

"Really?"

"God, yes."

"Show me," he said.

So I did.

Chapter 11

WE DROPPED our towels on the bathroom floor, and I led Milan by the hand to the sofa in the living room, where I gently eased him down. When he was sitting comfortably, I dropped to my knees between his legs and gazed up at him as I lazily ran my hands over his body. Exploring. Maybe laying claim a little bit. Thighs, stomach, chest, it was all prime real estate. There wasn't an ounce of fat on him, and the heat of his skin was delicious. We both reeked of green apple bubble bath, which I realized now had been a questionable purchase. Next time I should try one a bit less pungent. We smelled like a truckload of Granny Smiths.

The hair on Milan's legs was soft and fluffy from the bath. The hair on his head was still wet and had slipped into ringlets. Until now I hadn't realized how curly his hair really was. I avoided his towering cock for the moment, and I could see it drove him crazy.

Out of everything I liked about him, I really liked the fact that I could drive him crazy the best.

Or course, it worked both ways. Just by sitting there naked in front of me, legs spread wide and his dick in my face, he was driving me crazy too. I mean *really* crazy.

I pressed my lips to the inside of his leg, then rested my chin on his knee so I could look at him with what I hoped wasn't a moony-ass simper, but I suspected it was. His face molded itself into a one-dimple smile as he ran a finger over the bridge of my nose as if studying the contour of it. He shifted his hips slightly and spread his legs a wee bit more to make room for both me and his balls. Having the best seat in the house, I didn't mind at all.

Milan's balls were plump and round and fuzzy and nestled there under his erection as if they knew how tempting they were. Dragging my eyes a little higher, I could already see a teeny drip of moisture gathering at the tip of Milan's erect cock, and I was pretty sure that little drop of moisture wasn't bathwater. It took every last ounce of willpower I possessed not to scramble across his lap and lick it away.

He hugged me with his knees as if he knew what I was thinking. His one-dimpled smile turned sexy.

"So," he asked with a sly, conniving look in his eyes, "after this weekend are you still going to be a wise guy when you go back to work?"

I laughed. "Depends. Are you still going to be a glacial hard-ass?"

His jaw dropped in a parody of shock. "I was just trying to teach you your job as efficiently as I possibly could."

"No. You were trying to see how far you could go before I banged you in the head with that big fucking paddle you scoop bread out of the oven with."

His hand slid across my cheek. His voice was playful. That was sexy too. "I've liked you since the very first day you came to the deli, you know."

"You had an annoying way of showing it."

His smile broadened a little more. Both dimples were at play now, and God I loved looking at them. I wasn't sure, but I thought I felt a drop of precome forming at the end of *my* dick, and considering where I was huddled, why they hell wouldn't I?

"Your ex is a fool," he said. "Sometimes people don't appreciate what they have until they don't have it anymore. Do you think he's sorry he broke your heart and threw you out of his life?"

I didn't like the route this conversation was taking, but there wasn't much I could do about it. I was too drawn to Milan to want to pick a fight or simply back away. And maybe it wouldn't kill me to answer the question anyway. Maybe if for no other reason than to hear what I had to say.

"No," I said. "I don't think he's sorry. He's probably forgotten about me completely."

Milan's fingers caressed my hair. "Then he's an idiot."

I couldn't argue with that. Still, I wasn't comfortable with this line of questioning. I wasn't sure why. It's not like I wasn't over Dan. I was.

"So what about *your* ex?" I asked. "He dumped you too, right? Why do you suppose he did that?"

Milan eyed me with a quizzical expression. I stared right back as if to say "you started it, not me." After a couple of seconds, he appeared to come to the same conclusion.

"Really want to know?"

I interrupted kissing his knee long enough to nod.

Milan stared past me to the evening light outside the living room window. The day was almost over, and a red sunset lit the sky to the west, shimmering through the San Diego skyline. For a crappy apartment building, the Belladonna Arms had a million dollar view.

"He found somebody else," Milan said. "We had been together about two years. Then one morning he simply announced he was moving on. That was several months ago."

"And you still miss him?"

Milan shook his head. His azure eyes were bright and serious in his face. He stared at me for a cluster of heartbeats before he finally said, "No. I don't miss him anymore."

"Good," I said and meant it. I wondered why my heart was doing flip-flops. Maybe it was time to change the subject.

"Who's Julie?" I asked out of the blue.

Milan's face twisted into that quizzical grin again. "How do you know Julie?"

I told him. "The first day I went to apply for the job at the deli, your dad was on the phone with someone named Julie who was giving him a hard time about never getting out of the house and never having any fun."

Milan laughed. "Yep. That's Julie." He leaned forward and kissed my forehead. For some reason, it appeared to be something he really wanted to do at that particular moment. I closed my eyes at the feel of his lips on my skin. I opened them when he sat back and continued speaking. My heart was still lurching around inside my chest like a panicked cat trying to get out of a box.

"Julie's my sister. And she was right to be nagging him. He *didn't* get out enough. I have a feeling that's all going to change now, though. And I think maybe Pop has you to thank for that. You and Sylvia."

I reached up with both hands and stroked the bristle of beard on Milan's cheeks just to see what it felt like. He hadn't shaved all day, and I found it intriguing. The touch of his sprouting beard turned me on enough that suddenly I couldn't bear to remain where I was in front of all that perfect nakedness another minute. Milan was simply too handsome. Too sweet. Too sexy.

I leaned in and pressed my face to his stomach. His erect cock nudged my chin as if begging for attention.

"I'm so glad you're here," I mumbled into him. "I really like being with you."

"Come up here," he purred. "Let me hold you."

He helped me to my feet and smiled when I straddled his lap, resting my thighs on his and sliding forward into his arms until our two dicks were snug against each other's stomachs. He slipped his right hand around to my back and pulled me in to him. I wrapped my arms around his neck as his mouth covered mine, and, eyes closed, I let his kiss carry me away.

He slid his other hand beneath me, cupping my balls. When an exploring finger rested lightly on my sphincter, I gave a tiny gasp. He smiled and his finger did a gentle reconnaissance, probing my opening with a feather touch, making me shiver. I dragged his face closer to mine, and our tongues came together somewhere in the white-hot moisture of our kiss.

I could not remember the last time I had felt so hungry for another human being. Dan and I had been good together sexually, but this was different. There was something about the size of Milan, the looming strength of him and the gentle way he wielded that strength, that made me want to crawl inside of him—or have him crawl inside of me.

"Fuck me," I whispered into his kiss. "Please, Milan. Fuck me."

There was humor in his voice, but there was pleasure in the gentle groan of it too. "So that's the way it is, is it?"

With a gentle smile on his face, he eased me over onto my back on the sofa. My legs came up to circle his waist as he lay atop me. His mouth left mine, and he kissed me delicately downward, burrowing into the well of flesh at the base of my throat, taking a minute to worship first one of my eager nipples, and then the other, and finally sliding down to pull my cock into his mouth, causing me to shudder and buck beneath him.

But even that wasn't enough for Milan. He released my cock and laid his mouth over my balls, tasting one then the other, nuzzling into them with his nose, lapping at them with his tongue. I buried my hands in his damp curls and held his head right where I wanted it as I waited for what was coming next.

And when it *did* come, Milan didn't disappoint.

Taking a firm grip on the backs of my knees, he hoisted my legs as high as he could get them, and when I was totally exposed beneath him, he repositioned himself with his face alight with wonder like a kid in a candy store.

As his mouth found my opening and his hot tongue slid into me for that first exploratory taste, I craned my head back, mouth agape in a rictus of wanton need. A silent scream erupted in my head, but thankfully it didn't find its way to my voice. I didn't want to interrupt Milan's train of thought in case he had any other universe-shaking moves to try on me next.

Which he did.

"Wait," he whispered, easing my legs down to the sofa and once again taking my dick into his mouth. He held me there in that satin heaven for just long enough to make me want more, and then he slipped off the sofa and padded naked across the room to the bathroom where I heard him rummaging through his clothes. A moment later, I heard my medicine cabinet open and immediately bang shut again.

When Milan returned, still naked, his dick was as hard as stone, bobbing around in front of him. As he crossed the room toward me I could see what he held in his hands. A cluster of foil-wrapped condoms were in one fist, and a jar of moisturizing cream was in the other.

Milan was ready for bear, and I guessed I was gonna be Smokey.

With a wicked grin on his face, he stood directly over me at the side of the sofa so I would have a bird's-eye view as he stared down at me and slid the condom over his hungry cock. While he did that, I reached up to caress his balls and was rewarded with the sight of his legs trembling at the brush of my fingers on his skin.

"You're going to pay for that." He grinned down at me, his sheathed cock hovering over my face, my hands still on his balls.

"Oh, good," I said. It was all I could do to get the two simple words out of my mouth without choking to death on my own saliva.

Again, Milan lifted my legs high and positioned himself between them. His mouth found my opening once more, and I bucked at the sensation of it. I was just about to cry out when he pulled his mouth away and gazed up at my face, pressing my dick down flat to my stomach so he could see around it.

"You're the most beautiful man I've ever seen," he said, his voice husky and raw with desire.

And before I could speak, before I could do anything, I felt cool lotion pouring across my anus. I closed my eyes at the luscious feel of it, and when he slipped a finger through the lotion and eased it into me, gently and slowly, I pushed my ass against his hand and begged for more.

Taking my cock into his mouth one more time, he slipped another finger inside me, and I rocked against his probing movements, forcing myself to relax, allowing myself to be whatever he wanted me to be, take whatever he wanted to give.

When his fingers slid free of me, I felt like weeping because I didn't want them to go. But I forgot my disappointment when Milan rose up onto his knees between my legs. I muttered, "Yes," and he pressed his cock to my hole and gently pushed. I reached up to grasp the back of his neck and pull him closer, and when I did, I felt my anal ring open up, and Milan's cock slid deep inside me with almost no resistance whatsoever.

I cried out and opened my eyes to see his face drifting over me. I touched the stubble on his cheek and smiled as he carefully pushed his cock deeper into me. He watched my face, and I knew he was looking for signs of pain. But I gave him none to contend with, for in reality there was no pain to be had. Every movement he made, every slippery inch of the penetration, was sheer pleasure to me. His cock was hard and throbbing inside me, and it filled me up completely. As he began to move in and out, slowly, exquisitely, I dragged him down until his mouth met mine. With my tongue piercing him as he was piercing me, I slid my hand between us and gripped my cock because I simply could not bear to leave it be.

"You feel like heaven," he muttered into our kiss, but still I couldn't speak. I held him tighter, arching my back hungrily into his thrusts as I relished the feel of his fat stabbing cock entering and leaving me over and over and over again.

"Let me," he whispered between gasps, and easing my hand aside, he slid his lotion-wet hand around my dick and began to slowly manipulate it for me. Between his cock in my ass and his hand on my dick, I thought I was going to explode. And it didn't take long before I knew I was right.

I tried to push his hand away, but he wouldn't let me. He continued to slide his slick hand up and down my shaft, continued to slip his wet fingers around my glans until I knew I was going to come if he didn't stop pretty damn soon. He seemed to relish the idea of driving me to the very brink, and since I didn't have the strength or the will or the desire to stop him, I let him do it.

Which he did, with unabashed glee. As my scrotum tightened and my come gathered to erupt, I arched high against the thrusting of his cock. And still tearing me apart, just as I wanted him to do, Milan took a fistful of my hair and pleaded, "Look at me."

I opened my eyes to see him hovering over me, his cock buried inside me as far as it would go, the tendons in his neck taut and trembling as he neared climax himself.

And as my come spilled into his hand and I bellowed like a bull at the force of the eruption, Milan too gave a yell when his come exploded from him. We clutched each other and shuddered through our individual releases, but still we kept our focus on the other.

Gradually, Milan's body relaxed, and he melted over me. His cock was still buried deep inside me, and I could feel it throbbing to the rhythm of his racing heart. Our stomachs were pressed together, my seed smearing both, and when his hand came up to caress my face, I felt him spread my come across my lips, then lean in to kiss it away a second later.

My body burned at every point of contact we made, and the contacts were everywhere. Legs, bellies, lips, hands. And that one other contact, deep inside me where Milan's cock still burrowed, eager to stay right where it was—and where I was just as eager for it to remain. Forever if need be. Hell, yes. Even forever wouldn't be too long.

"Thank you," Milan breathed over me.

All I could do was nod as I pulled his mouth back down to mine. Smiling, I squeezed my eyes shut, locking the memories inside.

Chapter 12

WAS I going too fast? Should I slow down? What the hell was I doing?

One would think I was worrying about the burgeoning affair I had embarked on with Milan Burger, my boss at the deli. But no. At the moment I was too busy trying not to ruin the pumpernickel dough he had entrusted me with. Milan spouting orders and breathing his heavenly scent all over me while crowding up to me like a big-ass oak tree looming over a rose bush didn't help.

"Stir it slower," he said. "What's the rush? It's just yeast and water. Let it dissolve."

So I stirred it slower and let it dissolve.

Milan had done as he promised, you see. Now that my apprenticeship had gone on for several weeks and I had yet to scream "I quit!" and run out the deli door, Milan was teaching me a bit of the trade. Not that I cared about being a baker. I didn't. But I did like knowing every joint venture we undertook would serve to inch us a little closer to each other than we already were. And since I couldn't imagine being *too* close to Milan, I was all for anything that threw us even a little bit more together.

Milan poked his nose over my shoulder and rested his hand at the small of my back. Farther south, I felt his leg brush mine.

"I wish you were naked right now," I mumbled.

He nudged me with his hip. Subtly. After all we were in the middle of the deli kitchen, there were workers scurrying about everywhere, and Milan's dad was parked at his desk not twenty feet away trying not to look like he was watching us, but I think he was.

There was a smile in Milan's voice when he said, "Naked bakers and hot ovens are a bad combination. Lots of knives lying around too. I think it's best I keep my goodies tucked safely away."

I craned my head around to peek at him. "Until later?" I asked hopefully.

His dimples flashed. "You bet. Until later. Then my goodies are your goodies."

I liked the sound of that.

His strong hand came up to cover my spoon hand. He steered the stirring for me, and all I could do was think about how his skin felt next to mine. *All* of his skin. Every square inch of it. And his goodies. I seemed to always be thinking about Milan's goodies these days. I wondered how many other baker trainees stirred pumpernickel dough while sporting a hard-on and lusting after their boss's goodies.

"Now while I help you with this, stir in your ingredients," Milan said softly. He had been speaking softly to me at work since the day I called him a glacial hard-ass. I should have done it sooner.

I pointed to an array of ingredients he had brought me earlier on a steel tray. "This shit here?"

I didn't actually *hear* him roll his eyes, but I *thought* I did. "Yes, Harlie. This shit here. Molasses, caraway seed, rye flour, salt, and shortening."

"Just dump the shit in?"

"If that's how you want to look at it, yes." He rolled his eyes again. I *know* I heard them rolling around *this* time.

I did as he said and dumped the shit in.

He plucked the spoon from my fist and set it aside. "Now use your hands to make the dough. Squoosh it around real good."

I squooshed it around, trying not to groan. "Feels funky."

"Just keep squooshing. Knead it until it's smooth, then separate it into eight small loaves. I'll be back to show you how to bake it. Has to be done promptly or the dough is fucked."

"Ooh, I so hate it when the dough gets fucked!" I said it with a smirk too. Sometimes I fail to comprehend the concept of overkill. Sarcasm I have down pat. Restraint continually eludes me.

Apparently Milan agreed. He shook his head and walked away. I admired his ass as he went, then turned my attention back to the damn dough.

We were four days into our affair, and I had not spent a night alone since it began. We arrived at work together now, but since we were bakers, we arrived earlier than everyone else, so the rumor mill which is always alive and thriving in any work environment hadn't caught wind of our relationship yet. However, I figured if I kept walking around the kitchen with a hard-on someone would figure it out sooner or later. To keep our secret from the other workers, we left work at separate times, and Milan would join me later at the Belladonna Arms after he had cleaned up at home, although we still managed to sneak in a communal bath every now and then when the urge arose.

As I worked the brown glob of dough, which I must say smelled delicious, I saw Mr. Burger grinning into his coffee as he sat at his desk going through a stack of invoices. I think he liked the fact that Milan was seeing someone, even if it was a lowly baker's assistant. I liked the fact that Milan was seeing a lowly baker's assistant too. I especially liked the fact that the lowly baker's assistant was me.

Burger's eye caught mine, and he shot me a wink as if to say, "Don't worry, kid. Your secret's safe with me."

I winked back as if to say, "So is yours."

A flash of unease crossed his face the moment I winked at him, and I wondered if I had crossed the line as far as the boss/employee relationship went with me and Mr. Burger. The fact that I had crossed that line—and several others—with my *immediate* boss, Milan, went without question.

But still, Mr. Burger and Arthur were going gangbusters with their own burgeoning affair, and Milan and I were thrilled about it. While they still seemed the oddest couple imaginable, there was no denying they enjoyed each other's company.

So far, Arthur had kept his penchant for cross-dressing a secret from his paramour, but I know he missed it. I feared one day he would spring a surprise on poor Mr. Burger that might very well kill their relationship dead. Hell, for all I knew, it might kill Burger dead too.

On the other hand, finding new ensembles for Arthur was becoming a chore. So far in our sartorial explorations, we had channeled several of the Village People—cowboy, construction worker, even one stint where I stuffed Arthur into military fatigues just for the fun of it—but now I was running out of ideas on ways to keep him looking butch. A three-hundred-pound gay Indian in a loincloth and eagle-feather headdress was too outlandish to contemplate even for me, so I was reluctant to try that particular Village People.

Arthur was no help at all. He hated each new outfit I coerced him into trying on. He missed his chintz and taffeta and silk and lace and earrings and nylons and wigs and makeup and crap, and constantly balked at my suggestions of denim, wool, flannel, leather, work boots, and baseball caps.

On the diet front, I can report Arthur had lost a grand total of four pounds in the six weeks since I started nagging him about his weight. I suspected he was cheating when I wasn't around. No, wait. I didn't suspect it. I *knew* it. In fact, I had once caught him red-handed with a box of Ding Dongs in his Gucci knock-off purse. Besides, I had apparently been wrong all along thinking Arthur would never snag a boyfriend at three hundred pounds. He had indeed.

And looking up, I saw his boyfriend approaching me now.

"Ah, pumpernickel," Burger said, leaning companionably against the butcher block table I was working at and eyeing the fat glob of brown dough I had sunk my hands into up to my wrists. I kept thinking of the original version of *The Blob* when the nasty little alien who looked remarkably like a hunk of pumpernickel dough crept down the stick and swallowed the old homeless guy's paw in the backseat of Steve McQueen's car.

"Smells good," Burger added. "You look like you're getting the hang of this baking stuff. My son seems to be a good teacher."

"Yeah." I smiled wide. "He's taught me a lot."

Burger coughed up a chuckle on that one. "I'm sure he has, son. I'm sure he has." I guessed he had caught my double entendre. And here I thought I was being subtle for once.

Burger stood there, arms crossed, hip against the table, watching me as I proceeded to rip the blob of dough into eight equal parts and try to mold them into uniform shapes. It wasn't easy because the dough kept sticking to my hands.

"Sprinkle a little flour on your hands," Burger said. "It'll work better."

"Thanks," I said. So I plucked my sticky paws out of the brown shit and did as he suggested. When I went back to my sculpting duties I found the stickiness had lessened considerably.

"Wow! Thanks."

Burger chuckled. "I guess my son hasn't taught you *everything*."

I opened my mouth to spout another double entendre, then thought better of it. "He probably forgot about the flour trick," I said and left it at that.

Burger nodded. "Probably did."

While I did my "three-year-old with a ball of Play-Doh" thing, still trying to turn one big fat ball of dough into eight uniformly shaped smaller ones, Burger stood silently watching. I tried to ignore him, but frankly he was beginning to make me nervous.

Finally, I stopped what I was doing and asked, "Did you want to talk to me about something?"

Burger reddened as he gazed down at his feet. When his eyes came back to me, they were sober. *Uh-oh,* I thought. *He wants to talk about Arthur.*

"I want to talk to you about Arthur," he said.

Boy, do I hate being prescient.

As if his engine had suddenly started sputtering along on only one or two cylinders, Burger began speaking in practically a mumble. I had to lean forward over the eight little Blobs finally beginning to take shape on the table in front of me to decipher exactly what it was he was saying.

"Son, I know you and Sylvia had something to do with Arthur and me getting together. In fact, it's taken me a while to realize you two probably orchestrated the whole thing. Am I wrong?"

I hemmed and hawed and tried to act like I was still concentrating on getting the eight little Blobs to take the right fucking shape, which was a lie. I was hanging on to every word Burger was saying. I hoped to God he wasn't about to ask me to tell Arthur for him that their affair was over. Jesus, he wouldn't do *that*, would he?

"Well," I ventured. "I have to admit it was my idea first, but it was really Sylvia who thought of getting you two together at the party." I stoked a fire under my ass and forced myself to beam happily. "And aren't you glad we did? You guys are getting along great! Right?"

Again, Burger dropped his eyes to his feet, where even I could see they were about to start shuffling uncomfortably. His feet, I mean. Although in truth his eyes were doing a little shuffling too. His mutter dropped another decibel, and I had to lean even *closer* to hear what he was trying to say.

"Arthur's a wonderful man, Harlie. I like him a lot. It's just...." His mumble trailed away completely. I guess his engine finally died.

Since I didn't want to hear what he was about to say anyway, I looked around for Milan. The dough was ready to go into the oven, or as ready as it was ever going to be, and I thought getting back to work would be a good way to prevent Burger from telling me whatever he was about to tell me.

As it turned out, I wasn't the only one who was prescient.

"I sent Milan to the supplier for some things so we wouldn't be interrupted. He won't be back for about an hour."

Shit. "But what about the dough?"

"Fuck the dough."

I gave a soft whistle. "Wow. Milan *said* this dough might get fucked."

Burger was beginning to look a little grumpy. "I'm not even going to pretend to know what that means. Can I have your attention for a minute, while we talk about Arthur? Please, Harlie. It's important."

I idly patted the tops of my eight little Blobs like they were the Octotwins, but all the while I was focusing on Burger's face. While I focused, my heart gradually sank into my upper colon. I just knew Arthur was about to get dumped.

"Son, like I said, Arthur's a wonderful person. It's just that... well...."

Crap. Burger *was* going to dump Arthur. And here I was, stuck in the middle of it.

"Just what?" I almost growled. "Spit it out!"

Burger looked abashed by my tone, as well he should, I thought. But still he forced himself to go on. "Son, Arthur's a sweet man. It's just that he's so... so... *complacent*. There's no spark about him. No individuality. He just stands around plucking at his clothes trying to look comfortable when I know he's not. Maybe it's me he doesn't feel comfortable around."

Burger was looking guiltier by the minute. But still, he seemed determined to finish what he had started. He didn't look happy about it, but he looked... *determined.* "I don't think the man ever did a silly, spontaneous thing in his life. He seems to be trapped in this awkward well of insecurities, unable to escape, unable to just be himself and let himself go. Now, I admit I'm not the most exciting guy in the world. Look at me. I'm old. I own a deli, for Christ's sake. But I still know how to let loose. I still know how to have fun. I even know how to be goofy, if the circumstances call for it. But not Arthur. I don't think he's ever done one fly-by-your-pants, come-hell-or-high-water, eccentric thing in his life. Dammit, Harlie, he's just so bloody *normal!*"

By this time I was staring at Burger as if an array of breadsticks had sprouted off the top of his head. When I spoke, my voice was so high it sounded like a squeaky brake drum. It surprised even me. But not as much as what Burger had just said. "You think *Arthur* is too *normal?*"

Burger seemed decidedly upset now. His ears were bright red, and he had crossed his arms even tighter over his chest and buried his hands into his armpits as far as they would go. He looked like a mummy.

He had to clear his throat a couple of times to get the next words out. It was almost as if he had forgotten how to talk, as mummies undoubtedly do. "I'm sorry, Harlie. The man is just boring. Just flat out boring." He breathed a sigh of relief. "There. I've said it."

I spent the next five or ten seconds staring at Burger and blinking. Just blinking. When I did finally find my voice, it didn't sound any happier than Burger's. In fact, it was a flat-out snarl.

"And you want me to tell him you don't want to see him anymore."

If Burger's ears got any redder they were going to start seeping blood. "Well, yes, Harlie, if it isn't too much trouble, I'd really apprec—"

I punched one of my eight little Blobs with my fist and made an ashtray. The Octotwins were no more. "Well, it *is* too much trouble. If you want to break up with Arthur, you'll have to do it yourself. I'm not going to be a party to breaking the man's heart. He likes you so much!"

Burger did his own little round of incredulous blinking. "I know."

"And still you're willing to break his heart!"

"Well." This time Burger was so embarrassed he not only shuffled his feet, he practically went into a soft-shoe routine. I was tempted to sprinkle a little salt on the floor so he could get the full effect.

I figured the next time I opened my mouth I would probably get fired, but what the fuck. I was already sick of pumpernickel bread anyway. So there I stood, a foot shorter than the man, and suddenly doing what my heart told me to do, damn the consequences.

I stabbed a nasty-ass dough-smeared finger into Burger's chest and left a brown smear on his white shirt that looked remarkably like a tighty-whitie shit stain. "If you want to break Arthur's heart you can fucking well do it yourself!" I glanced at the clock. It was early afternoon. Arthur would just now be setting down to lunch in his Lucy Ricardo garb—maybe a sequined cocktail dress with two petticoats under it, a bright red wig slapped on his head with a chopstick or two sticking out the top for decoration, and his size twelve feet stuffed inside a pair of stiletto heels that made the man defy gravity and physics and maybe even molecular biology every time he took a step without falling down. If I was lucky, maybe he had even smeared on a pint or two of makeup, glued on his three-inch long eyelashes with the purple glitter, and screwed in a pair of big-ass earrings.

If Burger wanted a boyfriend who was anything but normal, he was about to get one.

"Go over there right now!" I barked. "Don't call him first. Just go and pound on his door. Poor Arthur deserves to hear his fate from the man who's dishing it out. And he needs to hear it right away before he falls for you any harder."

Burger seemed rather amazed that I was talking to him like he was a misbehaving three-year-old, but he also seemed to realize what I was saying was right. He really should take responsibility for his actions and let Arthur down personally.

Of course, after he had time to think about it, he still might fire my ass, but what the hell. I was pretty sure Milan would still see me, even if we were no longer making pumpernickel together and flirting in the storeroom.

"Go!" I barked again, pointing at the door, and damned if Burger didn't jump like I'd poked him with a needle.

He sucked in a great gulp of air as if it were hopefully laced with a shitload of fortitude, and still looking guilty, he reached out a hand in my direction.

I thought he was going to strangle me, but what he did was pat my cheek. That was a surprise.

"You're right, Harlie. I'll go over there right now." He looked down at the brown smear on his white shirt with a certain amount of dismay, gave a sigh as if he deserved nothing less, then turned and headed for the door I was still pointing at.

As he walked away, he mumbled, "Hold down the fort."

The minute he was out of sight, I dragged my cell phone out of my pocket and punched in Arthur's number. If Burger wanted a nonboring Arthur, he'd get a nonboring Arthur. I impatiently tapped my foot and glared at the seven perfectly shaped Blobs alongside the one fucking ashtray with the impression of a fist in it laid out in front of me as I waited for Arthur to pick up the phone.

When he did I barked at him too. "Are you dressed?"

I knew he was in drag by the tone of his voice. When Arthur was in high drag he sounded like Lauren Bacall. When he was out of drag, he sounded like Tallulah Bankhead and Bluto singing a duet.

"Hi, Harlie. Oh, yes. You should see it, honey. I'm in a little number I picked up at the Salvation Army the other day. Sort of a Suzie Wong, slit up the side, tight as hell silk number that shows off the dimple in my one knee. Remember the dimple in my knee I told you about? Of course, you do. Ha-ha. You little scamp. Oh, Harlie I just know you'll *adore* this new outfit. I even found new high heels and a black wig to go with the Oriental flavor of the dress with chopsticks that stand up in the back and everything. Oh, honey, it just makes me look so-o-o-o sexy!"

Holy shit. I was right about the chopsticks.

"Well, that's great, Arthur. Don't change a thing. I'll be right there to take you out to lunch. I'll be knocking on your door any second now. Don't sing out. Don't ask who it is. Just yank that fucking door open and let me in. Got it?"

Arthur giggled. "Are you drunk?"

I screamed, "Just do it!"

There was a faint tapping sound in the background. Arthur cried, "You're here already?"

"Yep," I lied. "That's me. Open the frigging door."

Arthur giggled again. I heard a clatter as he either dropped the phone to a tabletop or stomped on it in his new high heels. "Oh, this should be fun," I heard him say in the distance.

I wondered if Arthur was right. I wondered if what was about to happen to him would be fun at all. I also wondered whether I had saved Arthur's and Burger's embryonic relationship or slaughtered it completely, and then I wondered how in the world I was going to scrape all the sticky pumpernickel dough off my fucking cell phone and what temperature I was supposed to bake the damn baby Blobs at.

THAT EVENING, Milan and I were lounging naked and sated between two pizza boxes on my sofa. We had just consumed both pizzas, followed by a spirited round of sex, and as we were beginning to relax after all the exertion and good food, we heard footsteps and the rustling of paper at my door. We looked over in tandem and saw an envelope slide under the door and shoot halfway across the room.

Since we couldn't very well answer the door naked, we didn't even try. We just went for the envelope.

I got there first, studying the envelope in my hand. It was pink stationery with no recipient mentioned on the front and little petunias printed on the flap in the back. I ripped it open, killing the petunias, and with Milan reading over my shoulder, we curiously gobbled up the handwritten message inside.

Dear Harlie, (You little cupid, you,)

Thank you so much for making an old queen very, very happy. Tom and I have decided to take our relationship one step forward so we are heading off to San Francisco in the morning for a romantic getaway. (Tom is such a doll, and my God, the dick on that man! Ooh, he just slapped my ass for writing that.)

We'll be gone for a week so tell Milan the deli is in his hands until his daddy (and mine) gets back.

One more thing, dear Harlie, do you have an extra suitcase lying around? Theseball gowns are a bitch to pack. Let me know. We're leaving at dawn. Toodles.

Love and smooches,

Lorraine (My new drag name, tee hee—don't you love it!)

P.S. Tom said to tell you he's giving you a raise. Isn't he the sweetest thing? And what a dick! Ouch. He slapped my ass again.

Milan slipped his bare arms around my naked waist and rested his chin on my shoulder as we proceeded to read the note *again.* And then for the third time.

"Excellent penmanship," Milan commented drily.

"No shit."

"What the hell did you do, if you don't mind my asking?"

I nestled back into the heat of Milan's body and tried not to purr. "I made your father see that Arthur wasn't boring after all."

"He thought Arthur was boring?"

"Apparently."

"So how did you make him think otherwise?"

"I just took a risk and introduced him to the real Arthur. The one I'd been stupidly trying to cover up all this time."

"Which Arthur was that?"

"The drag queen Arthur."

"Arthur's a drag queen?"

"Not a very good one, but yeah."

"You know," Milan chuckled, his whispering lips tickling my ear. "Pop's last lover was known to don a dress now and then."

I squirmed around in Milan's arms until we were face-to-face and dick-to-dick. "You might have told me that a long time ago and saved everyone a lot of drama."

He shrugged and hugged me tighter. "I was too busy trying to get in your pants."

"Well, you've gotten there now."

He grinned. "Yep. Several times. And now we're so far along you don't even wear them anymore."

I laid my lips to one of my favorite spots in all the world—the V-shaped hollow in Milan's throat. "Don't I know it," I mumbled into his skin, cooing like a pigeon. "With you around, clothes are superfluous, a waste of time, and just plain annoying."

He snuggled closer. "It's fun taking them off, though."

"That it is."

His lips were on my forehead and his hands were on my ass. "Maybe we should do what Pop and Arthur are doing."

"What's that? Go to San Francisco?"

"No. Take our relationship one step forward."

My breath caught. I leaned back an inch to gaze up into Milan's face. He was staring down at me with both dimples on full display. While his mouth was smiling, his eyes were not. They were watching me carefully. As if expecting me to panic and make a run for it, his hands took a wee firmer grip on my ass.

"Really?" I asked, trying to speak loud enough to be heard over the thudding of my heart. "Is that what you honestly want?"

His smile finally reached his eyes. "You know it is. Besides, how else will you earn the extra money Pop is paying you? As a baker's assistant, you pretty much suck."

I dropped my head to his chest and groaned. "I know."

He laughed. Tucking a finger under my chin, he dragged my face up to where he could see it again. "So what do you think? One step forward? It won't kill you, will it?"

"It's killing me already."

"In a good way, I hope."

I rose onto tiptoe and planted a kiss on his chin. "Yes, Milan. In a very good way."

He lifted me off the floor completely, shook me like a throw rug, and mashed his mouth down over mine. By the time the kiss was over, we were both as hard as andirons.

Two hours later, I wiped the come off my chin, threw on some clothes, and scurried down the stairs to loan Arthur my one and only suitcase. On the second knock, with a giggle, his naked arm snaked through the door and snatched the suitcase out of my hand.

Then the door clicked closed and Arthur and Tom sang out in unison from inside the apartment. "Thank you! Everybody's naked. Can't ask you in right now."

"Thank God," I mumbled to myself as I headed back up the stairs to the man who had asked me to take our relationship one step forward.

And wasn't *that* the most romantic thing ever!

Chapter 13

MILAN AND I were enjoying a casual dinner with Roger and Stanley in 5C. It was just the four of us. Oh, wait. I'm sorry. The *five* of us. Gizmo (or Studley, as Roger and Stanley called him) had dropped in unannounced and decided to stay for the duration. He was lounging on the kitchen floor with a plate of roasted chicken and a little dish of gravy. He wore a smug expression on his face, as if celebrating the fact that he had hit the mother lode this time, what with being served honest-to-God food and not some crap that came from a can. Maybe I was reading too much into his expression, but I wouldn't bet on it. Gizmo was a supercilious little shit.

It was well into spring now, and the weather had grown balmy. The winter rains were apparently over. A mild breeze scented with the honeysuckle blossoms that grew along the railing of the Belladonna Arms's front porch wafted through Roger and Stanley's kitchen window and made us all breathe a sigh of relief in knowing summer was on the way.

We were at the pleasant stage of dinner where one is still picking at the food and sipping at the wine, but the immediate feeding frenzy is over. Conversation was beginning to creep back into the proceedings.

Sylvia's surgery had been performed two days before our little dinner party in the same hospital where Roger worked as a registered nurse, so he had all the dirt for us.

Roger was talking and gnawing on a chicken femur at the same time. He could have been gnawing on a tree trunk and he would have still been gorgeous. Stanley seemed to know it too. He watched Roger with what could only be described as absolute devotion. With all their physical differences, I had never seen two gay guys who fit so well together.

"Sylvia's doing great." Roger grinned. "She's got a lot of guts. I don't work in the ward where she's in post-op, but I drop in to see her when I can. Pete hasn't left her side, of course. They set up a bed for him in her room, but I don't think he's been in it yet. He just sits in a chair by Sylvia's bed and holds her hand. Even when she's sleeping, he sits there whispering soft words into her ear. He told me he didn't ever want her to think she was alone."

Stanley plucked his geeky black glasses off his nose and wiped his eyes with his napkin. "Geez, Roger, you made me tear up."

Roger reached over and brushed his fingertips over the blond hair on Stanley's arm. "My baby's a big softy."

From the corner of my eye, I caught Milan smiling at the obvious affection flowing back and forth between our two hosts. The next thing I knew, his hand had slid beneath the table and found a home on my thigh. I was finished eating, so I weaved my fingers between his and left them there. Milan's face softened when I did. Stanley wasn't the only big softy sitting at that table.

"Is she comfortable?" I asked. "I don't know much about that kind of surgery. Is she in pain?"

Roger dropped his chicken bone onto his plate and wiped his fingers on a napkin. "Minimal," he said. "They give them a morphine drip on the first day, but by the second day an oral analgesic usually works just fine to alleviate any residual discomfort. She's probably more uncomfortable from the tube drains and the urinary catheter than she is from the actual surgical procedure. They'll leave the tubes in for about five days."

"So she's stuck in bed," Milan said.

Roger smiled at him. He seemed to enjoy the fact that Milan was holding my hand under the table. I hadn't known Roger long, but I was already convinced he had a romantic soul. He was also, without a doubt, the kindest man I had ever met. As was Stanley. Somebody in Planning and the Bureau of Romantic Entanglements knew what they were doing when they threw those two together.

Roger slipped his hand under the table and loosened his belt buckle. "I ate too much," he said, looking slightly embarrassed. Then he turned to Milan again. "They'll probably try to get her up tomorrow if the incisions look good. Then they'll also begin her bladder training."

"Golly," I said. "You mean she has to learn to pee again?"

Roger nodded. "Pretty much. It'll be uncomfortable for a while, what with the vaginal packing and the tube drain and the catheter, but those will come out on the fifth day in order for her to have a better shot at remaining clean and free from infection while the natural healing takes over."

"When can she come home?" Milan asked.

Stanley jumped when Gizmo leaped into his lap, and then, with a giggle, he went to work rubbing Gizmo's ears. The cat's purring filled the kitchen like the sound of raindrops on a roof.

"Barring any unseen problems, she'll be able to come home on the sixth day."

"She'll like that," I said.

And Roger laughed. "Her and Pete both."

Stanley cleared his throat and politely squeezed his way into the conversation. I had a feeling Stanley was shy, but I wasn't sure. He couldn't be *too* shy, or he would have never had the courage to woo the most handsome man on the planet. I wouldn't know until many months later, and it would be Sylvia who told me, that Stanley hadn't wooed Roger at all. It was Roger who did the wooing—and winning.

Stanley's question was for Milan, and he asked it with a gentle smile on his face. "I see your dad all the time now. Scurrying in the front door, scurrying back out again. I take it things are going well with him and Arthur."

Milan swelled up like a peacock, even while his ears turned a startling cherry red. His fingers gripped mine a little tighter under the table. Not many people knew it, I suspected, but for a six-foot-four hunk of man who was a powerhouse in bed and who looked like an Adonis when he was naked, Milan wasn't immune to shyness either.

"Pop's never been happier. I think they're going to make it. I mean him and Arthur. They are almost inseparable now. Jeez, Arthur's even trying to run the deli. The other day he was giving me cooking tips on the best way to bake sourdough biscuits. And dammit, the man's cooking tips were right on the money."

Everybody laughed.

"Nobody knows food like Arthur does," Roger beamed.

"Or loves it as much or eats more of it," Stanley threw in for good measure, and everybody laughed again. Even Gizmo meowed happily.

"And here I was the one who told him he'd never find a man unless he stopped going in drag and started losing weight," I groaned. "Shows you how much I know about love."

Milan's hand came up and stroked my jawline. It was just a gentle, warm touch of camaraderie, but somehow it made my toes curl. Milan was good at doing that.

"You know plenty about love," he whispered teasingly, and I froze in my chair. We had been seeing each other for almost five weeks now, and not once had the L-word crossed either of our lips. If you wanted to get technical about it, I knew it hadn't crossed Milan's lips now either, not *really,* but it sure seemed like it was coming close.

Happily, Roger picked up the conversational thread. It's a good thing too, since I sure as hell didn't know what to do with it.

"Nobody knows anything about love," Roger said. "It just happens or it doesn't. You can be with somebody for fifty years and never feel a thing, or you can take one tiny glimpse into a person's eyes on the very first time you meet them and you're lost forever." He turned to Stanley and flashed a smile hot enough to ignite paper. "I know because it happened to me."

Stanley blushed, but he didn't look embarrassed. He simply looked happy. He brought Roger's hand to his face and pressed it to his lips. "It happened to both of us," he whispered back.

Watching these two made me want to run right out and rent a couple of tuxes, then call a church and hire a minister. That couldn't be good.

Milan was watching me carefully when I said, "Arthur told me the first day I met him that there was something special about the Belladonna Arms and that anybody who lives here will—"

"Will what?" Milan asked.

"Nothing," I said.

Stanley grinned. "He told you about the love pollen, didn't he?"

I glanced at Milan and saw an odd expression on his face as he carefully studied me sitting there beside him still holding his hand. I knew I was blushing, but there wasn't much I could do about it, so I simply nodded.

Roger groaned. "Ah, the old love pollen theory. Yeah, I have to admit there's something about the Belladonna Arms that bestirs matchmaking." He ran his fingers through Stanley's reddish blond hair and gaily messed it all up. "Some of us still had to batter down a few walls to get in, but even Stanley finally came around."

"It was a conspiracy," Stanley joked. "Everybody was against me."

Roger laughed. "They weren't against you. They were just in favor of me." He turned to Milan and me and said, "Sometime I'll tell you guys the story of how the whole building conspired to throw Stanley into my arms."

Stanley dropped his head to the table with a thunk. "Oy, this story!" He twisted his head around just enough to give me a wink. "Don't tell anybody, Harlie, but it was my idea all along."

Roger slapped his arm, startling Gizmo. "Yeah, right!"

All four of us shifted out attention to the ceiling when a flurry of bumps and thuds and angry yells suddenly interrupted the evening.

I saw Stanley and Roger exchange resigned glances before Milan asked, "What the hell was *that*?"

Stanley released Roger's hand and poked his black glasses a little higher up on his nose. He didn't look like he wanted to answer Milan's question, but he did. "It's ChiChi and Ramon. They're in 6D. They've been fighting for weeks. Real knock-down-drag-outs."

Roger studied Stanley's face, nodding all the while. "It's getting worrisome. We've almost called the cops a couple of times." His eyes turned to Stanley and there was sadness in them. "We don't know what happened between those two. They used to be so much in love. Now I think maybe things are falling apart between them."

Stanley ran his hand over Roger's close-cropped hair, and at the first touch of his hand, the sadness in Roger's eyes was quelled.

"Does Arthur know?" I asked. "Maybe if he told them to cool it—"

I noticed a glower on Milan's face which hadn't been there twenty seconds earlier. "What?" I interrupted myself. "What's wrong?"

Milan glowered all the more. "Nothing. It's just…."

I wondered what had pissed him off. Milan was always so easygoing. But now he looked like he was ready to knock somebody's block off. "Just what?" I asked. "Why are you getting upset?"

Milan cast embarrassed glances at both Stanley and Roger, and then he turned an abashed expression on me. "I just don't like ChiChi much, I guess. He put the moves on me once. He knew I was with you, but he put the moves on me anyway. I don't like people who do that."

I growled. "Neither do I." I felt a tightening in my chest, and I knew immediately what it was. I was mad. Damn mad. The ferocity of that sudden surge of anger surprised me. Only after reflecting for a minute did I realize what the anger was all about. It was jealousy. Plain and simple. And I had always thought there wasn't a jealous bone in my body.

Apparently that was before Milan came along.

Before I knew it, my brain was teeming with really cool scenarios of me pounding the crap out of ChiChi in the stairwell of the good old Belladonna Arms. In one scenario I even dragged the little shit all the way downtown by the scruff of his neck and tossed him into the deli oven. I liked that scenario the best. I didn't let it go until Milan snapped his fingers in front of my face to bring me back. He had an odd expression on his face when he did, as if wondering where the hell I'd gone.

"Poor Ramon," Roger and Stanley were saying in one breath. Stanley had taken Roger's hand and pressed it to his lips again.

I took Milan's hand and did the same, stilling his snapping fingers at the same time. His frown reluctantly flipped over, and he offered me a hesitant smile. "Sorry," he said. "I thought *I* was mad about it until I just saw you slip off to Murderville."

"You could tell?" I asked.

Milan grinned. "Oh yeah. You were looking a little crazy there for a second. I guess I would have been mad too if he had been putting the moves on you."

"Well, actually he did," I said. When Milan's eyes opened wide and his frown started to make a return engagement, I headed it off with the truth, which I should have done to begin with. "He cornered me in the park one day when I was jogging. Invited me into the bushes for a little one-on-one. But calm down. That was before I was with you. Still, I was mad at the time because even if I wasn't with anybody, *he* was." I gave Stanley and Roger an apologetic shrug. "Sorry. I don't like cheaters."

Stanley giggled. "Guess not."

The thuds and bangs over our heads suddenly reached a crescendo, and then the noise quickly abated. We heard a door slam. And silence. I couldn't help wondering if Ramon was now standing in his apartment all alone, crying his heart out. Perhaps it was unfair to assume the problem was ChiChi's fault, but from what I had seen of the guy, he had shown me nothing to make me believe otherwise.

Poor Ramon indeed.

After listening to the fight upstairs, our evening with Stanley and Roger never quite recovered. The four of us made plans for the next day to visit Sylvia together, and after saying toodles at the door to Gizmo, Milan and I then turned our good-byes to our hosts.

Roger shook our hands at the door and Stanley gave us each a kiss on the cheek. I noticed that, like me, he had to rise up on tiptoe to plant one on Milan. Milan balanced him with a touch to Stanley's arm when he did.

"It's nice having another couple in the building to get together with," Stanley said to both of us, stepping back into Roger's arms.

Roger snaked his arms around his lover's waist and clasped his hands over Stanley's belly so as to better rest his chin on Stanley's shoulder. His green eyes were alive and friendly and sweet, all at the same time. "Stanley's right. You guys belong together, I think." He gave me a tiny grin, and leaned forward to brush something off Milan's shoulder.

"Cat hair?" I asked.

"Pollen," he said.

And nobody laughed.

"Good night, guys," Milan said softly. "Thank you for dinner." And taking my hand he pulled me toward the stairs.

Two landings down, he stopped and pinned me to the wall. Towering in front of me with his hands against the wall to either side of me, hemming me in, he ducked his head and leaned in to give me a soft kiss on the lips. He held the kiss until I began to feel my knees buckle. My hands came up and clutched his waist to hold myself up.

"I can't wait another minute," he whispered, his warm breath stirring my eyelashes. His big gentle hands slid in to lay themselves against my waist, holding me in place.

My heart began dancing a jig, and I felt the little hairs on the back of my neck kick off their shoes and join in like a bunch of drunken Irishmen.

"Wait another minute for what?" I managed to ask after a couple of false starts to get control of my voice. But I thought I knew. I thought I already knew. At least I hoped I did.

Milan's blue eyes were as pleading as I had ever seen them. They were so locked into my own I couldn't have looked away for anything. A troop of elephants might have sauntered past, topped by a bevy of naked mahouts, and I couldn't have turned my head an inch.

Milan pressed his warm forehead to mine, and at the touch, I watched his blue eyes close. When he spoke, he said the words into the darkness behind his eyelids. He also said them to me. But not *to* me really. He said them *into* me. I could almost feel his words burrowing into my thudding heart. I closed my eyes too, to hear them better, to lock them away in my heart where they belonged.

"I can't wait another minute to tell you I love you," Milan said, his hands tightening almost imperceptibly on my waist. I wasn't sure, but I thought I felt them shaking a little bit. He leaned in closer and pressed his cheek to mine. His lips brushed my ear, his urgent words spoken so softly they were little more than a disturbance in the air. "Don't say anything, Harlie. Please. Let me talk. I've loved you since the second night we were together. That night, after we made love, I managed to get past the beauty of your outside and start to see you for what was inside. I started to see you for who you really are. And don't get me wrong, the sex is *great,* but it's you as a person that's even greater. I took one of your books last week, did you know that? It's the first one you wrote, I think. I loved it. And I knew for sure the minute I finished it I was in love with you. Don't ask me why. I just knew. I knew reading your words like that finally let me get the entire picture of who you are. And I love that person, Harlie. I never want to be away from him. I never want him to be away from me."

He laid his broad hand to my chest, covering my thudding heart with the heat of his palm. His tender touch was just enough to keep me upright. My knees were shaking so badly, if he had let go I think I would have fallen flat on my face. I leaned into him, laying my cheek to his chest. And there, I heard the hammering of *his* heart.

He gathered me into his heavenly, strong arms and pressed his lips to my hair. His words were a gentle rumble in his throat. The vibration of them stuttered through me like electricity. "Please tell me you feel the same way about me, Harlie. Please tell me you love me too."

We both waited, breathless, wondering what I would say. Even I didn't know. For a moment.

But then I did know. And I knew it with all my heart. I spoke into his shirtfront, fearing to move away. Fearing to lose the sound of his racing heart matching the rhythm of my own. Those two heartbeats pounded in my ears like a couple of jackhammers tearing up a street. And they sounded so right together. As if one had been waiting all this time for the other. Waiting to finally... *join.*

I sighed and took a shuddering breath. I inhaled Milan's sweet scent even as my words came pouring out with no hesitation at all. They sounded rehearsed, as if I had been planning them for weeks. And maybe unknown even to me, I had. But I was surprised to hear those words too. As surprised—and relieved—I think, as Milan seemed to be.

I had to wait for a lump in my throat to dissolve before I could say the words. But then they came gushing out. "The first time I saw you in the deli, I wanted you. And now, after every day that we're together, after *every single day*, I find myself wanting you more. Every time we make love, every time we see each other first thing in the morning after waking up, every time you take me into your arms and bury me in your heat, I can't imagine ever wanting to be anywhere else."

Suddenly, I couldn't speak anymore. I pressed my face to Milan's chest and felt the tears start up. Jesus, what was that all about? Why was I crying? Why were my knees shaking? Why was my heart racing? Why were *both* our hearts racing?

Milan hooked a finger under my chin and pulled my face up to his. He bent forward and kissed the tears from my cheeks. I slid my hands under the tail of his shirt because I couldn't bear not to feel his skin beneath my hands. His stomach was warm and welcoming. As enticing as ever. God, I had never known a man whose skin felt the way his did. Even now, in the midst of our most important conversation, I wanted him more than ever. I hungered for him.

Through a blur of tears, his face was as somber, as pleading, as I had ever seen it. His voice, barely audible, wrapped itself around me and lost me in its need.

"Then say the words, Harlie. Tell me what you're feeling. Give me that much. Please."

I nodded. I was trembling all over. But I was smiling, too. I could feel it.

"I—I'm sorry. I thought I did."

"No, dipshit. You didn't." But he smiled when he said it.

I took one more deep breath, and I knew at that moment nothing could have stopped the words from coming out. "I love you too, Milan. I think I've loved you since the very first day I saw you. I never want to be apart from you either. It's like you said. Exactly like you said. I don't want to be apart from you for even a minute. Not one fucking minute. I love you so much my toes hurt," I finished lamely.

Milan scooped me off the floor as if I weighed nothing at all. He nailed me with a ferocious stare, but there was laughter in it too. "You're a writer and that's the best you can come up with? I love you so much my toes hurt?"

I wiggled in his arms like a fish on a hook. "Well, they *do*, dammit!"

I wrapped my arms around his neck and his mouth found mine, probably to shut me up. At the feel of moisture on my face, I opened my eyes and saw he was crying too. His dimples were flashing and his white teeth were sparkling, but hovering above all those tokens of happiness, his blue eyes were awash with tears. Just like mine.

I took a ragged breath. "Take me home," I whispered into his kiss.

"Yes," he whispered back. "Home."

And once again, he took my hand and led me down the stairs.

NAKED, WE tumbled onto the bed and wrapped ourselves in each other's arms. I pressed my face into Milan's broad, welcoming chest, and with our legs tangled together and our leg hair scraping merrily at each other's skin, he folded me into him. Having slept together for so many nights, we were experts at this cuddling business now. I fit inside Milan's embrace like a key in a lock. I knew, of course, I had not once grown tired of the gentle sense of security he gave me when he held me close, but somehow it wasn't until a few minutes earlier, when we spoke those words in the stairwell, that I really understood what that overwhelming impression of security really meant. It was part and parcel of the whole thing, you see. Love. It was love all along. I just hadn't voiced it yet. Not to myself. Not to Milan. But now the truth was out in the open, I understood it completely. God, I'm clever. Slow. But clever.

Our hearts were calming down now. I was beginning to think they might not actually explode and render us deader than a couple of tuna sandwiches. And that was certainly a step in the right direction.

"Do you really love me?" he asked softly, his lips buried in my hair.

I slid my hand over his ribcage and felt a rush of desire. Tilting my head up, I kissed his throat. "Yes, Milan, I really love you. And if you ever ask me that question again, I'll be forced to beat you to a bloody pulp."

"Should be interesting to watch," he mumbled into my scalp.

I gave him my best growl, sort of like a hamster threatening a Great Dane. "You think I can't?"

He laughed. "You've already pinned my heart to the mat. Isn't that enough?"

"No. With you, nothing will ever be enough."

"I think I like the sound of that. Although I'm not quite sure."

"You know," I teased, "just because you said the words first doesn't mean you did the actual loving first. I did. I just didn't want to tell you until I knew for sure you weren't a raging asshole. It took me a while to figure that out."

"Thanks."

"Don't be snippy."

We let the silence of the night move in to quiet us. Looking lazily over Milan's shoulder, I could see a sprinkling of stars in the late-night sky outside my bedroom window. There was a eucalyptus tree out there at the side of the Belladonna Arms, and I could hear a night bird singing a song in its branches. Maybe he had just professed his love too. Maybe to a little hen two trees over. Or to a sparrow nesting in the rusty old neon sign far above our heads.

"We can be like them," I whispered, snuggling closer, no longer in a teasing mood, feeling Milan's nipple against my cheek, relishing its supple stiffness and what lay buried beneath it: Milan's heart. The heart I had somehow been lucky enough to win.

"Like who?" he asked in a sleepy voice. "We can be like who?"

"Stanley and Roger. Did you see how in love they are?"

Milan trailed a gentle finger down my spine, sending a delicious chill through me from my balls to my ears. "And Roger saw how in love *I* was, Harlie. That's why he brushed the imaginary pollen off my shoulder. Remember?"

I smiled. "Yes. The infamous Belladonna Arms love pollen."

Milan's voice mellowed and deepened. It was no longer sleepy, and he was no longer teasing either. "It was like an epiphany for me when Roger did that. When he spoke that one little word. Pollen. It made me see the truth like I'd never seen it before. It made me realize I was in love with you, and there was no reason in the world why I shouldn't tell you. At least, I hope there wasn't a reason."

I scooted up in the bed until our faces were aligned. The hand that had been at my spine now rested lightly on my ass, making me shiver. God, I loved Milan's hands.

"No, Milan. There can never be a reason for you not to tell me what you're feeling. Ever."

"And you'll be the same with me?"

"Yes. I promise."

He kissed my nose.

"Do you want to make love?"

I groaned, too comfortable and satisfied to move. "I want you to hold me just like you're holding me now. At least for a while."

He kissed each of my eyelids, and his hand clutched my ass more firmly and dragged me closer to him. "That's what I want too. And it won't just be for a while, Harlie. I plan on holding you like this forever."

"Baby," I murmured into his skin. And with my heart revving up to set off at a gallop one more time, I said, "Tell me again, Milan. Just so I can hear you say it."

He smiled, and every inch of him pressed itself a little closer to me. Arms, legs, lips, and cock (which was now as hard as mine).

"I love you, Harlie Rose. And I'll take care of you. You make me feel complete."

At those words, I started. I lifted myself up on one elbow and looked down at him. "Yes," I said, grinning. "That's exactly right."

Looking bemused, he brushed a fingertip over my cheek. "What's exactly right?"

I tried to explain. To do it, I had to study the stars outside the window. Somehow the answer was written out there. Not here inside this room.

"A while back I told myself my life was like an unfinished novel. A work in progress. Arthur's too. When I was stupidly trying to make him into someone he didn't want to be, and never *could* be, I imagined him as a work in progress too. But now, thanks to you, I'm not a work in progress anymore. For the first time in my life, I feel *complete*. You *make* me complete. Like you said I do to you."

I could see Milan watching me in the moonlight. He smiled a dreamy smile and laid his hand against my face as I still lay there propped on one elbow looking down at him. "Do I really make you feel complete?"

"Yeah," I said. "You do."

"And what about Arthur?"

I interrupted our conversation long enough to taste his lips. They were scrumptious, as I suspected they would be.

"I guess Arthur's completion is up to your dad. I still hope he doesn't break Arthur's heart."

"He won't," Milan said softly, soothing me, kissing me back. "I have it on the best authority that Pop is currently head over heels in hots for his new boyfriend, the voluptuous Arthur."

I stiffened like a Weimaraner pointing at a pheasant in a cornfield. "He told you that?"

Milan laughed. "Yep. And pretty much verbatim."

"Holy shit."

"Daintily put." I could sense him struggling for words. "I guess maybe I've never been complete before you came along either, Harlie. But I feel complete now. I feel like one of those split heart-shaped lockets that is always seeking its missing half. But then you came along, the worst baker's assistant ever, and suddenly the other half of my locket is right here." He pulled me closer. "Right here in my arms."

"The worst baker's assistant ever with a *raise*," I reminded him delicately, and he grinned.

"If you think about it," he said, his voice growing husky again with sleep, "we're all works in progress. Me, you, Arthur, my dad. And Sylvia! Sylvia's *really* a work in progress. She's getting a new transmission and everything. Hell, she's jumping into a whole new demographic."

"I'm happy for her," I said. "She's finally going to be the person she was meant to be."

Milan smiled gently. "I know."

"I'm happy for her and Pete both," I sighed.

Milan nodded. "Me too. The pollen got them too."

"The pollen gets everybody in the end."

"Thank God," we said in unison.

Contented, we lay in silence, letting the implications of everything we had talked about settle over us. And while it was all soaking in—like pollen—we fell asleep, still wrapped snugly in each other's arms.

So, oddly enough, our first night together after proclaiming love for each other was also the first night we slept together without making love. It was an oversight properly remedied the following morning with great abandon and a great expenditure of bodily fluids.

And then, since we were late, we threw ourselves together, grabbed a couple of bagels from the refrigerator, and raced out the door to visit Sylvia.

Thus beginning our first day on the planet as honest-to-God lovers.

Chapter 14

STANLEY MET us in the hospital lobby. Halfway up to Sylvia's floor the elevator jerked to a stop, the door beeped open, and Roger jumped in to join us. He was on duty and wearing scrubs. He wore a stethoscope around his neck and looked delicious. Stanley beamed when he saw him. Apparently he thought Roger looked delicious too. I gazed up at Milan to see what *he* was thinking of Roger in his sexy-ass scrubs, but Milan only had eyes for me. How could you not love a guy like that?

Since there was an old guy in a neck brace on the elevator with us, Roger merely smiled at the three of us in turn—shooting for a little professional decorum, I suppose—and, after the elevator jerked back into operation, turned his back to us while waiting for the door to open on nine.

We traipsed two by two down the corridor to Sylvia's room, leaving the old guy in the elevator to whatever horrible fate awaited him. Roger laid his hand on Stanley's shoulder while he filled us in on Sylvia's progress.

"She's doing great. Like I told you, they'll start bladder training today. She was standing and moving around earlier for the first time since surgery, but then Pete insisted she go back to bed because he thought she looked tired. She pooh-poohed him, but he insisted. For an accountant, Pete can be pretty bossy when it comes to his girl."

We laughed.

"Pollen," Milan muttered into my ear.

Roger steered everyone toward a door just off the hallway, but before pushing it open and ushering us inside, he studied Milan and me standing there patiently waiting. I was holding a spray of lilies in one hand, Sylvia's favorite flower. My other hand was lost in Milan's massive paw.

Roger's green eyes caught the fluorescent lights overhead and damn near sparkled like fireworks. Suddenly I noticed Stanley was eyeing us too.

"What?" Milan asked. "Do we still have come on our foreheads?"

I whapped him with the lilies, but lightly so I wouldn't ruin them. Then I turned to Roger. "You're looking mighty inquisitive. Is there something you want to ask us?" I might have been a wee bit too lackadaisical about it since I was pretty sure I knew what the two of them were getting at.

Roger cocked his head to the side and took Stanley's hand as Milan had taken mine.

"Let me be succinct and cut right to the chase," Roger grinned, "is there anything you two want to *tell us*?"

"I can't imagine what you mean," I said around a big phony yawn, checking my nails, studying the ceiling, acting like a putz.

"It *is* the come, isn't it?" Milan asked, sarcastic as hell, dragging a handkerchief out of his back pocket and patting his face as if it was still dripping with jism. (Which, by the way, it had been less than two hours earlier.) This time I didn't bother whapping him with the flowers. They'd cost twenty-three dollars, after all.

I snapped my fingers as if I suddenly remembered something. Then I schmoozed up to stand a little closer to Milan's side. A trio of nurses walking by gave us a look but, smiling, immediately turned and went on their merry way after Roger shot them a wink as if to say he had the situation under control.

I snapped my fingers again. "Oh, maybe you're referring to the fact that Milan and I are lovers now. Truly and unstintingly lovers. Just like you guys. Is that it? Is that what you were inquiring about? The fact that we are committed to each other for better or for worse, and so far the 'better' is way ahead and still gaining? Well? Speak up. Is that it?"

"You little shits." Stanley beamed, jumping forward and scooping us both into his arms. A moment later, Roger joined in, all but bonking our four heads together like a pack of Keystone Kops in an old Mac Sennett comedy. "That's *great*, you guys! That's *super!*"

"Yeah," I simpered for Milan's benefit. "The big lug finally admitted he couldn't get along without me."

Milan barked out a laugh. "And the little lug will pay for that comment later."

A lot of hugs and backslapping ensued, and when we were done congratulating each other (Milan and I on getting together, and Roger and Stanley on being smart enough to figure it out), we straightened our clothes and brushed our hair out of our eyes, and I tried to resurrect my poor lilies, which suddenly appeared to have been run over by a train.

Still giggling and wrapped in each other's arms, the four of us barged into Sylvia's room to greet the newest, and only actual, female tenant of the Belladonna Arms.

Sylvia was sitting up in bed with a breakfast tray in front of her. Pete was sitting in a plastic chair beside the bed eating her toast. They looked up when we stormed into the room, and Pete guiltily stuffed the rest of the toast in his mouth as if we'd caught him shoplifting.

Sylvia was pale, but her eyes were alive and vibrant. She had her hair pulled back in a scrunchie, and there wasn't a speck of makeup on her face. She was beautiful. She held her arms out to the lot of us and motioned for us to come give her a communal hug.

"Gently," Pete ordered, but Sylvia rolled her eyes and flapped a hand in his direction to shut him up.

"Don't you boys be gentle at all," she cried. "Each of you give me a hug and act like you mean it!"

"Ah, but we *do* mean it," Stanley crooned, kissing her cheek and pulling her into his arms, although I noticed he was indeed extremely gentle about it as Pete had suggested.

The rest of us took our turns and Pete scooted his chair out of the way so the four of us could plop our asses down on Sylvia's bed, surrounding her completely.

"So it's done," Stanley said, gazing at her fondly. "Three days out of surgery and you've never been prettier."

Sylvia blushed and reached out for Pete's hand. She pulled him to her, and he perched himself on the edge of the bed beside her pillow.

Her blush deepened as she studied us each in turn. "Yes, it's done. I'm finally who I was born to be."

I smiled at her glow. It was a beautiful thing to see. "I'm glad," I said.

Roger cackled. "And by the look of him, so is Pete."

Sylvia executed her little laugh, the one that reminded me of tinkling silver bells. "I know," she said. "My man can't wait to go spelunking."

Roger cleared his throat professorially. "Um, Pete, it'll be a while before you can do any *invasive* spelunking. You know that, don't you?"

It was Pete's turn to blush. "Yes," he said meekly. And turning to Sylvia, he droned, "Jeez, woman, can't we have *any* secrets?"

Immediately, tears lit her eyes and her chin puckered up. She turned to him and clutching his shirtfront, pulled him close. Pressing her face to his chest, she said, "You called me woman."

Pete appeared uncomfortable with the lot of us watching him, but a smile still split his face as he pressed his lips to Sylvia's hair. "That's what you've always been to me. Now you'll have the plumbing to go with it. Not that I didn't love the other plumbing too."

"Now *I'm* starting to blush," Milan said, and *everybody* laughed.

Sylvia wiped the tears from her eyes, clapped her hands, and said to me, "Ooh, are those lilies for me? I *love* lilies. Even—um—battered ones."

"Sorry about that," I said. "They ran into a wall of faggots in the hallway."

Pete and Sylvia eyed Milan and I with renewed interest. It was Pete who asked, "What's going on here? You two look different." He waved a hand in front of his face. "Phew. The smell of devotion is almost palpable. Are you two together now for good? Have commitments been made? Oaths of love declared? Are we shopping for curtains? Looking to adopt? Wedding date set?"

I waved my ring finger in their faces, even though there was no ring on it. "Guilty as charged. We're not married, but we might as well be. Ain't love a hoot?"

Milan chortled. "And if we want to adopt, we'll adopt Gizmo. He eats all our food anyway."

Sylvia winked and poked a finger in my ribcage. "You like tall men just like I do."

I shot her a wink in return. "We shorties always do."

Sylvia peeked around us toward the door. "I was sort of hoping Ramon and ChiChi would come too. Are they all right? I'm worried about them."

Roger and Stanley both looked uncomfortable. It was Roger who finally commented. "I don't know what's going on there, Syl. They've been fighting an awful lot."

Pete frowned, his chin still resting on Sylvia's head. "Poor Ramon," he said softly, and everybody nodded. It was good to know I wasn't the only one who thought the problems in that relationship could be laid squarely in ChiChi's lap.

The five of us were still perched on the edge of the bed surrounding Sylvia. She gazed around at each of us in turn with a wondrous smile on her face. "At least the rest of my friends are happy." Her gaze homed in on Milan and I. "Are you two moving in together?"

Milan and I both jumped. Unless Milan had been having secret thoughts he hadn't shared with me, that possibility had not yet entered our heads. Or so I thought.

"Yes," Milan breathed in my ear. "Harlie doesn't know it yet is all."

I twisted around to face him. "I don't want to leave the Arms."

Milan reached up and pushed my hair out of my eyes. "Neither do I," he said gently. "I love the place. After all, I found *you* there. Besides, I hate the apartment I have now. It's too far from work and too far from… you."

I felt my heart kick into overdrive again. Funny how many times it does that when you're in love. "In point of fact, you found me at the deli, Butch, not the Belladonna Arms."

"Don't get technical, sweetcakes." He waggled his eyebrows. "And I like it when you call me Butch."

Sylvia clapped her hands. "We'll have to throw a party!"

"No can do," Stanley said. "There's a party planned already."

Roger dragged his lover into his arms and slapped a hand over Stanley's mouth. "*Secret,*" he hissed. "*Secret.*"

Stanley's eyes opened wide over Roger's hand. "Oops," he mumbled into Roger's palm.

It was the first Milan and I had heard about a party, but Pete cast Sylvia a suspicious glance as if he might know a thing or two about it, and hopefully Sylvia didn't. That was all it took for me to understand. The party was for Sylvia. We simply hadn't heard about it yet.

Everybody on the bed began talking at once about the weather, the Russians, the hospital food. Anything to put the specter of Sylvia's once-but-no-longer-surprise party to rest while Sylvia tried to pretend she didn't know what was going on. But she didn't try very hard.

Roger growled good-naturedly at Stanley, "I'll rip your tongue out later."

Stanley straightened his glasses, which Roger had knocked askew when he was trying to shut him up. "No need," he muttered, still embarrassed. "I'll probably rip it out myself."

Sylvia eyed us deviously. "A party is Arthur's idea, I suppose." It wasn't a question. She seemed to already know.

"Yes," Roger groaned, "but for God's sake don't let him know you know. He thought it only fair that since you threw us a party before going *into* the hospital, he should throw a party for you—and your new plumbing—when you come *out*."

Before Sylvia could comment, and while Pete was whistling silently up at the ceiling and trying to look innocent of all knowledge of any such party, the air was suddenly sucked out of the room when a red, rustling mountain of fabric swept through the door. A clatter of crimson stiletto heels tapped and pecked their way across the floor, and a mouth painted as red as a quart of fresh blood opened wide in a great O of excitement. Above the blood red O, and the two-inch long glittering eyelashes hovering above it, sat an upswept wig of such intricate design it must have taken a team of architects and a necromancer or two to create the fucking thing.

Of course, buried somewhere inside all this rustling, sparkling, shimmering splendor, stood Arthur. And behind Arthur trailed my boss. Mr. Burger was beaming proudly and carrying a bouquet of yellow roses of such magnitude he could barely gather them in his arms. To this day I can't remember what he was wearing. After Arthur's entrance, how could I?

I wondered if all hospital business, brain surgeries, MRIs, and the lot, had stopped on a dime when Arthur and his mountain of crunchy red silk flounced through the lobby, snagging the attention of every single soul in the joint.

Milan said, "That's one noisy-ass dress, Arthur. What's it made of? Crepe paper and aluminum foil?"

Arthur gave him a playful slap that would probably have knocked Milan over and rendered him unconscious if he hadn't been sitting on the bed already.

"It's Georgette silk, you heathen," Arthur laughed. Turning to Mr. Burger, he sang out, "Isn't our boy just a *heathen*, Tom!"

Milan and I turned to each other, and in unison mouthed the words, "Our boy?"

Mr. Burger, I must say, did not look embarrassed at all. I personally would have been chewing my way under the floor like a termite.

"Fashionably speaking," Burger warbled fondly in Milan's direction, "my son is a heathen indeed, Arthur. But look how happy he looks sitting there with his little baker's assistant." Then he seemed to remember where he was. "Oh, hello, Sylvia. Hello, Pete. Quite the little conclave you have going here."

In a rustling swirl of what I now knew was Georgette silk, Arthur retraced the steps he had taken back to the door and hauled Burger forward like Mama Rose dragging Gypsy Rose Lee onstage for her very first strip. As soon as they were in the middle of the room, Arthur scooped Mr. Burger into an embrace with one arm while with the other he held his huge hand aloft, fingers down, and flashed a glimmering diamond ring for all to see.

"Engaged, darlings! Isn't that scrumptious?"

I was thrilled, but I must say no one in the group appeared more stunned than Milan.

"Well, gee, Pop. Uhh, way to go." He didn't sound particularly sincere, but give the man credit. If *your* father had just been outed as the fiancé to a three-hundred-pound drag queen in fifty yards of Georgette silk and stiletto heels, it might take *you* a while to establish sincerity too.

Everyone, including Sylvia, swooped in to gather Arthur and Mr. Burger into one big massive hug. In the midst of it all, Arthur squealed,

"Don't crush the silk!" Shortly after that, I heard Pete bellow, "Don't crush Sylvia either!"

Another mountain suddenly stormed through the door. It was one of the wing nurses, and she didn't look happy. Her eyeballs were big and round and flashing white in her dark face, and she wore what must have been five hundred dollars' worth of braided hair weaves sewed onto her scalp. As if that wasn't enough, she also wore almost as much makeup as Arthur, although not quite. She stood in the doorway, erect and glaring, with both fists sunk into her massive hips. One orthopedic white shoe tapped the floor menacingly as she waited for silence. She reminded me of my first grade teacher, Mrs. Anderson (God, what a bitch *she* was).

The moment the room stumbled to silence, and the mob of huggers and revelers had separated by sheer force of will (the nurse's will, that is), she clapped her hands like a gunshot and everybody jumped.

"This is a hospital! I'll have you know we have rules here about noise." The nurse spotted Roger and wagged a finger in his face. "You should know better, sir. Abetting such behavior is inexcusable. I may have to report this."

Roger laughed and snapped a finger in her face. "Oh, blow it out your ass, Jasmine. These are my friends and we're celebrating Sylvia's new womanhood, Arthur and Tom's engagement, and Milan and Harlie's—uh—moving in together!" He waved a dismissive hand in Stanley's face. "This cutie's just here because he's my lover and where the hell else should he be?"

The nurse said, "Harrumph!" and pulled the door closed behind her to seal us all inside. "Well, shit, Roger, why didn't you say so?"

The next thing I knew the noise level was jacked up about fifteen decibels as the crowd split off into chattering, laughing groups, all congratulating each other on one thing or another and doing it with no small amount of glee and racket. The nurse gathered up Mr. Burger's massive bouquet of yellow roses and stuck them in a wastebasket filled with water from the bathroom sink. Pete held Sylvia close and protectively while Roger and Stanley, also in each other's arms, chatted about the surgery and how lovely Sylvia looked in her newfound role as an honest-to-God female. Mr. Burger stood with his hand at Arthur's waist, claiming possession. They were the two tallest men in the room, aside from Milan, and I had to admit they looked more in love than anybody. The moment everyone but Milan and I were occupied with someone else, Milan leaned in and planted a kiss on my cheek, causing a delicious shiver to shoot up my spine. I fended off a rising hard-on by sheer will, and even then I wasn't completely successful.

"I love you, Harlie Rose," Milan murmured sweetly into my ear.

I couldn't help it. I misted up again, hard-on and all. I murmured back, "I love you too, Milan Burger."

And as if I wasn't blushing enough already, I blushed even deeper when Milan's dad winked at us from across the room. He had a smile on his face so broad and so toothy, if it had stretched itself a wee bit wider I was pretty sure the top of his head would have slid off and landed on the floor.

Milan chuckled at my side. "Look how happy Pop is."

I rested my head on Milan's shoulder, and took in everything before us. All the happiness. All my new friends. All my new loved ones.

I gave a tsk. "I think the pollen's particularly bad this year. It seems to be nailing everybody."

Milan folded me into his arms and tucked my face against his chest. "Well, it certainly nailed me."

And about then, above the fray, Nurse Ratchet, or whatever the hell her name was, asked Arthur where he had his wig done, and when Arthur told her, she pulled the clipboard off the foot of Sylvia's bed, tore off an empty sheet of the statistics chart, and jotted down the name of Arthur's stylist.

Arthur jealously eyed the nurse's braids while she did it.

PETE FINALLY threw the lot of us out of Sylvia's hospital room on the pretext that she needed rest, but we all knew the truth. She had a rough day ahead of her, what with the bladder training and all, which none of us fully understood, and in truth, none of us really *wanted* to understand.

Arthur and Mr. Burger toddled off down the street, arm in arm, to dig up lunch somewhere since it was Sunday and the deli was closed, which was a shame, for I would have loved to have tagged along to catch the other employees' reaction to their boss's new love interest. However, I did notice that outside on the street under the wide California sky, Arthur did not seem like quite the mountain of drag-queenliness he did in a confined space. Of course, even the broad blue heavens above couldn't disguise the fact that, when all dolled up, he made a really big woman. *Nothing* could have disguised *that* fact.

Stanley was off to class at Beaumont. His enthusiasm for his studies was admirable, don't get me wrong, but he could get a little carried away sometimes. Before he left, he explained to Milan and me at length—and I mean *leeeenggtthh*—that he was working on a thesis pertaining to the Incans' practice of bookkeeping using the *quipus*, a series of knots on strings. He explained at even greater length how the string of each *quipu* was unique, and how the keepers of the *quipus*, or *quipu camayocs*, used various colors and lengths and groupings of knots to indicate different values.

By the time Stanley finished explaining this all to us as we stood outside the hospital entrance hopping impatiently from one leg to another, waiting for a lull in his lecture so we could hotfoot it out of there, we were ready to gather up all Stanley's *quipus*, braid them together into one long fucking rope, and hang ourselves from the nearest lamppost.

Just as I was about to throw myself in front of a passing bus so I wouldn't have to hear any more about *quipus*, Stanley let us go.

Finally alone, Milan and I looked at each other and sighed.

"Thank Christ," I said.

"No shit."

"He's a sweet guy, but all that Incan stuff is boring."

"No shit again. Who cares about a bunch of fucking knots?"

My eyes lit up. "Unless, of course, we were tying each other up with them."

Milan's eyes lit up a little too as he considered the possibilities. "Hmmm. Sex with *quipus*. Intriguing."

We let that sink in for a moment; then I forgot about Stanley and his knots completely. "Would you really move in with me at the Arms?" I asked, studying his face closely for any sign of hesitation.

"If you'll have me," he said. No hesitation there. Nope. Not a smidgeon.

"I'd like to think I will always have you, Milan."

"Then you will. Until I'm old and doddering and peeing in the petunias."

"Well, maybe not that long," I hedged.

We found my old Buick right where I'd left it, much to Milan's chagrin. He seemed to think my Buick was a threat to the globalized depletion of fossil fuels, and even I had to admit it was doing more than its fair share to obliterate them. But I still loved it.

"Darn," he said. "Nobody stole the thirsty beast."

"Oh, shut up."

In a cloud of exhaust fumes and another quart and a half of depleted fuel stores, we headed back to the Belladonna Arms and the beginning of the rest of our lives together.

Milan's hand stroked my thigh as I drove. "Are you sure you want this?"

"You mean us living together? I want it more than anything."

"It's not a very big apartment."

"All the better. You'll never be more than a dick's length away."

He smiled at that. "I love you."

I gave him a cocky grin. "I know."

What I thought was a witty retort seemed to work in the opposite direction. His face twisted up in worry.

I rushed in to repair the damage. "Oh, God, Milan, I was kidding. I love you too. You *know* I love you too."

He shook his head and pointed through the windshield. "No, Harlie. It isn't that. Look!"

I was just pulling the car up to the curb in front of the apartment building. When I followed to where Milan was pointing, I knew immediately something was wrong.

Ramon was sitting on the Arms's front steps, all hunched over with his face buried in his hands. Even from where we were seated at the curb, I could see something was wrong with his T-shirt. It wasn't hanging right. Then I realized why. It was torn in the front from neck to hem and barely covering him at all.

Wary, Milan and I climbed from the car and approached. When we came to within a couple of feet of him, Ramon lifted his face from his hands and stared at us.

"You've come," he said.

This close, Ramon's appearance was disconcerting, to say the least. I hadn't seen him for a couple of weeks, and his shocking pink hair was now faded and sat upon two inches of black regrowth. He had obviously not been taking the trouble to keep it colored properly, which was odd, since Ramon was a hairdresser and spent every day of his waking life in a beauty salon. What had once been a glaring head of hot pink hair, whimsically silly and somehow suiting Ramon's childlike personality, now appeared simply sad and pale and unkempt.

But his hair was the least of his problems.

Ramon's face was swollen, and one of his eyes was blackening even as we stood there looking down at him. With his torn shirttail, he continually dabbed at a seepage of blood coming from a torn lip. The lip, too, was swelling, and a bruise was rising on his cheek.

Milan and I immediately dropped down to sit at either side of him. Ramon didn't seem to mind us there. He didn't really seem to register us there at all.

Milan pulled a handkerchief from his back pocket and pressed it into Ramon's hand. "Use this," he said softly.

Ramon took it, but held it in his hand as if he wasn't quite sure what he should do with it.

"Where's ChiChi?" Milan asked softly.

No response.

I laid my hand on Ramon's knee to get his attention, but quickly pulled my hand away. The leg of his jeans was soaked with what looked like spaghetti sauce. Then I realized maybe it wasn't spaghetti sauce at all.

Fear stuttered through me.

Ramon turned his eyes to me, and I had never seen an emptier pair of eyes in my life. It broke my heart a little bit just looking at them.

"Ramon," I said. "Where's ChiChi?"

Roman sucked in a shuddering breath. "He's upstairs," he whispered.

"In the apartment?"

Ramon nodded a vacant nod. Again he looked at the handkerchief in his hand as if wondering what it was there for. "He's been there awhile," he said. "He's getting cold, I think."

A chill shot up my spine, and I could see those words had frightened Milan too.

We both leaned in. "It's a beautiful day," Milan said softly, his worried eyes focused on me, even while his words were directed to Ramon. "Why would he be getting cold? Ramon? Why would ChiChi be getting cold?"

With a weary groan, Ramon pulled himself to his feet. Taking our hands in both of his, he led us up the steps.

"I'll show you," he said quietly. And with sinking hearts, Milan and I followed him into the Belladonna Arms.

RAMON LEFT the building long before ChiChi did. Arthur and Milan's dad arrived as the squad car with Ramon in the backseat was pulling away.

Milan and I were standing on the porch talking quietly at the railing when the two rushed up to us. Arthur was so distracted, he had pulled his wig off and was holding it in his hand like a bag of trash. Wigless, but still in his red silk dress and stiletto heels and makeup, Arthur looked unfinished, and somehow *wrong*. Even Mr. Burger, standing helplessly at his side, seemed stunned by what was happening. Melancholy lay so heavily on the air it seemed to deaden the sound around us. Everyone was whispering as if afraid to disturb the mood.

Arthur's hand came out to gently grasp my arm. "One of the tenants called me on my cell phone to say the place was swarming with cops, but they didn't know what was wrong. Where are they taking Ramon, Harlie? What's happened?"

I was still in shock, I think. Somehow the events had not yet soaked in. Milan too seemed subdued.

"He and ChiChi had a fight," I said quietly. "ChiChi's... dead, Arthur. Ramon stabbed him."

For the hundredth time, I remembered ChiChi's still body lying on the kitchen floor, the knife handle poking up, as out of place as anything I had ever seen in my life. ChiChi's eyes were opened wide in surprise. There was a dusting of white powder on his nose and a pile of half-chopped vegetables on the kitchen sink. A huge pot simmering on the stove told me someone had been making vegetable soup. I reached over and turned off the stove.

Milan and I stared down at the lifeless body, too stunned to say a word. Ramon cried softly between us, dabbing softly at his lip with Milan's handkerchief.

Somehow, Ramon's childlike weeping seemed the worst of it all. I wondered if the memory of it would ever go away, or would it be there in the back of my mind forever, always waiting to grab me when I least expected it.

I shook that thought away and brought myself back to the present.

We were still standing on the porch. Milan pulled his dad closer and the four of us stood there in a tight cluster, our eyes glancing from one to the other as if in a continual worried dance.

Milan cleared his throat. He reached for his handkerchief, then seemed to remember he had lent it to Ramon. "The police think it was self-defense, Arthur. Ramon was beaten up pretty bad. They think it might have even been some sort of accident. We told them Ramon would never intentionally hurt ChiChi, and I think they believed us. They also found cocaine on ChiChi's nose. Ramon was clean. At least he said he was. And I think they believed him."

Arthur's hands were at his cheeks, like the little kid in *Home Alone*. But when Arthur did it, it wasn't cute. It was merely sad. Sad and horrified.

"I'll get him the best lawyer I can," Arthur said. "He's a good boy. We'll make them understand that."

I nodded and gave Arthur a gentle hug. "I think they already do, Arthur. Ramon's injuries pretty well told them everything they needed to know, I think."

Arthur stared off into space absentmindedly, as if he didn't have a care in the world. "That's good," he said to no one. "That's good."

Only when Mr. Burger's arm slid around his waist did Arthur turn to him and, through sheer will, twist his mouth into a weary smile. "It'll be all right, Tom," he said. "You'll see."

And Mr. Burger brushed a hand over Arthur's balding scalp. "I know it will, baby. I know."

An hour later, we were still standing on the porch, afraid to go inside, unwilling to disturb the police, hoping someone would come and tell us what was going on. When a flurry of activity drew our attention to the lobby door, we stood silently as ChiChi left the Arms for the very last time. He was tucked inside a black body bag on a gurney. The gurney had a squeaky wheel, and the body bag was tented from the butcher knife still protruding from ChiChi's chest. The somber faces of the policemen and the stillness of the bag told us everything we needed to know. Men from the coroner's office carried the gurney down the front steps, rocking its silent load. On the sidewalk, they rested it back on its squeaky wheels and the gurney rattled and squealed its way to the curb.

Arthur broke into tears as the coroner's van pulled away, ChiChi's still, silent body tucked neatly inside.

Chapter 15

"YOUR NOSE is whistling."

Milan was sitting at the kitchen table in his boxer shorts, reading my second novel, while I stood at the stove preparing dinner.

"I love you too," he grunted back.

It was a week since ChiChi's death. Ramon was staying with his parents while awaiting the outcome of the police investigation because he couldn't bear to set foot in the Belladonna Arms again. At least he wasn't in jail, and so far it appeared he never would be. The prosecutor was definitely leaning toward self-defense, as ChiChi was high on coke at the time of his death, and Ramon obviously was not. Fueled by drugs, ChiChi had attacked Ramon as Ramon stood at the kitchen sink chopping vegetables. As he tried to defend himself, Ramon's knife slipped, and that was the end of ChiChi.

Ramon's facial injuries were also a supporting argument in favor of a self-defense decision. ChiChi's irrational behavior during the last few weeks of his life did not go unnoted either during the course of the investigation. A fact that, for Ramon's sake, thrilled us all.

Poor ChiChi, yes. But it was the living we were worried about now. And I, for one, figured Ramon had suffered enough.

Yet life goes on, as they say.

Sylvia was home, which meant Pete was happy. To all outward appearances, she was the same as she always was. But I thought I could detect pride now, where before there had merely been an almost palpable sense of incompleteness. Sylvia was whole now, and she knew it even if no one else did. Yet somehow the knowing showed through.

Milan was all moved in with me, and his stuff that wouldn't fit into our tiny second-floor apartment, which was a lot, was in storage in his dad's basement across town.

And last but not least, Arthur and Mr. Burger were still so crazy about each other it was a little disconcerting to watch. I hadn't seen Arthur out of drag all week. That was a little disconcerting too. Needless to say, my battle to butch the man up had fallen by the wayside, and I expected it would lay there in the ditch forevermore. Right where it deserved to be.

Feeling a desperate urge for praise, as is too often my wont, I eyed Milan reading my novel and blithely asked, "How's the book?"

Milan didn't look up. "S'okay."

"I want a divorce," I said.

He smiled at that one. "You can't have a divorce. We aren't married. Yet."

I dropped a potato and watched it roll across the floor. Then I turned to stare at him. "Did you say 'yet'?"

"It sounded like it," he grunted again, his eyes still trained on my fucking book but dancing happily anyway. He knew he was pulling my chain. Even I knew he was pulling my chain. Time for me to take matters into my own hands. I imagine he knew that too.

Since I was naked already, I didn't have to undress to get a little skin on skin action going. I wiped my hands on a dish towel, dumped the rest of the unpeeled potatoes in the sink, and plucked the book from Milan's hand, setting it aside. Without asking permission, I simply straddled Milan's lap and plopped my naked ass down on it, at the same time wrapping my arms around his neck.

His warm hands pulled me close. "Feeling needy?" he asked, kissing my forehead, then my nose, both cheeks, my chin, and, after a little wrangling around to get in the proper position, my nipple.

My dick stood up and saluted, brushing Milan's belly button when it did. Milan's dick was suddenly doing a bit of saluting too. I could feel it nuzzling my balls. It seemed to have escaped his boxer shorts without any help from anybody. I love a clever dick.

Milan shifted his ass around in the chair until his erect cock was in a more comfortable place; ergo, not being sat on so my hundred and forty-five pounds might at any moment snap it off like an icicle.

I guess he decided to relent on the whole "wont" thing. Writers can be such a trial. "Your book is wonderful and you know it. Your baking sucks, but you sure know how to write a novel. Not that I've seen you doing much of it lately."

An old, familiar guilt bubbled up inside me. Milan was right. I hadn't written two sentences of late on the new book. I had been far too busy being in love.

I blushed, which had nothing to do with the book comment. Or the slur on my baking talents. I was blushing because it was broad daylight and my dick was smearing a snail trail of precome over Milan's stomach. Although, to be honest, neither of us seemed to mind. Still, I was blushing anyway. I do that sometimes.

"Ramon called this morning," I said, "when you were at the deli. He's coping as well as can be expected. He still blames himself for not getting ChiChi help earlier with his drug problem, but I told him it wasn't his fault. I think ChiChi had a lot of demons working against him. Drugs was only one of them."

"Did you tell Ramon that?" Milan asked, his finger dragging a slow heat across my sphincter.

"No," I said, with a shudder. A *good* shudder. "And I never will."

"Good."

His finger continued to do its magic and my dick continued to drip. I was quickly becoming so turned on my eyes were crossing, and I suspected the goose bumps on my back were as big as marbles.

"Harlie?" Milan asked softly, his lips brushing mine, his dick balancing one of my balls on top of its head like a trained seal.

"Hmm?" I purred.

He laid his forehead against mine. His breath was warm against my face. It smelled of the orange he had eaten a few minutes earlier. When he spoke, his voice was lazy and deep and sexy as hell. "I've never felt like this about anybody. I love you so much my... my...." His words trailed away.

"Yes?" I asked, opening my eyes to study the bottomless depths of his. "You love me so much, what?"

"I love you so much my toes hurt."

I bonked his forehead with mine. "No fair. You wouldn't let me get away with that line. Why should I let you get away with it?"

He looked uncomfortable. "I don't have a way with words like you do."

"Oh, bullshit. Try again."

I pressed my dick against his stomach, which probably didn't do much for his concentration, but it did wonders for mine. "I'm waiting," I said, depositing a teeny, glistening swirl of precome into his belly button.

He finally smiled. "You're a bitch."

"Thank you."

He gazed around me toward the top of the refrigerator. "The cat's watching us."

"Fuck him."

"He's creeping me out."

"Don't let him. He's just a cat."

Milan dipped his finger in his belly button to moisten it with my juices, then pressed the moistened finger to my opening once again. I forced myself to relax and he worked his finger in up to the second knuckle without so much as a by-your-leave. I couldn't have been happier.

When Milan spoke again, his voice was husky with desire, which made me shudder all the more. His finger slipped to the third knuckle, and I gave a teeny grunt.

"I love you so much," he whispered with his lips to mine, "that I think we should do something fun."

"Like what? Go to Disneyland? Take a cruise? Buy some sex toys?" I lifted my ass a fraction of an inch so I could have the pleasure of lowering it once again onto that very talented finger digging its way into my innards.

"No," he moaned. I could feel *his* precome as he slid the head of his cock between my balls, juggling them now, like a really *talented* trained seal. "I think we should get married. It's legal in this state, as you damn well know. There's nothing stopping us from doing it. If you want to, I mean. Only if you want to."

Still straddling the chair, I rose up on tiptoe and reached down between us to grasp his iron cock and point it in the right direction, as if it wasn't pointed there already. "Move your finger," I muttered.

I gasped a second time when Milan removed his finger from my ass. That gasp was quickly replaced by a *third* gasp when I pressed the head of his cock to my opening and held it steady while I slid myself over it like a glove. I didn't stop until he was buried to the hilt.

We both sat there, clutching each other and shivering at the sensations pummeling through us.

"Oh God," I said. "Yes."

"Yes, what? Sex toys? Disneyland? A cruise?" His mouth was at my throat and his hands were cupping my ass, raising me, lowering me, almost leaving me empty, then filling me to the brim once again with his stabbing cock. Gently, but not so gently either. Milan was a good fucker. No pun intended.

"Yes, I'll marry you. Oh God, yes! Right there, baby. Right there!"

Milan's teeth nipped at my Adam's apple while his dick set off in search of buried treasure, or whatever the hell it was doing. As far as I was concerned, the *dick* was the treasure, and I was the lucky treasure hunter. I didn't want to let it go either. This was an excellent treasure to have buried in me.

His hand circled my cock. "Come for me," he breathed into my ear. "Come for me while I'm fucking you."

"Yes" was all I could say, and I almost swallowed my tongue trying to say it.

He spit into his fingers and slid them over and around my cock until I was shaking like a leaf. While he did that, his cock repeatedly pounded me from below.

And as the cat leaped onto the table all the way across the kitchen from the refrigerator to see what was going on, scaring us both to death in the process, I came. My seed gushed into his hand and he caught as much of it as he could. Bringing his fingers to his mouth he licked it away like cream, and the moment he did that, he let out a groan of his own.

I pushed the cat away; he was really getting interested in what was going on, and why the hell shouldn't he be? There are more wonders in the world than tuna. Where was I? Oh, yeah. I pushed the cat away, and the minute I did, something about the way I twisted my body made Milan clutch me tight and bury his cock into me as deep as it would go. We both gave long moans, and for the first time ever, I felt his sperm shoot deep inside me.

My God, I only then realized we'd forgotten to use a condom!

But this was no time to quibble over forgotten condoms. I rode Milan until his well of come ran dry, and then I rode him a little while longer. He held me in his arms with his face pressed to my throat until the last shudder escaped his body. Then, slowly, we both relaxed.

When his cock slid free I wanted to cry. I missed it so.

Still clutching me tight, Milan reached over to the chair next to us and plucked something from the seat of it that was hidden by the tabletop.

A tiny velvet box.

With one hand holding me in place above him, he flipped open the box with his thumb and offered it to me with wide, beseeching eyes.

"Marry me, Harlie. I love you so much. I never want to be without you."

I tore my eyes from his pleading face and tried to focus on the velvet box and what it held, but I was too late. The tears were already blurring my vision. I hastily wiped them away and tried again.

As my vision cleared, I realized there was more than one ring in the box. There were two. Two simple gold bands. One for him, one for me.

I plucked one from the box while he still held it there before me. Slowly, with shaking fingers, I tried the ring on. It was way too big.

"I think that one's mine," Milan sweetly said, holding out his finger. "Slip it on me."

So I did.

"The other one's yours," he said, and before I reached for the ring I closed my eyes for a moment to better hear the gentle thunder of our two hearts racing inside us. My tears starting up again, I lifted the second ring from the box and handed it to him. "You do it," I said.

With a delicate smile on his handsome face, he took the ring and slid it over my finger.

It fit perfectly.

We held our hands side by side and simply sat there staring at our two rings.

"Yes, I'll marry you," I said. "You know I will."

I buried my face in the crook of his neck and savored his heat as my tears let loose.

He made shushing noises in my ear until my crying stopped, and when I looked at him again, he was smiling.

"Forever," he murmured into a kiss.

"Yes," I murmured back. "Forever."

And Gizmo walked away as if he had never been more bored in his life.

The little shit.

THE PARTY was being held in the basement party room at the Belladonna Arms, a dark dusty dungeon that all other days of the year the tenants avoided like the plague. But tonight it was decked out to perfection, with arrangements of lilies on every table, a spinning disco ball hanging from the ceiling and spraying sparkles of candlelight everywhere, and ropes of white garlands draped around the walls and suspended from overhead. With so much white everywhere, the party room reminded me of the snow-encrusted interior of the country house in *Dr. Zhivago*. And since the lights were dimmed to the point where no one could see the unpainted walls or the mouse droppings in the corners, it was romantic as hell. As long as you didn't look too closely.

Milan and I had escaped the decorating committee but were coerced into catering the shindig, along with help from Milan's father. This time, since the three of us were a little busy with our blossoming love affairs and not in the mood for much of anything else, we simply spent a couple of hours at the deli slapping together some party trays of cold cuts, cheeses, veggies, and breads and called it quits. Since Arthur was in charge of liquor, there was no shortage of that, so no one seemed to mind they were not being served hot food. In fact, within thirty minutes of the party beginning, most of the attendees were well on their way to being sloshed anyway.

Milan and I, still fresh and smiling from our little rumble at the kitchen table and the vows of love we had spoken there, arrived early to set up the trays. I'm afraid my mind wasn't on business, however, because I kept staring at the gold band on my finger, as well as the matching one on Milan's. True, we weren't married yet in the eyes of the state of California, but in our hearts we were. And as far as I was concerned, that's what really mattered. Milan agreed completely.

The band was just setting up, and I'm pretty sure I've never seen a motleyer collection of humanity in my life. They were dressed like bums, and not one of them was under seventy. When they tuned up—bass fiddle, guitar, keyboard, and drums—they sounded cacophonous. But when they began their first set, I realized they were actually a jazz quartet. And a good one too. Maybe the night wouldn't be so bad after all.

As party time rolled around, people began to wander in. In twos. In threes. The first ones to arrive were Charlie and Bruce, the resident kleptomaniacs. I was hoping they had taken their medications, otherwise the band, who at their age were likely blinded by cataracts anyway, might discover their instruments gone before they ever finished their first set.

Gradually the basement filled up, and as it filled up and the stock of alcohol began dwindling, the noise level ratcheted up to near frenzy. It was fairly obvious from the get-go it was going to be a raucous party, although most of the people there I had never seen before in my life.

Roger and Stanley arrived arm in arm and, after snagging a couple of cocktails from the bartender—a luscious hunk of manhood dressed in red Speedos and nothing else—made a beeline for the corner where Milan and I were standing in each other's arms.

"So what's the surprise?" Roger asked. "Have you heard yet?"

Milan and I gazed blankly at each other, then shot the same blank expression back to Roger.

"No idea," I said. "Why? Did you hear there's going to be a surprise?"

Stanley chuckled. "Yeah, heard it from Arthur. That man never could keep a secret, although apparently he's managed to keep this one."

"Well," Milan said, "whatever it is, I guess we'll find out about it when it happens." He made a big show of pushing his hair out of his eyes with his ring hand, so I dove in to help him with *my* ring hand, both of us flashing the gold in the candlelight as best we could, and finally Stanley and Roger got the hint.

"Are those wedding rings?" Roger asked, grabbing our two hands and pulling them up to his nose.

Milan and I both had the good grace to blush. "Oh, you noticed."

Roger laughed. "Hard not to, guys." He studied the rings for a second, muttered, "Beautiful," and swooped in to give us a hug. Stanley swooped in right after him.

By the time we broke the huddle, Stanley was beaming. "We've been talking about that too. Getting married. Legally. Like real people."

Milan leaned in and ruffled Stanley's hair. "I hate to break this to you, kid, but we *are* real people. With the same rights to happiness as all the *other* real people on the planet."

It was Stanley's turn to blush. "I know that."

"Oh, sweet Jesus!" Milan suddenly exclaimed, staring off across the room. "Please tell me that's not who I think it is."

Roger, Stanley, and I looked to see what he was talking about and spotted Arthur, in full drag, making his grand entrance into the party with another drag queen on his arm. They were without a doubt the tallest two drag queens I had ever seen in my life.

Milan looked as if he had swallowed a bug. "What's wrong?" I asked. "Who's that with Arthur?"

Milan opened his mouth to speak, but nothing came out.

"Holy shit!" Stanley cried. "It's your dad!"

"*Whose* dad?" I asked.

And with a horrified expression on his face, Stanley pointed to Milan. "*His* dad."

Roger muttered, "My God, I think it is."

I looked closer and realized Stanley was right. The second drag queen, the towering dude in white evening gloves and a skin-tight, floor-length, sequined, strapless, baby blue stripper's gown with a slit in the front up to the knees and a bundle of lacy stuff poking through the slit in the back at his heels and a back-length blond wig with a deep wave covering one eye like Veronica Lake and a plunging neckline that exposed two bulging mounds of newly-shaved flesh even Veronica Lake hadn't sported in real life, with or without the hair—yes, *that* second drag queen—was Milan's dad. My boss. Arthur's boyfriend. Mr. Thomas Fucking Burger. In person.

And he didn't look half-bad.

"He must be taped up to within an inch of his life to make his tits pooch up like that," Roger mused, which apparently wasn't what Milan really wanted to hear at that moment.

"I'm gonna need a bigger drink," Milan mumbled, downing his cocktail and heading off to the guy in the Speedos to grab another. Or maybe two.

Arthur spotted us from across the room and flapped a jewel-bedecked paw in our direction. In horror, I realized he had somehow managed to acquire eight or nine hundred teeny tiny braids that were either glued or stapled to his head and which flung themselves all over the place every time he jerked his head. He looked like a cross between Bo Derek in *10* and Monstro in *Pinocchio*. I remembered the nurse we had met in Sylvia's hospital room and her hair weaves and figured the mystery was solved.

"Girls!" Arthur screamed, hauling his drag partner along behind him like an overly ornate pull toy. "Look who I've got here! Isn't she lovely?"

In all fairness, I have to say Mr. Burger didn't appear to be embarrassed. He didn't look particularly feminine either, but then neither did Arthur. He did look like he was having fun, though. I had to give him credit for that. The man had balls, although at the moment they were certainly not on display.

Up close, the only recognizable bit of the man I thought I might have seen before were his baby blue eyes, the color of which exactly matched his gown. I had seen those eyes before because every time I looked into Milan's face to tell him I loved him, those same blue eyes gazed right back at me. Milan had his father's eyes, you see. Right down to the gold specks in the irises and the long black lashes.

And speaking of Milan, I looked around to see him approaching now. He had a drink in each hand, and I'm pretty sure neither one of them was for me. In fact he was sucking on each of them in turn, going from one to the other without missing a beat. He seemed to have developed a powerful thirst all of a sudden.

Milan stopped a couple of feet away and looked his dad up and down like a man buying a horse. A really *sick* horse.

He shook his head and turned to Arthur. "You've ruined him. You've taken my dad, who used to be butch, and you've turned him into a woman. I may never sleep again."

Burger laughed a deep throaty laugh that sounded completely out of place coming as it did from between that sexy blond wig and those voluptuous taped-up tits.

"Chill out, son," Burger said, chucking Milan on the chin, which made Milan jump and spill both of his drinks down the front of his shirt, which Milan didn't seem to notice at all. "I simply drove a hard bargain is all. Desperate measures and all that." He gave me a wink when he said it.

Milan eyed him skeptically. "To get you like this? How fucking desperate were you? What'd you have to offer in return? Huh? Your soul? I hope to hell you got something decent in exchange for making yourself look like this." Then he backtracked just enough not to hurt his dad's feelings. "Not that you don't look lovely." The words might have been wrenched from Milan's throat with a pair of pliers.

It was Arthur who answered, and he didn't seem too happy about it. "Oh, he did." Then even he backtracked, suddenly eyeing his partner up and down one more time. "He *does* look lovely, doesn't he?"

Burger made a shushing sound and pulled Arthur to him, ball gown, train, fur wrap, evening bag, and all. Arthur's face softened and Burger kissed the man's bright red bee-stung lips, but gently so as not to smear Arthur's lipstick. Or his own.

I was watching Milan closely. When he saw how happy his dad was, his face softened too, as I knew it would. Before he could stop himself, he pulled me into his arms even while he continued to study the two gigantic drag queens in front of him, one of whom was his biological father and wasn't that a major kick in the fucking head (which, if I was any judge, was what Milan seemed to be thinking).

"So, Arthur," Milan finally asked after he had downed what was left of his two spilled drinks, which wasn't much. "What did you have to promise Pop to get him to come to Sylvia's party in drag?"

Arthur glowered. He looked like he was suddenly besieged with gas. Or rickets. Or was about to pass a big fat kidney stone.

"He made me promise to quit… to quit…." Arthur growled and grumped and groused around, but he couldn't seem to get the words out.

In a mellow, babying voice, Burger prompted, "Tell him the rest, Arthur. Don't be shy now. Buck up. Spit it out." He appeared to be having a real good time.

Suddenly Arthur didn't appear to be having a good time at all.

"He made me promise to quit smoking!" Arthur blurted out. He blurted it out with such force and with such ill-humor that his wig slipped when he did it, and Roger reached out to straighten it for him before it slid down his back and landed on the floor.

Stanley stepped in to give Burger's bare shoulder a couple of congratulatory slaps. "Well done, sir! Congratulations! We've been bitching at Arthur to quit smoking for over a year!"

Roger was all teeth and dimples. I'd never seen him happier. "Year, hell! I've been bitching at Arthur to quit for as long as I've known him! This is wonderful news!" He gave Arthur a hug which was so enthusiastic it dislodged Arthur's wig again, which Roger *again* took a moment to straighten.

"Finally!" I declared. "The stairwells won't smell like spit-soaked tobacco!"

"Yeah, that *is* a plus!" Milan piped up.

"But I'll die without my cigars!" Arthur groaned.

Burger tapped Arthur's nose with the tip of his finger to get his attention. "No, my love. You'll live *longer*. And that means I'll get more time to be with you. The way I see it, I'm the big winner here, not you. So stop complaining and tell me you love me."

Two spots of color blossomed under Arthur's pancake makeup. His bee-stung lips formed a perfect little O. "I love you, you big galoot," he said sweetly, and Burger patted his own chest, taped-up tits and all, as if to say his heart had just skipped a happy beat.

Arthur cast a critical eye on Burger, from the Veronica Lake wig to the skin-tight stripper's gown to the sequined slippers peeking out through the slit in the dress. Wistfully, he sighed and said, "I wish I had your figure, Tom."

"Do you?" Burger asked.

"Yes." It was perhaps the saddest "yes" I had ever heard.

Burger took Arthur's hand. "Then we'll work on it together."

Arthur's eyes misted up as he brought Burger's evening-gloved hand up to his lips. He gazed around the room, at all his friends, at all his tenants, at all the people I knew he cared about in life.

"Before things went wrong between them, Ramon and ChiChi would have loved this. Now ChiChi is gone forever, and I doubt I'll ever see Ramon again either." Arthur's eyes were melancholy as he cocked his head for a moment and listened to the band. When they traveled back to Mr. Burger's face I saw the love he felt for the man shining through the glitz and the makeup and the god-awful glittered eyelashes.

Arthur heaved another sigh and looked about the crowded room. "Over the years, a lot goes on in a building like this. All of it isn't good. But all of it isn't bad either. Friends are made, love is found, people lose their way, but still—life has a way of moving forward. Always forward."

At the tender, wise words, I saw Stanley dip his head to Roger's shoulder just as Milan's hand took a firmer grip on mine.

"Arthur," I said, "you're a philosopher."

Even through the pancake, Arthur blushed. "No, I'm just an old softy."

Burger snuggled up close to him and smiled. "I happen to love old softies."

Arthur blinked back a tear at the same time his bee-stung lips formed a gentle smile. "Do you?"

And Burger thumbed a tear from Arthur's cheek. "You bet I do."

A communal gasp rang out across the party room, interrupting the tender moment between Arthur and Mr. Burger, which Stanley and Roger and Milan and I were in the process of eating up as much as they were. We looked around to see what was happening and saw everyone looking toward the entrance off to the right.

Without warning, the lights dimmed and the band fell silent.

"Oh, poop!" Arthur exclaimed.

As if suddenly remembering where he was and what he was supposed to be doing, Arthur snatched a glass from Milan's hand, gathered his skirts around him, and climbed onto the seat of a chair, with Mr. Burger holding his other hand to keep him balanced.

Arthur raised Milan's glass high in the air and cried out for everyone to hear, "To the bride and groom!"

Milan gave me a look that said, "Huh?" and we both turned to see who was coming through the door.

I heard a chorus of confused "Cheers" and halfhearted "Many mores," but no one really appeared to know what was happening.

I did, however. And I also knew now what Arthur's surprise was turning out to be. And it was a flat-out, romantic-as-hell doozy.

The band broke into the "Wedding March" as a tall older gentleman in a black suit holding a Bible in his hand stepped up onto the stage. At the foot of the stage stood Pete, materializing out of nowhere it seemed, all decked out in a bright blue tuxedo with a small boutonniere of white lilies pinned to his chest. He looked tall and lean and as handsome as any man I had ever seen. Except for Milan, of course. No one compares to Milan.

Pete turned to face the door at the back of the hall as Sylvia stepped into the room. She was wearing an empire-waisted wedding gown of snow white silk and lace, and her beautiful face was barely visible beneath a crisp white veil that hung all the way down her back and trailed across the floor behind her as she stepped forward to the rhythm of the music. Before her, in her folded hands, she clutched a spray of lilies held together with a blue ribbon that perfectly matched the blue of Pete's tux.

The partygoers parted like the Red Sea to afford Sylvia a path to the stage, and I watched on tiptoe with Milan's arm around me, both of us smiling like loons, as Pete took one look at his approaching bride and clutched his heart in pride. Even from where we stood, I could see a tear sparkle on Pete's cheek as he stepped forward and took Sylvia's hand to lead her the rest of the way to the foot of the stage where the preacher waited, smiling.

Pete and Sylvia came to a halt in front of the man with the Bible, and immediately the room fell silent, but for the music of the band, which had grown progressively softer as Pete and Sylvia approached the stage. Now, with the music so soft it barely registered on the ear at all, it was almost as if two hundred people were holding their breath, waiting in awe for what was to come next.

Pete still clutched Sylvia's hand just as Milan was clutching mine.

With Mr. Burger's hand at the small of his back, Arthur pulled a teeny handkerchief from his bodice and quietly dabbed at the tears streaming down his face, while Roger and Stanley stood in each other's arms, both of them holding their fingertips over their mouths in stunned silence, waiting for events to unfold.

"Look at them," Milan whispered softly into my ear. "Look at Pete and Sylvia. Look how happy they are. One day that will be us."

As I edged closer to him, because closer was where I always wanted to be, I ignored the growing lump in my throat and listened with growing reverence as the music waned one last time and finally fell to silence. Through a blur of rising tears I saw the preacher open his Bible and smile a forbearing smile at everyone present, including the silent, expectant couple standing before him.

Delicately, he intoned the words: "Dearly beloved, I bring you this man and this woman...."

And silently, hands clasped, Pete and Sylvia stood perfectly still as the preacher's soft voice recited the old familiar litany and their lives became forever joined.

Milan held me tight, his sweet breath stirring my hair, as we waited and watched, wishing the moment would never end.

At the first "I do," I buried my face in Milan's shirtfront, and he held me gently in his arms.

I listened intently to the words being spoken by the man on the stage, and at the second "I do," *Sylvia's* I do, Milan and I gazed at each other and smiled. For Sylvia and Pete, a cheer broke out across the room.

And not once during that long, raucous cheer did Milan's bottomless blue eyes leave my face.

Not even once.

JOHN INMAN has been writing fiction since he was old enough to hold a pencil. He and his partner live in beautiful San Diego, California. Together, they share a passion for theater, books, hiking and biking along the trails and canyons of San Diego or, if the mood strikes, simply kicking back with a beer and a movie. John's advice for anyone who wishes to be a writer? "Set time aside to write every day and do it. Don't be afraid to share what you've written. Feedback is important. When a rejection slip comes in, just tear it up and try again. Keep mailing stuff out. Keep writing and rewriting and then rewrite one more time. Every minute of the struggle is worth it in the end, so don't give up. Ever. Remember that publishers are a lot like lovers. Sometimes you have to look a long time to find the one that's right for you."

You can contact John at john492@att.net, on Facebook: http://www.facebook.com/john.inman.79, or on his website: http://www.johninmanauthor.com/.

The Belladonna Arms Series

Serenading
Stanley

THE BELLADONNA ARMS
JOHN INMAN

http://www.dreamspinnerpress.com

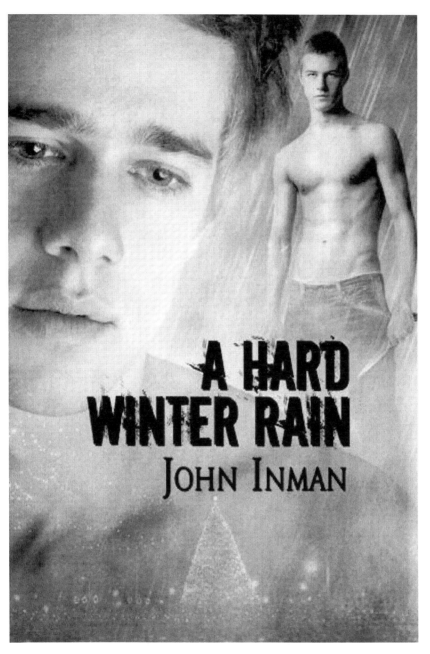

A HARD
WINTER RAIN
JOHN INMAN

http://www.dreamspinnerpress.com

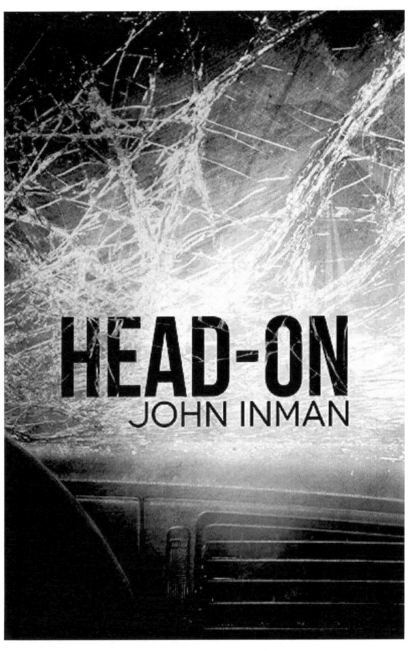

http://www.dreamspinnerpress.com

http://www.dreamspinnerpress.com

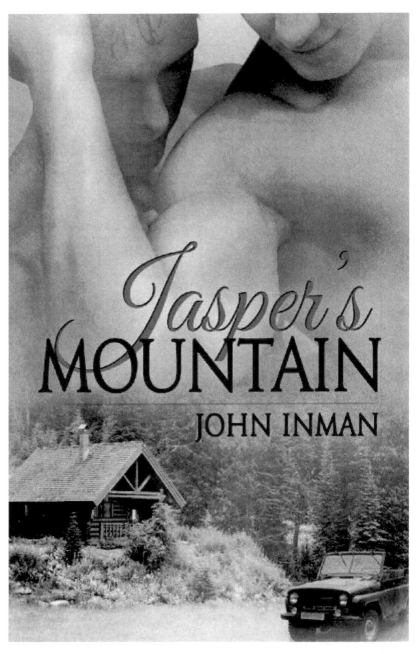

Jasper's

MOUNTAIN

JOHN INMAN

http://www.dreamspinnerpress.com

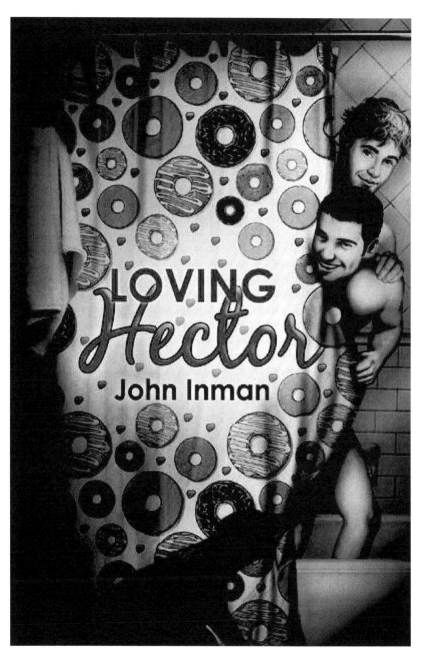

http://www.dreamspinnerpress.com

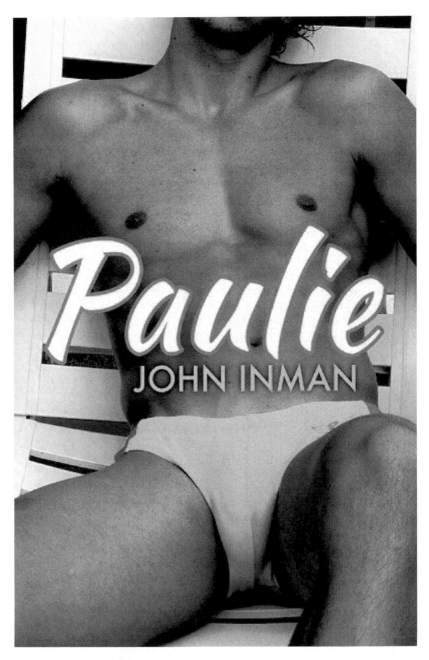

http://www.dreamspinnerpress.com

http://www.dreamspinnerpress.com

http://www.dreamspinnerpress.com

SPIRIT
JOHN INMAN

http://www.dreamspinnerpress.com

http://www.dreamspinnerpress.com

Wade Kelly

Names Can Never Hurt Me

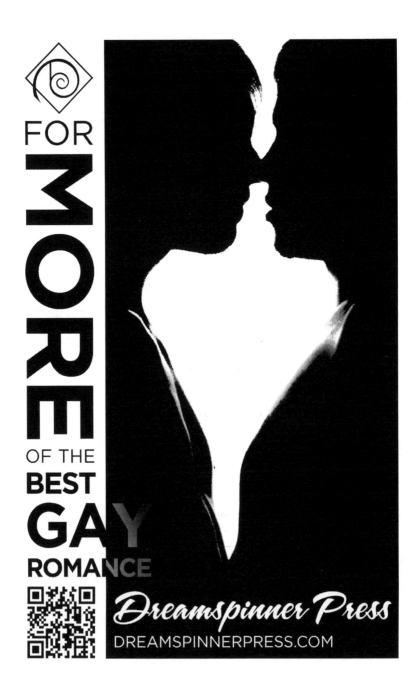